Alexei

and the Second Empress

Fred Nolan

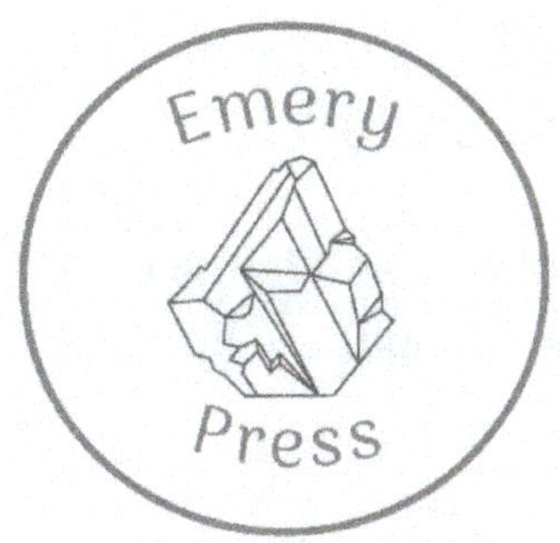

Emery Press Books
Fort Lauderdale, FL
www.emerypressbooks.com

First Edition – November 2018

ISBN (Trade): 978-0-9992047-8-8
ISBN (eBook): 978-0-9992047-9-5

Cover Design by Billy Gino Johnson
Editing by Grammar Goddess Editing

For Demitri

Note on Russian names and the use of "tsesarevich"

In Imperial Russia, as in Russia today, the patronymic was a legal component of the name, appearing before or in place of a surname. Masculine patronymics ended with the suffix –ovich, for example. Feminine patronymics ended with the suffix –evna, among others.

Three contemporary examples may be illustrative. The tsesarevich's patronymic Nikolaevich indicated that Alexei was son of Nicholas. On the contrary, his oldest sister was named Olga Nikolaevna, or Olga, daughter of Nicholas. The Russian count Yusupov, whose father was named Felix, was known formally as Felix Felixovich Yusupov.

Tsarevich was the title for any son of a tsar until 1721, when Peter the Great conferred the title of tsesarevich (heir-apparent) upon his son Paul Petrovich.

In 1797, the Pauline house law formally discontinued the title tsarevich, replacing it with tsesarevich, for the heir-apparent alone. His younger brothers were known simply as Grand Prince or Grand Duke.

**Saint Petersburg
November 1741**

THE TSAR was 15 months old when he lost the throne.

There had been snow the week before, but the Winter Palace grounds were thawing. Instead of blizzard was a field of countless ugly ponds. A landscape of mud, difficult for boots.

Yet Elizaveta Petrovna, a Romanov daughter in cavalry gear, had enough boots to make do.

She came with 300 men, her father's old guards, fine pedigrees. It was after midnight, dark, only a small moon. As they rode, with the occasional lantern glint from war helmets, the sight would have been of fireflies with great shadows underneath.

They dismounted in clear view of the palace, and had to negotiate, although briefly, with the entry guards. "My children, will you follow me?" The defending soldiers were wise enough to kneel, praying mutinous things. In only minutes Elizaveta's force grew by two score, now three. Some of the recruits went into the city to make arrests. Those who stayed accepted it, the chance of drawing swords on brothers.

The tsar and regent apartments were upstairs. By this time it was noisy, almost a farce. Elizaveta had dozens of men inside, climbing stairs to overturn three pitiful rulers: the emperor Ivan VI, his mother Anna, his father Prince Anthony.

The apartment garrison let the coup inside without blood or protest. The parents of the tsar were snoring in bed, mouths open. The intruder put a hand on the sleeping regent's skin.

Elizaveta's voice was unsteady. The words did not satisfy, considering the claim. She said, "My sister, it is time."

Anna said, "We are finished." She had long arms, which rarely took sunlight. She liked fiction and warm bodies instead of ruling.

Cavalrymen led them out, to a carriage. Anthony had bare legs and Anna was never quite dressed, nor did she arrange her hair, even for official work. For now she spoke of her elephants, which a Persian gave her at the start of their regency. She said, "Do not kill them, mama. They are gentler than they seem."

Mama: she already used the deferential word for empress.

It was not dawn, and Elizaveta ordered men to stay by the tsar's crib, to let the baby wake on his own. The intruders stank of wet underclothes and socks, were forbidden from speaking. Ornate rugs hung on each of

Ivan's four walls, and walking toward one was like falling to the floor, a step at a time.

Because they could not stare or converse, they spent most of the hours with eyes at their feet. At last, the deposed infant came around with a stretch. He made a contented noise.

The court doctor took the frail tsar to Elizaveta, who said, "Little one, you are not guilty of anything."

That was it. By taking a happy, swaddled boy into her arm, she took all of Russia.

The parties to the coup rushed out to greet the rising sun, a happy omen. From today their nation had a new crown. Elizaveta, the loving autocrat.

Part One

May 1896:	Russia crowns Tsar Nicholas II
March 1898:	Amid poor living and working conditions, illiteracy, hunger and strikes, the Russian Social Democrat party is formed
February 1904:	Outbreak of Russo-Japanese war
August 1904:	After announcing four daughters, the tsar and empress deliver Tsesarevich Alexei Nikolaevich Romanov, the heir apparent
January 1905:	Russian infantry opens fire on a peaceful workers' march, killing 92
February 1905:	The tsar's uncle is assassinated by a member of the Socialist-Revolutionary Party

October 1905:   Unrest and mutinies culminate in a general strike of more than 2 million workers

April 1912:   Russian infantry opens fire on striking gold mine workers, killing 270

July 1914:   Germany declares war on Russia; World War I will claim 1.8 million Russian lives and increase the national debt by 8 million rubles

August 1914:   Germany defeats the Russian Second Army, resulting in the suicide of Alexander Vassilievich Samsonov, the General of the Cavalry

July 1915:   Heavy Russian losses in Poland

August 1915:   Nicholas II assumes military command

September 1915: Two in three members of the German Army are deployed to the Eastern front

June 1916:   A new wave of protests in response to the huge Russian offensive along the Romanian border; the front spans 400 kilometers

January 1917:   Heavy fighting in northern Romania

Chapter One
February 1917

IN THE CENTRAL-WEST of Russia are a dead lake and a house. Alexei was born here, and never goes far, or leaves for much time. He is stricken with hemophilia and when he is away, his mother is eaten up by worry.

Not Alexei of Petrograd. This one's name is Alexei Karlovich Shafirov, and he will come to know today as the first day.

For a boy with his condition, a small cut on the skin is enough. Once as a toddler he slipped while rinsing off, cracking his mouth on the rim of a tub. He bled for three days, licking at the wound, nourishment that always came. At the moment he fell his mother was there, readying dinner. She put her knife down, took him up, listening to him bawl, shushing him as she ate. Years later he told her she could have ended it there, the same knife.

Worse than outward cuts is the inner bleeding, which does not clot, either.

The pressure is terrible, an egg in every joint. Knees, elbows, shoulders. When the pain is the worst it feels as if the eggs will hatch and birds will come out. On that day, Alexei will pop open at every stitch, lay on his back, or what is left of his back. Once a boy, now a flock of cardinals.

He can only wonder if the chicks will know better health than he does, but he has no hope in that. There is nothing as frail as a newborn bird. Small wonder, then, that his joints are made of yolk, not real blood.

#

This is how it starts. Alexei climbs to the roof, overlooking the lake and the bland acres. Beyond that, a neighbor's producing farm. He means to drop to the entry gable below, some eight feet down. The moment of jumping from a height is a thousand pinpricks in the stomach, some as high as the underarm. No boy can resist that.

Yet he catches a toe in the gutter and lands jaw-first, planting with his forearms and head, snapping his chin up. The private grunt would be funny if he could hear it, hidden within his lungs and bones. But he blacks out instead, wakes to the clouds straight up, his thoughts a stew. Somehow he has not fallen from the gable but now he has to scale down the metal spout to grade level. He has a smeared-away feel. His jaw and hands are shaking. His wrists, feeble.

There are bruises but no blood—his mother does not need blood to know. As she leads him to bed he is crying, or rather he tries to, with sobs chopped into fine exhales, mostly empty.

When the blood does not clot the hours do. He waits and waits, warming at the neck. His knees throb as if they are filling up.

Mama sits bedside with an arm over his feet, which they have propped up on blankets. She is tall, almost the same height as papa. Her arm, bent in such a way, looks like one of his adolescent legs. Yet the elbow is too healthy to be his.

She says, "Here is a question for the lake. What could have possessed you? You could've died. You still—" but no mother would finish a warning like that.

"Sorry, mama."

"My two lunatics, you and your father. My reckless little army man and his son, who is just like him."

She tells him this in Russian although he would have preferred to hear it in French, like the aristocratic kids do. Instead of child she would call him *l'enfant*, the infant. And instead of warrior it would be *l'infanterie*, the infantry.

He can only say it again, "Sorry, mama. Sorry."

If she could quiet him she would start with the inflammation, which is turning his legs blue, the color of ether, ocean, anything wide and dispersed. And yes, he feels as if he is scattering, becoming unwhole.

As the days pass his breath comes back, yet the masses in his joints are unbearable. He walks less and less until, on the fourth night, he is bedridden. His mother reads, whispers, speaks in scattershot. She mumbles on about God, clocks, the bitter taste of seeds, what his father likes to drink. More than not she speaks to him about a careless one named Alexei Karlovich, and the way he needs to behave from now on, if he walks again.

Tonight, late, she is out of admonishments. Her eyes are blue and red, like a sea bound by fire. Her attention stalls and spreads, also like fire.

She says, "Did you hear what happened in St. Petersburg?"

Their country is all news anymore. Stampedes, strikes, war. She knows she will have to be clearer than that and she says, "There is a monk, or there was one. He was a friend of the empress and he was attacked. He did not make it."

Yes, Alexei has heard of the man, through Anastasia, who one day will be his lover. But they are not 15 yet, and they are Orthodox. For now Anastasia forbids it.

He says, "Who attacked him?" They are speaking of Grigori, from Siberia, the land of the exiles.

Her answer: "Maybe it was one of our princes, Felix Yusupov. No matter. The empress will have him killed and then the Bolsheviks will have her killed, and all will be settled."

Alexei knows about both of those. Yusupov is the richest man in Russia. His wife wears the veil of Marie Antoinette and that old ghost is ready for blood, to be sure.

As for the Bolsheviks, Alexei learned of the movement at school. They are the library revolutionaries who murdered the grand duke and the tsar's grandfather. They will bring literacy and bread but not true law. Only a Romanov can properly rule. Yet Alexei secretly pulls for the Bolsheviks because, if they come to power, it could mean the end of war. His father will be home and Russia will still be Russia. No one has to give a damn about the means to production.

He says, "How did they do it?"

"That's not what interests me and I would never talk about it with a boy. Father Grigori was my friend, too, from years ago. I am sure we are safe, but it disturbs me that the prince sought him out."

"I am sure we are safe, too."

"If anyone tells you of Father Grigori, ask me first, before you go on believing what they say."

Alexei ought to reply, 'You and papa taught me to never believe,' but he knows better.

She says, "What interests me is after the attack. There were gunshots that night and, the next day, a barrel's worth of salt was in the river, frozen hard. Maybe someone put it there, even the British could have done it. But the point is that no one bled to death, and no one was drowned."

Alexei nods and she strokes his knee. The joint hurts the wrong way, in the wrong color, and that distresses him.

She says, "In the morning when the people of the city knew who it was, they scooped water out by the bucketful."

Alexei believes he understands and says, "To take up Father Grigori's blood?"

"Not his blood, Alexei. His salt. What some are saying is he died and turned to salt. Every pound, tissue or bone, all of it was salt."

"And those who scooped it out will cook with it?"

She laughs, touching, now discoloring, his cheek. "My pigeon."

Time is a crawl, yet the sun jumps across the sky during his naps, which are many. It is a flip-book view of sunlight, by a child who is too clumsy to draw well, and whose mother cannot afford aspirin.

Alexei has been this way before, even heard last rites once. He knows that, when he is the weakest, dreams are sad, faraway. Colors are burned through to white, or maybe black. You have to wonder if paradise is not the coming together of loved ones but instead the endless rotations of sad day, sad night, sad day again.

He dozes through until late afternoon, and when he looks up again the sun burns red from across the evening lake.

There is a certain madness in dreaming of dark, but waking when it is still light out. In his confusion, the wall is in flames with reflected sun. He says, "What is it?"

"It was a bird, love. Only a bird."

He was not referring to any sound but to the look of the wall. Anyway he fears she has answered him right, and there is a great bird of myth brought indoors, a wingspan on fire. He sleeps again, thinks of Anastasia. That the girl has not come means she is not worried yet, and because of that he will not worry, either.

#

Hours later it is as bright as day, with the glow of a perfect moon and its image on the lake. Which are the two lunatics now?

He should tell Anastasia of the earlier lesson in words, which pertains to them whether she would accept it or not. *Infant, infantry.* Russian forgets how similar they are, but in some languages the connection is evident. The suffix *–fant* comes from the Latin *fari*, to speak. To create fables, fabulist tales, to offer fame. It is rooted in the Sanskrit words *bhanati*, *bhane*, which mean greeting, speech, moral wisdom.

Seen this way, an infant is one who cannot speak. An infantryman is one who is paid to not-speak. Trained for and commanded to silence. Alexei could tell her, No matter what mama says I am neither of those, yet you never let me speak of our marriage.

Anastasia is fluent in French, she will know what he means.

When he is well, he sits with her, his left shoulder to her right, and she might let him reach over with one leg and leave a knee between her knees, as long as she is wrapped in bedlinen. It does something to their inhales they do not understand. They pant, gasp as if they were climbing. Yet it is an unmoving act, no reason for short breath. Soon one of them has to stand, to be rid of the tautness in the chest.

Afterward, he might dream of bringing her in close. If he does, the sound of her whispering makes him piss, or something close to piss. Blood and yolk again. For this, Alexei does not believe they need to wait. His hair and voice have come, and his life may be short.

Anastasia is moon-touched every 28 days exactly. A more regular cycle, she says, than that of her mother. The pleats in his slacks are always taut, but still they do not play.

Not before we are 17, she says, and it is not a good promise. His parents say they were married at 17.

He wakes some time before morning. Panting again—pain this time—with his mother's hand reaching across. The woman snores like a retriever.

#

There are sounds in his sleep, and he is aware that every inward breath makes him frown. Some time later, in the dull hours after midnight, his chest turns to ice. The sensation knifes under his back in frozen lines.

He wakes in panic, but his mother's panic is more. "I'm sorry, pigeon. Your fever. Jesus, Mary, pray, your fever." She repeats and repeats until the words are mumbles: so hot, so hot.

Hot? Impossible. He is freezing, no chance of fever. She will murder him with cold, the stupid woman! This is something an older brother would do, splash you with water while you slept. Yet when she puts a hand to his forehead her palm feels cool.

"Blankets." Is that the sound of his voice? It cannot be, it is too soft, haggard. His father sounds like that after tall glasses of whiskey, but rarely his mother. Alexei, never.

If she recognizes her husband in the plea she does not say. The room stinks of vomit and digestive gas—which one of them threw up? She has the back door open and the moist, breezy smell from outdoors is in, making his throat taste of bile. A child turning to battery. There is his answer.

She says, "Blankets? You're engulfed. I'll drop you in the lake with all of those slates. I brought some in from outside but you've already warmed it back up. Feel."

True, the water is hot and has the blue oxidized smell of their property. Soapy, alkaline. His mother calls the pond Galilee but Anastasia has unwisely rechristened it Bay of Alexei.

Lake water. He is becoming that, and his mother has just vowed to pour his remains into it.

"Mama, no. I'll be well soon. I'm better." It is a lame oath. With the pounding in his heart comes nerve and vascular pain all over. She took the blanket in his sleep and his wet clothes cling hard, baring him. He does not dare look. He says, delirious, "Send for papa."

"Love, he's at the front."

"Just send."

"Send who? He wouldn't get the letter for weeks and he couldn't leave. What of Father Rauf?"

"Anastasia."

"She's a lovely girl but she's no surgeon."

Alexei is coming around, able to reason again: "Father Rauf is no surgeon either. You only say him because the gospels will calm me. Anastasia would calm me, too."

In the end they agree to walk out into the lake until he is waist-deep. Anything more than that, he assures, will consume him.

The clay under his feet is hard but not slippery. His mother has brought him to the shore in her cart. He is as light as vegetables tonight, like unharvested barley. University students used to come here, check the water all along the bank and in the middle at depths of one, five, and twenty feet. The samples were all the same, half-solid from bits of mineral floating around.

Nor is there rot, it is too infertile for rot. Only the joining of water and stone. Moreover, dead lake is not the proper term. This is a place that has always been without life.

Mama stays back more than two feet, to keep from wetting her stomach. She has come out to keep him upright, but hyperventilates with cold, swimming in the Russian steppe in winter. It is precious energy, what they lose from shivering arms. The pond is ringed with ice at the bank. Precisely level, exactly white.

They could use the researchers again now, what with their state-of-the-art methods of fever control, pain control. Her peasant way will only kill both of them.

He stands, frail with spasms. Here, outside of the house, the minutes are slower than ever. At last mama says, "Is that better? Alexei?"

"Why? Are you better?"

They stand, always waiting. She is watching the red patches of skin on his cheeks and will not haul him in until the patches are gone. While they are here, he knows she will ask about the slates and at last she does. It has taken her 15 minutes to bring it up. Even her thoughts are freezing to ice.

What she says is, "You could tie off another slate. You could ask papa about Tulcea."

#

Here is a question for the lake.

Before the war started the boy took knives and dug from the earth square, clay pieces, cutting questions into the flat parts, leaving them in the water with a rope.

The inquiries were brief, primary: Am I five years old? Am I a child? Is the sky good? When he turned his back, which was often, his father would pull at the rope and dry the slate, carve in the answers: Yes, yes, yes.

After a time, Alexei grew smart to the trick and they spent a year asking and answering in the same way, but openly. The son would find a slate and tie it off, scraping his problem into the clay. The father would in a day or two notice the taut line: a boy fishing not for carp but for insight, each inquiry sharper than the last: What is grass? What is kindness? Why are there different kinds of love? Soon his father only had space for symbols, not words, oracle runes that Alexei could interpret as he liked. Young boys do that anyway, with all but our most direct answers.

It was just as well, because Alexei had started tossing in pieces of slate without tether, those matters he knew papa would never answer, or responses he didn't want to hear: Is Genesis bollocks? If we reach paradise together will you be young again? If I am older than you in life will I be older after life? How can anything be eternal?

Tonight mama says, "Wouldn't you like to know what he's at?"

"He doesn't answer the slates from afar. He does it right from the dock."

"But it could be waiting for him here. Waiting for both of you."

Alexei will only tell her if she asks, that there is a piece of rock already, at the dock-end, near the bottom of his ladder. The piece is fully submerged, held in a leaning position by the last rung, which none of them use. There are no snakes on the bottom, but he jumps from the middle rung as if there were. All of the family does.

They fear the water more without plants and serpents than they would if there were. There is a heavy weight to the surface that he does not care for. And because there are no observed creatures here, there is full room for the imagined ones. Make-believe animals in centrifuge water.

As for the slate, he wrote the question during the summer of 1914, when the ceramic pond was ionized in sun. He walked straight in from the bank, no need for the dock. He did not shiver at all. The question was: Will there always be a Russia?

He chose a difficult one on purpose. He is quite convinced of it, that if a son has unanswered questions the father will live on. Uncertainty will act as a shield, no matter how many of Karl's cavalry brothers fall around him. No need for second questions, the first will do.

You could tie off another slate. If Alexei gives in his mother will suspect and if he continues to resist, she will press on. He can end the discussion with only one word, an exact one, and he does: "Maybe."

She presses lips to his head. Affection, yes, but mostly to ensure that his fever is less. The mineral lake is unmoving and it would be a horrible sight if you came on them now. A woman and her stricken son, both miserable and half-buried. A last kiss before the telegram.

#

Breakfast in the morning is beets, for the inflammation, and lemon, for better health. There is no bread and it would take his mother all day to buy more. Sugar lines, wheat hoarding, black-market food, no herbs, these are the tsar's ideas for a better Russia.

The beets are a gift from the neighbor, who saw them standing in the glacial water and grew worried. The lemons, mama bought in January. They have jars of pears, too, but those are papa's favorite. If they open a jar they will have to eat all of it, one fewer for Karl.

Alexei is too weak to enjoy the meal. The voltaic mix leaves him scraped up, tongue to stomach.

Mama sees the circle of red on the outside of his mouth and gasps. The impression is of blood, and when he spots a mirror, he understands. The crimson beet residue makes him look like a boxer with a jab to the mouth.

Later in the day, his first piss will look like blood, too.

Thoughts of toughs make him act like a tough and he spits a lemon seed onto the rug without knowing. His mother sees and chides him for it, "I will leave that where it is and you can clean it up when you're well. I hope that day comes before a tree grows out of my floor."

"At least we would have food again."

Good, they are taking swats at each other, starting to act normal again.

The pain and fever are back at dusk; the boy cannot deny that last night's frigid bath restored him. They repeat it tonight and he sits in what for her is hem-deep water, letting it fully cover his legs. He leans forward, elbows in, troubled by the nagging slowness of the world, and by that no one else seems to know. Shivering or not, Alexei cannot hold the pose for long. He lies back, partially buoyant, the taste of rusted metal lapping at his mouth.

"Does it feel better?"

Her voice makes him lurch. As premonitions go it is a lousy one: the young, bleeding man sleeping in water, waking to the sound of his mother's voice. She is distant, worried, above ground.

Anastasia comes in the morning and his mother, who would have disapproved a week ago, is glad to see her. The woman wants sleep, needs to try the food lines in the afternoon. She brings the girl to Alexei's bedroom: "Look who has come!" When she shuffles away, it is with a foot turned at an angle and dragging behind. Now that she has a chance for a brief nap she is all but asleep already, still upright.

His girlfriend is half-pretty but, the way Alexei understands it, her mother is quite beautiful. Nor is Anastasia made for horses the way her father is. A long path, more seam than scar, runs from ear to cheekbone, where it splits. One branch is high, toward her lip, the other aims at her chin. It is the result of a saddle fall.

The outline and size make him think of a scorpion, with its stinger buried under the hair near her temple. Hard for him to describe her face beyond that scar although if he considered it, he would note the cinnamon hue, lackluster chin, healthy cheeks. "Mixed blood," his mother said, not too long ago. "African mother, Russian father, French mother." He was not sure how to respond about the second mother.

He has named the scorpion Alexander IV and tells Anastasia that it is her chastity guard. But the way he understands love play, a sting would only press him forward.

She offers their normal virgin greeting: hand up, flared out, meant for him to reach and interlace fingers. Doing it hurts every one of his knuckles and he tries not to wince. She says, "I saw that, Alexei Karlovich." He will not think of himself as Karlovich for long.

They only sit and watch. The trees are not doing anything until you look far off, past the lake, which is high today. It makes her remember something from her studies and she says, "I heard this week there is a basement kitchen in Alexander's Palace, with a tunnel to the main building and a drain." She is always telling stories about Tsarskoye Selo, as would a traveler who will visit it soon.

"A drain? Because of submerging?"

"The underground rooms at Winter Palace flooded once. Or it was Alexander Palace, I don't know."

Forget her answer, he will enjoy thinking of it his way. Floods before a meal, as the empress prays for nutrition.

Her palm is on his leg, deliberate in that it is safe from knee joint, from hip joint, which are visible through the blanket. Normally her touch would rouse him but his blood is pooling elsewhere, all around, over a dozen pockets that fill with coins. Money he can count but never spend.

When she says, "How did it happen?" he is mute. The roof climb was too rash to tell. Let his mother say it if the girl has to know. She leaves by kissing in the direction of his ear. Very French.

Days come without food, letter or healing. But the room smells of discarded lunch.

Because of his father's rank and friendship with the tsar, two imperial officers come to tell the family, before the telegram arrives. The news causes his mother to flinch as if they smacked her with a loud hand. She bites at the announcement and swallows it whole; a mouthful of rancid beef.

Karl and Revekka lost two children before Alexei was born and mama is not close to her family, which is small, lives elsewhere. Paris, maybe.

She will never remarry. But she seems to refuse it, her best chance at grief.

When the men leave she closes Alexei off with a door. In another hour she will be at his bed again, making a duck-wing out of her hair, running both hands through, over and over until it stays. "What will we do, Alexei-bear? What are we going to do?"

But there is no questioning it. They will continue to starve and then move to Moscow, where Grandfather Konstantin is. The proceeds of selling the house—this lakefront with mud in the well, no fish or crops—will barely cover the transfer south. Alexei's grandfather is, ultimately, a good man, but his mood can be a spectacle. Every one of his ideas is bad.

"I'm so sorry, Alexei. I cannot imagine."

She will dry his face by pushing outward, moistening his hair. He will rest and ache, try not to blame his mother for a war death.

#

With so much talk of his internal bleeding he would think, if only once, mama would say something about internal scarring. No doubt his hollows are as battle-marked as anyone's, with line-shaped wounds that skew, converge, run parallel, in more than not a prevailing direction. Or instead, letters becomes words. Shapes become visual arts. It is a novel Anastasia would have to murder before she could read it.

#

Here is an odd realization: Alexei did not stand during the news of his father and he has not stood yet. Every time his mother cries the skin around her eyes looks peppered with chili grind. The worse, the redder, so much that tonight she looks ready to dissolve into curry. She must have sobbed again while he dozed.

This is what Anastasia tells him about the monk: his name was Father Grigori Novykh, no patronymic. He was a strannik, drunkard, politician, con artist. Anastasia says, "There was no salt, no body. It was nothing to do with a river. A cave opened under his bed and he was swallowed whole."

"Then what of mama's fear? That the empress will have a prince murdered?"

The girl says, "Grigori speaks only Russian, and poorly. The empress speaks French, English, German, and a little Russian. Forget the rumors; I do not believe they converse at all. It seems impossible that he has any control."

"But the scriptures are in Greek, do they not share Greek?" That much has always nagged at him; that his bronze-age faith was written in the same language as the pantheon of myths, fates. And those are ridiculous.

Anastasia says, "The scriptures are the word of God and the word of God transcends language." When she talks like this he knows he is arguing not with her, but with her mother, who is mad and thinks of everything.

Today he and Petrograd-Alexei share more than a name and ailment. One has a dead father and the other, a dead Father, both killed, in a way, by aristocracy.

Chapter Two

GIVEN THE CONDITION of the body, the Shafirovs must settle for an empty funeral box. Rarely do you see mama protest like this: "Sir? My Karl will not rest until we bury him fully."

To believe this response is to accept that a ghost, her murdered husband, will make the trip from Tulcea and find his way home. Karl will wait in the streets, visit Alexei at school, or here, when the boy sits with Anastasia. Revekka and her son will know the shadow on sight, hear his voice in the leaves.

Not a haunting, necessarily, because each side will haunt the other.

It is an army officer who has come to tell her but he is mostly forced to listen. He somewhat resembles admin as well as military command, what with the high shoulders, grave expression and so little color anywhere. His skin, clothes, hair, all within the grays.

An overcast man. Even the Russian winter is not sure what to do with him.

What the officer is trying to avoid saying is that the body of Alexei's father is gone, including the face. Busted in, blown off, turned to splash, taken as souvenir, who knows. Perhaps the man does not read the death reports as a matter of policy, for better negotiating with the widows.

All he has left to say, to each of her statements, is, "Lady, you would not recognize your husband. No characteristics."

"If I may speak with some candor, I wonder if he was killed at all. If Karl Shafirov was dead the tsar would not report it to me this way. Officers, telegrams. A simple visit."

"I assure you."

"Then assure me with his remains, in whatever their state. When a government returns a body the family takes comfort in it. Small comfort, whether they know it or not. It is their reassurance they were not told in error."

"Then what I am saying is you would not be reassured. Not to talk explicitly, but there is nothing you could identify."

"If my husband's appearance is so grotesque I will close the casket. That much is easy."

The officer looks away to gulp, as if she has spoon-fed him something mealy.

She says, "And you forget a woman's ability to recognize her husband. Now I am the one who is going to be explicit because I could tell from a patch of skin. I have spent enough time looking at it. I would know from one scar, any birthmark, whether you had sent me the right man."

The visitor is trying not to blush and he removes his eyeglasses, now returns them. He says, "It was a terrible battle. There were too many dead to count and one of our own has confirmed the casualties."

"You say there were too many to count. Then you say it is one man doing all of the counting."

The officer's hands are shaking and he pats at four pockets. Both hands, two pats each. Is he looking for tobacco or, just as likely, is it mere symmetry that calms him? He says, "The man is one of our princes and there is an infection in his leg. He will recover at Tsarskoye Selo. The empress has set up hospitals there and works with her daughters as nurses. You can visit him when he arrives."

"What is the boy's name?"

"Prince Vladimir Mikhailovich Bey, of Crimea."

"You will notify me when Vladimir Bey returns to Petrograd?"

She has refused the honorific and patronymic, and the officer rightly understands the conversation is done. But does he want to mention something else, or correct an earlier remark? All at once his attention is divided.

"Sir? You will notify me, yes?"

So many pitiful gestures in so short a conversation. Is this the best whom the tsar could enlist?

And before the officer leaves he sees that the widow has struck herself with furniture, let blood trickle down her shin. It is likely that she does not know. The man gets the handkerchief in his trouser pocket and gestures for her to take it. "Here. Please, here."

"What?"

"The blood. Under your—" He means to say under the knee but cannot think of the word. Now, given the look on her face, he will never think of it.

"The blood under my what, sir?"

When she notices at last, she bends at the waist, cups a hand and collects it as she would a bird. Somehow it dislodges what the man was trying to tell her and, as she stares into her palm, he says, "I left a footlocker by your door. Some personal effects, although there may be more. It is so heavy that I assume—do you need me to bring it inside?"

"Do not assume. I need only one thing from the army."

"I must ask you, please do not dispose of the contents."

Mama ignores the case until late at night. The last Alexei hears before he sleeps is the woman grunting with effort, dragging. Grit across grit.

She whimpers after her first look inside.

They were not supposed to say goodbye to Karl like this. When the man died the moon should have been yards away, and dogs were to always howl his name.

\#

Services are in two days. Alexei is in too much pain to go, but no matter. With an empty casket, their church may as well be burying the shovel.

Mama knows the event will take hours and invites Anastasia to come, to watch the boy, along with her mother. They are to arrive at daybreak, but it is full light before the girl is here. She is on her own; her mother could only send regrets.

Alexei hears them talking at the door, their voices changed by walls. "It is a lovely dress. You look just like Alix."

"That's kind, Anastasia. I suppose I will meet her soon, at the hospital. Then we will know if I favor her or not."

"She is the ideal, and of course you favor her." The girl has said it before, exactly those words. But Russian suspicion of the German-born empress has grown since the start of war. Alexandra's friendship with the last of the monks made sure of it.

The girl seems happy; Alexei likes the way hair falls out of place and covers her eyes, makes her smile. She forgets herself, forgets the reason she has come, and drops on the foot of the bed, bouncing all of his joints. She tries to apologize, but he has quacked with pain, a ridiculous sound that makes them laugh. She stands, now collapses with laughter, her head bouncing him at the lower abdomen, an inch from the rooster. He should know little about that, but, when he was a boy, he spied on his mother taking his father into the mouth, her body above Karl's in almost exactly this way.

There was an electrical storm that night, and every flash was a moment of daylight. The colors, surprisingly vibrant, and his father's jowls were bright red.

A myth born of lightning, like all the best myths are.

After they collect themselves Anastasia lifts her satchel high for the boy to see. There is the good word first, also Paul Verlaine's word, and a novel in English, *Dorian Gray*. She speaks some of Wilde's mother tongue, but Alexei does not speak it ever. She would have to translate and, because neither is in the mood for that or for scriptures, the choice is old French poetry again.

She begins, following the words with fingers, as if reading a map. That is perhaps the best description of poetry he could offer, a map of meaning instead of cities.

Both could recite the first line by heart: "*Melancholia*, for Ernest Boutier."

Not so many pages in, she puts the book down, her eyes clouding over. Her voice has not started to break but he is sure of it, she has not recovered from the dedication. He says, "What is it?"

"I would rather you not go back to Moscow."

What he ought to say is, —There is no money here. No bread or order. We can stay and starve alone or we can go to Moscow and starve with my grandfather.

But there is both, bread and money, you only need to convince the wealthy that they are too ill to keep it. That sounds like a bizarre sickness, yet if Anastasia and Alexei could unravel it they would never be without.

What he says is, "I have to."

"Then we have to, too."

He shrugs, leaves his next question unsaid.

#

She is the ideal.

Will the girl never outgrow her affection for the Romanovs? She holds fanciful conversations about them, a new favorite every time they speak, all manner of inventions. But talk of the imperial line makes Alexei sick with worry, for reasons he does not see. Catherine forced her husband Peter III to abdicate then ordered him hauled off in secret, likely killed while resisting. Catherine's son, Paul I, was strangled by officers. Alexander II was killed by a bomb, his legs and groin blown away. The tsar's uncle was killed years later, another bomb. One surname, so much violence.

More than just the Romanovs. Among the slain advisors, Pyotr Stolypin and Father Grigori shock him the most, although there were two attempts on Minister Witte. Why does Alexei fret? Because if Russian cruelty can reach all the way to the emperors, he and mama are helpless against it. But the girl is retelling the House of Romanov as a thing of magic.

The way Anastasia says it, Grand Duke Kirill did not sink with his warship, but was in fact north at the time, in the Arctic Circle. The vice-admiral and Kirill made sure of staff loyalties by breaking ceramic scream jars, of all the cooks, guards, dressers, grooms, infantrymen. In each of those pots was the hair of the staff member, a thing of the suspect's essence. When the grand duke shattered the jars one by one, the terracotta cried out, from which the name. It caused the staff pain, hemorrhage, vomiting. No one who had given hair was exempt from it, but those who were not faithful to the tsar would die.

"The church forbids them," Anastasia said once. "This is why Kirill sailed to the pole."

"The church cannot forbid it if it doesn't exist."

"Why wouldn't they exist? Of course they do."

Better are her tales of Grand Duchess Olga, who wakes early and intoxicates herself with bee stings. The girl is drunk all day, the way a windy orchid is drunk. In her stories the grand duchess keeps a hive in the stable, and has grown quite dependent.

Also, her citation of Grand Duke Paul, whom she claims was not exiled to Paris, but woke one morning to an elevator car in the plaza. On the far end of the car was Montmartre, and he simply walked through, nothing to do with banishment. Anastasia says when a Romanov dies, he leaves a vast crater in place of a corpse. And when he returns it will be in an underground current of water.

The girl's namesake, the youngest grand duchess, Anastasia, can speak to others from her sleep, yet she never betrays the most scrumptious of gossip. One of the Romanov counts wakes from poem-dreams and writes the verses out, word for word.

More than the rest the girl is taken with the empress, whom she calls mama, or Alix. Not because the woman is beautiful or enchanted, but because she is not.

Alexei only responds one way, telling her that his favorite Romanov is Alexander IV, the scorpion drawn into her cheek. When he does, Anastasia will smack him on the arm and they will consider it finished.

#

The funeral is not over until late. When mama returns she checks her son's forehead, kisses each child on the hair and shuts them out. They can only whisper but Anastasia's plan is formed anyway: there is a market near where she can buy Molokai red salt, and volcanic salt. They will mix it, heat it, season it if they have to. Work until the flavor is new.

Alexei resembles faith medicine already, the gaunt child who shivers when he breathes. He does not know much of healers and their herbs, he thinks of them as he does of the blizzard over a frozen well. The snow melts first and you are quenched while standing on ice. But then the ice melts and you are drowned.

Men of healing drown, and drown their patients, much the same way. He does not have a single example but he believes it to be true.

Revekka will be gone more than ever, looking for sewing work or, like today, only closing herself off in the bedroom. Even if Anastasia brings patients inside his mother will rarely see them. On the times that she does, he will tell her the guests have come to pray.

That will be enough for now. When money starts to add up mama will forget her questions. More likely she will play along.

Anastasia has a first patient in mind: a childless aristocrat woman within a month of 30. The patient cites a number of things, "listless, anxiety, panic, hypochondria, nostalgia, boredom," as if any of those were different from the rest. The children agree on this much, it is better to start their new clinic with a hysterical case than one with pathogens. And who can say the best cures for a mood aren't spices, advisors, scriptures?

Alexei says, "How do you know her?"

"She sent for me."

"Sent how?"

There is not much to prepare, the girl insists they are ready for a prompt visit. Yet events may forbid the patient's travel. In Petrograd, International Woman's Day turns into an uprising. It is not his mother who tells him, but the officer, the one who brought the footlocker. Mama greets the visitor coolly and says little. He has to state his reasons again, and she has no interest in hearing.

The man says, "Have you been through the crate?"

Her eyes whip toward Alexei and back, and the sting is hardly different. More painful, too, because she does not answer. She responds to a different question instead: "I will never be finished with it." To what does she want the boy ignorant?

The officer says, "I should have asked, would you like to know more of any of the contents?"

"I am his widow, I should hope so."

"In that case you will remember we spoke of Bey, who can give you an account of the last battle. I only come to suggest you visit him soon, fate being as it is."

"Fate?"

"The defections and uprising."

"Defections!"

"It was such a racket you must have heard it from here. Nicholas has abdicated for himself and for his son. As it happens, he is the last of the tsars, but, even in light of it, the empress is committed to her hospital."

Mama sits, tries to find her mouth with fingertips. Yes, they have heard of mutinies, and the anonymous death threats to General Brusilov, even during his victories. Russian soldiers walk away from the front, troops fire at empty cognac bottles in the street.

But this is wholly another matter. The Romanovs have held thrones for centuries, have become Russia herself. One does not cut away the throne of Russia without also cutting away Russia.

She says, "The last of the tsars? Who is governing?"

"The empress has asked those troops with imperial loyalties to remove the badge, for their protection."

"I ask to whom Nicholas has abdicated. Who is on the throne?"

"There is no throne, lady. There is only the Duma, but you know of the Duma."

"I should, yes."

"There are no phones or trains. The supplies are dry. Some personnel are leaving Tsarskoye Selo but others are garrisoned there. They seem hostile to the tsar."

He falls into that dance of hands again and says, "I keep calling Nicholas the tsar where I shouldn't. The Romanovs are prisoners in their home. The men jeer at him, they blow smoke in his faces and do not salute. His paintings are all removed. I fear Tsarskoye Selo will not be for long. You must come soon. I could make arrangements for us to travel in the morning, if you would."

In his stammering the officer has said faces instead of face and days ago that would have been sedition.

Revekka says, "My son, his knees." The impression is that mama has added to the old curse—my Father, His nails; my son, his knees—but she is pointing in the boy's direction, too. Despite his frail health, he does not believe she would profane him.

She says, "Alexei cannot go. But I wonder something."

"What is it?"

"It has been two weeks since you came. This prince was in a bad state then, about to come back from the front even with war and strike. Now that we have no tsar, and there is no food at the hospital, this trip took him, say, a week. Or 10 days. But in the best conditions, if he were healthy, it should have been more than that. However, the transfer was never delayed or once reconsidered?"

"My apologies, which one of those was your question?"

"Please do not feign. You told us that Prince Vladimir was wounded in the same battle that took my husband. The boy was going to make his way to Petrograd and, when he was ready, he would receive me. Now all at once he is here, and well enough to meet with survivors."

"My first visit was February, as you say. In the meantime the prince has come."

"Impossible, sir. Much too fast, given everything that is happening in Europe."

The officer searches for an answer up and to the right. Alexei has seen his mother do the opposite, casting her eyes high and to the left. At least this way, when they face each other, they will find their responses in the same place.

The man says, "My apologies, lady. It is difficult to keep track of so many. You are right, by the time of my visit the prince was at Alexandra's hospital."

The officer's lie is clear, only his intents are not. The behavior tastes to Alexei of vinegar, but in the dark of the throat, where there is no hope of spitting it out.

His mother says: "Fine, then. We will go."

"Everything is fleeting. Today's lieutenant is tomorrow's peasant. For that, today's peasant is tomorrow's baron."

She says, "I agreed, yet you continue to ask? Come for me at daybreak, the morning after next. I will spend tomorrow making arrangements."

Alexei does not want her to go alone but she is right to forbid his travel. His skin is yellow and his joints tight; they pinch at any angle.

Mama says, "It is an overnight trip, I suppose?"

"Do you think it would be less? For every hour you plan to spend on the train, we will be two."

But she will not return after one day or two days; it will be four. When she comes home, she will speak of a place that should have still been beautiful.

#

Anastasia's mother has failed to show up again, and it is time for Revekka to leave. The girl says, "She'll be here soon. She begs so many pardons, mama. Daybreak comes early for our home. I can only imagine what you think of us."

Mama says, "I am beginning to wonder if my son's friend is an orphan." But she cannot wait, the officer has come and is impatient.

Revekka leaves an adieu for each child and the man says, "If you think of speaking English or French you must not, at least outside of the home. Those are not the languages of the aristocracy anymore. They are considered the code speech of resistance. Nationalist fevers are quite high."

Alexei and Anastasia pass the first afternoon with her purchases, tasting the combinations of salts. One of the reds feels the same as needles, while this dark one here tastes of fertile ground. After a few combinations they cannot taste at all and Anastasia unpacks bread, now ill-prepared cocoa, which fills his mouth with chalk.

She says, "Try again. One ounce of Vasili, one ounce of Vachot, a bit less Jeanne Marie." She has given each salt weird nicknames. The girl is always playful. Play and poetry.

She licks her finger and dips it into the blend, now points it toward his throat as if it were the mineral that needed directions. The flavor does not settle and his mouth changes around it. The impression is of discomfort.

A vibrant flavor, thick residue. It is perfect and he says so.

Anastasia says, "Good. I will bring your first patient. Remember the one I told you about? Natalia Baratova?"

"Bring me a patient? You mean this week?"

"Which week is better? Mama is gone until tomorrow, late. We have the mix and our Bibles. Natalia will come inside, we will pray, it is mostly done. We will tell her the remains of the father are here. She is a storm of feelings but nothing too bad. It is not as though she is sick in her body."

"I can still hardly move."

Anastasia checks the lake from indoors, once with and once without her eyeglasses. Is her perspective improved in myopia? It seems a highly mystical act and he wonders if she should be the one to heal the Baratova woman, not him.

She says, "How about a walk into the pond? I'll be with you."

He would do it for only the glimpse of Anastasia's leg, but no, she is not as strong as his mother. With so much shivering they would both fall, succumb to cramps. Drown in chest-deep water. He refuses.

"Go find her if you have to. I'm not swimming again today."

He regrets the curt response because in 20 minutes she is out, looking again. Without her powdery scent there is only the everyday whiff of manure, which he does not get until there is nothing else to smell.

Chapter Three

THANK PROVIDENCE, for all of them, that Natalia Baratova is as anxious as she is. It better conceals Alexei's poor nerves.

Or would it have been better if she were loud and indulgent? If so, he could have picked one of the short verses and fed her a tablespoon of mix. From there he might have yawned, feigned exhaustion, which would not have been difficult to do. They would have collected his earnings and sent her on.

But Natalia is tall, with large hands and a full neck. Vulnerable in the way of a high building. Alexei has heard of blacks serving on the Russian court, earning their place among the aristocracy, and he discounted it. Yet her skin is dark, too dark for Mongol blood—as rich as ink. A peasant? Impossible, look only at her clothes. Anyway her French is effortless. The boy considers himself a part of the modern world, but he expected her accent to be coarse, agrarian. Russian at least. It is as fluent as Anastasia's and, when he accounts for different girths and ages, he sees a resemblance between those two.

Whenever he speaks to Anastasia of her heritage, this is her answer, or something close to it: "All of the places where the sky decides the music. Sudan, Siberia, Japan."

Sudan is always first, and she seems to know about sandstorms, too. The way she tells it, they are the rivers of earth and our bodies are trout.

They scarcely have time to introduce before Natalia speaks of Russia: "I fear for her, turning from God and the law. Such a lie, these elections. A Romanov is taught from birth in the matters of ruling. Nicholas has brothers and cousins in high office all throughout the army, and in other nations, too."

Alexei agrees with her but is tempted to dispute it. Elections are a lie? he would say. There are democracies the world over that would contest that.

He can only name a few and for this he keeps it to himself.

The Baratova woman goes on, "They hope to call it Soldatskoye Selo, now. But did you know? Those dogs chased Tatiana up a ladder, onto the roof of Catherine Palace. She has been sick, very sick. She has no voice to scream and the brethren knew nothing of it."

"Brethren?" Now the guest is speaking to Alexei like they were old friends, as if they knew each other, and knew other things together.

"Imagine, a score of men against only one girl. But before they could touch her they splashed."

It is rare for him to doubt so much all at once. Yet he is not as proficient in French as she is and the last of it, *ils éclabousser*, could mean anything. It could be one word or five.

The more, the better. Alexei has found that those speaking in one word, or only a few, are telling the truth.

He says, "Pardon?"

"They splashed, soiled. Turned to hot wax. It was well deserved, too. And when Tatiana was ready to climb down the ladder, the ghosts were dead lamps, and they helped light the way."

He shrugs, dismisses the news as distant, too strange to be true. But she is not finished. Natalia says, "They are seizing farms. The nation will starve. The same way the tsar is born to rule, a landowner is born to farm. Now the mob has taken the land and will make ruin of it. We will starve from the lack of throne and lack of bread."

Alexei did not prepare any remarks for her, inwardly or on paper. He had plenty of time to; Anastasia left yesterday evening, after preparing lunch, dinner, today's breakfast. The girl set up an array of chairs leading from the bed to the rear of house, for if he needed to empty a chamber pot.

But when he used it—that is, her path of unsteady handrails—he toppled over, banging his knee with full weight, spilling a container of piss on the floor.

He soaked up the urine with a towel, sobbing, then throwing away the towel, which seemed precious for that reason alone.

Anastasia was gone until morning, finding the boy thirsty and inflamed, angry in his sleep. Natalia did not come for another three hours and despite so much time alone, he never rehearsed for the guest. He regrets it now, because the woman has positively taken over:

"Do they think ours is the only country with wind? Drought? War? Every place on earth has those, but only Russia chooses Bolshevism instead of laws."

"My friend, please."

"I know. I apologize and I know. We are here to talk about my problems. I suppose a shared illness is not what you can cure."

Alexei does not like the word cure and sends it off. Now the woman says, "Your friend tells me you have come across the remains of Grigori Novykh. And that you will administer it with a prayer."

"We have the yearner's salt, yes. And we can suppose what his favorite prayers were. Mostly verses about love."

One of the many succulent details of French is its renown word for love, *amour*. The singular form of the noun is masculine and the plural form, feminine. It is a riddle Alexei will consider at length before he knows if he agrees.

It will take him a year, and two bouts with coma, before he says the gendered forms of *sel* ought to be the same as *amour*. Masculine in the singular, feminine in the plural.

Natalia says, "I would think, nourishing my body with Father Grigori will do nothing about my husband's time away. A prayer will do nothing about his time away."

"Not true. What is the difference between the strength to endure and the strength to refuse to endure? It is only strength." Anastasia stands where he can see her and Natalia cannot. The girl nods with a lovely smile, gestures him along.

Natalia says, "I understand. But I have endured it this long. I have not once refused him."

"But have you endured? The arrangement has made you sick. You have come here from Petrograd, which is a risk and a terrible inconvenience, and you ask help from a soldier's orphan."

The woman bows. His is a rhetorical win, and only by chance.

Alexei had time to commit the prayer, at least, to memory. He says, "The heavens vanish like smoke, the earth will wear out like a garment, and they who dwell in it will die in like manner; but my salvation will be forever."

Their visitor has started to cry a little, although she puts no sound to it, and it does not change her voice. She says: "Am I the sky turned to smoke? Or am I the fabric of his clothes too old to salvage?"

When Anastasia hands the salt to Alexei they cannot help the appearance of ritual. He feared the moment would cause him to laugh, ruin the game, but no, terror makes him reverent. Grains fall through his skinny fingers as he pinches with the opposite hand. Natalia gasps, says, "Careful with it, love. Careful. I cannot imagine the cost."

"It came to us as any salt would."

The woman eats greedily, pushing her tongue out, her mouth aimed up.

When the ceremony is done she stays and asks the children of their lives, schooling. Alexei is distant, expects his mother soon and does not say much, hoping the visit will be short. In time he dozes, often makes adjustments from one hip to the other. The hours in bed are as painful now as standing. But Natalia is content to chat—at times is nearly treasonous—and Anastasia seems to welcome it. They speak like sisters:

"You say it was drought that caused the famine and unrest? Child, do you think Russian weather is different from other weather, from the rest of the world? The famine was because of policies, and it was made worse with policies. Nicholas should be ashamed."

"We shouldn't impugn the Romanovs any more. Nicholas is no longer tsar, the Duma is no longer the thing of an emperor."

"No, but the Bolsheviks will fall into the same hole. Worse than the same." Her clumsy metaphor, which is also stumbling into a hole, seems to have followed both of them in. She says, "Whether nations or plains again, I still mourn the world."

"And why is that?"

"We have forgotten how to turn wheat to bread. In either case it is wasted."

"Yes, I have heard the old songs."

"Putting it to rhyme does not make it a lie."

Later, of art preferences, they clash a second time: "Newspapers today go on about Picasso, Picasso, Picasso. His work reminds them of physics and how the universities love ignorance. Blueshift, pinkshift, the mechanical atom!"

"No, mama. I am no admirer of Picasso, but I hate his work on the opposite terms."

"Much better the paintings of my youth, my father's youth. Monet, Manet, Gonzalès, but *s'il vous plait* never Van Gogh. Too obscured."

Natalia has choked on the name as she would on phlegm in the throat and Anastasia says, "By Van Gogh you mean Vincent?"

It has been over an hour now. Before Natalia opts to leave Alexei has slept, woken up, and thought of sleeping again. She says, "Thank you, loves. I must say, I am improved. I feel cured, medically cured."

Anastasia wears a victorious face. It makes Alexei grin and, when Natalia is gone, the girl says, "An anxious woman, some prayers, a little sacrament, and look how much she has given us!" The girl fans a stack of rubles into a poker-hand and Alexei only glances. His mother is the one who buys things. Whether the pay will feed them a day or a month, he could only guess. But tonight it is he who decides how they fit their legs together.

The second visitor is not as kind.

Already Revekka has been in Petrograd for three days and the children are starting to doubt. The knock is loud, impatient. You sense he is coming inside no matter what.

Alexei hears his friend speaking in the foyer. Her voice is low and stressed. It is clear from her meter that she has to explain a great deal, is forced to make up things. Now there are boot steps on the floors, which are dry and flat from winter. During other seasons the boards turn moist from lake air and footfall throughout the house is low-register, muffled. Not this time.

Two men follow the girl in. One of them is short, thin, lovely, but such fine attributes are menacing here. It is impossible to look away from him: the one-week beard, soccer hair, rather Italian eyebrows. The other man, who will not speak at all, is normal height, narrow at the shoulders, wide at the stomach. His nose was broken when he was young and, with time, the cartilage has healed back into an awful shape. No doubt it pains him to inhale and the man holds in his breath, words.

Neither introduces himself but the handsome one says, "Sitting in pajamas with brother? In the afternoon?"

"He has been sick. I watch out for him while our mother looks for food. That takes all day, you know."

"Yes, people are hungry. You have land, you never plant?"

"The land is not fertile."

"All land is fertile if you treat her well." He turns to his companion and they both grin. "Tire her out. Make her rest while sin finds the soil."

Sin and soil. The metaphor leaves the boy mostly without, yet he has a preliminary idea.

Anastasia makes a show of rolling her eyes. The men are not dissuaded.

"Treat her well. We treat her well."

She says, "Papa would have grown crops if crops could grow. If you invited yourselves through the back of the house, you also would have seen the sterile lake."

"You say papa now? Just before that, you say mother waits in lines for bread. Also, new flowers in front. Flowers for sadness, no man in the house."

He points at Alexei. Even the arcs of dirt under his fingernails are beautiful. "You are man of house, no? It is your decision. You invite guests here to show you to plant? There are many farms around, only yours is forgot."

"I am not the man of the house and it is not forgotten. If you need better fortune we could pray together."

"Pray! We look like harlots to you?" The visit, this first of three, is done, although the kids spot them on the property now and again for an hour. Pointing, surveying, backing away from snake holes. Their movements are faraway and slow.

#

What will it feel like to bed down with her?

For as much as he resists superstition, Alexei has some of his own, and knows his are the worst. Of at least one of these beliefs he is convinced, yet it is so absurd he does not say it to anyone.

Just what is it? It is that dreams, while inexact, give voice to truth, no matter how difficult to grasp. A dream, he has decided, is never wrong.

He has made love to Anastasia in those, at least he believes he has, although her coquettish look, or no more than a quick hand to the trousers is enough to be finished. He will wake, cover himself with both hands while spasms—uncomfortable but in a way a relief—fill his palms with liquid confection.

The thought makes him spit: Do not put it that way, Alexei! He would never taste it, although it looks sweet, some kind of mix between cane sugar and milk.

Relief. If that is the best he can say about intercourse it will not be worth the effort, certainly not worth so much waiting, asking. After one of those dreams the bed is damp, soon cold, too big for just him. The sex looks to be exhausting, and from what he has heard it is 10, even 20 minutes of shared calisthenics, all for a release and, maybe, a child.

Yet when he dreams of Anastasia, the girl is prettier than she is in life. Or she comes to Alexei's bed with another face, someone unscarred, say Lidiya, from school, whom he does not mention for just that reason. She is quiet, no, all is quiet. She does not bother with heating him up, she only strips the clothes from his skin and brings him toward her with a foot, which is clean every time. The act is warm, brief, like a perfumed bath with water turned to body, and it ends in the most ecstatic of cramps. He cannot put it in any other words than those although today's intruders made him wonder if it has anything to do with loam.

#

Tomorrow she will be back. She is going to say, "Tsarskoye Selo is lovely, except for the awful cold and the weeds. If it were kept up it would be remarkable." She will tell him of manmade hills, an island with a miniature cottage, built only for children. A great and empty palace for Catherine, and the bustling, hated Alexander Palace, where the imperial family is convicted.

She will speak of a garden city from which the gardeners have fled. There used to be water ceremonies there: long, cold, exquisite rituals of church and tsar, but no more. Or if there are, it will only be the secular drowning of royalty by an insurgent priest.

She will mention, almost in passing, the delays for rail and rain, and the danger in Petrograd: strikes, a military scattered, prison convicts loose. There are belligerent infantrymen surrounding Nicholas in his home: drunk revolutionaries, filthy men wearing red badges and chewing on seeds. Often they are knee-deep in pond water, chasing fish, having already poached the swans. There is vile graffiti on benches, and without fail, an obscene interest in Alix and her four daughters.

There is talk of Grigori's carnal sway over the empress, and over the aristocrats' wives.

Mama will nearly cry about the tsesarevich's wooden rowboat, soiled with feces. There are fistfights, men stripped of their clothes, a black market for visitors to glimpse the tsar, the empress, the Romanov children.

Above it all, a rather deep hunger for Grand Duchess Tatiana. She is an adult now, and striking, yet unspoiled the way a child is.

Of papa's end she will say little. Only, "It was best the casket was empty," and then make that look of hers which means no questions. She will conclude that Prince Vladimir is kind, has been through a great deal. She will confess that it was too soon, that Bey had only just arrived and had not sorted out his thoughts yet. Her visit, therefore, put the man in an impossible bind.

She will speak at length of Alexander Sergeevich Mamontov, or Little Sergei, who is building a metal golem with bits of armor, casing and small parts, as he can get his hands on them. The description will give Alexei the idea of a slapdash, almost vulgar work but his mother will insist it, the piece transcends that. "She is beautiful," the woman will say, then repeat.

Every time she speaks of the golem it is not it, but she.

"Her name is Freyja and I will be sure to see her again."

Is mama, as she claims, infatuated with the metal sculpture, barely five feet tall and unfinished? Or with the sculptor? The boy would not blame her if she was; so much time in bed has left him feeling nostalgic, too. Friendless, and with so many unwanted memories. It will take him years to realize there is only one memory.

It was Anastasia who proposed the word yearner. Alexei loved it at once. It seemed to already mean something to the girl.

#

Once when Alexei walked with the neighbor child, Mikhail, the two trapped a pigeon. It was the abandoned church close to where mama bought plums and dates, a place by now humble with weeds. He does not remember how Mikhail succeeded, but it could not have been simple. That other boy was 14 and thick, thickheaded. Alexei was 11 and smarter, but did not help much. No doubt Mikhail left out seeds and had to wait.

The catch left the bird mostly dead and they decided a kill was the most humane way. Mikhail snapped a small branch into a blade and put it in the bird's chest. The thing was flipped on its back now and made a dreadful, unchirping motion with its wings. A macabre swim across dirt.

The younger boy cried out, looked away. He asked his friend to end it. Mikhail, and later papa, assured him it was already done—that the pigeon was dead and the spectacle was only reflex. But Alexei knew better. What they had seen instead was how death was a watery realm, which we never glimpse until it is our time. The living mostly continue to believe, that the land of dying is one of the dry realms.

#

At last, the next afternoon, his mother is home. Her white scarf is gone and her black woolen coat smells of minor adventures.

Anastasia is ready with another lie. So much deception is unbecoming of her but the girl does it for the wheat, or at least money. She says, "My mother left a few hours ago. She is not feeling well again. She asked I give you this." The girl pushes a handful of bills toward Revekka. These are not all of the proceeds; Alexei made sure she took some.

Mama says, "What is it?"

"She has been fundraising for you," Alexei says, expecting her to claim dignity, or indignation. But the woman smiles faintly, the trip has been long. She accepts it with a nod and says, "That was kind of her. Please pass along our sorrows that she felt poorly. I trust she will recover soon."

They are the words of dismissal and yes, it is time for Anastasia to go. Both of them smell—Alexei would have been too ashamed for her to bathe him, so they did without. More than that, the steady burden of two souls in one room has left his jaw aching.

It is the first he has ever wished her to be off.

The woman offers this, that if Alexei's poor health lasts a month, they will wash him clean at Sarov, and Anastasia is free to come along. It is a holy place, with no walls, and men walk around with stomachs out, their jackfruits bare. She and Alexei would bathe together.

Anastasia has told them the waters there are curative. That, before the rise of the strannik, the empress suffered a Frenchman's curse, a hen-egg pregnancy. Alexei recalls the idea of birds hatching in his joints and thinks, See? I share more with the imperial family than a simple name.

What the boy fails to see is that no name is simple.

#

They rest from mid-afternoon until morning. Alexei wakes only one time, at what would normally be an hour after dinner, and hears her loud, rough inhales, prolonged like waves on sand. Several more hours of sleep and then, at breakfast, she says, "Do you have any questions for me, from when we spoke of Father Grigori?"

The conversation, weeks ago, is a struggle to remember. He has nearly died since then, spent most of the time in wincing pain on a bed, finding some relief in the lake. He says, "You only told me Yusupov attacked him. That he was shot and drowned and frozen."

"And after?"

"After that you poured lake water into my bed."

She laughs, pushes a tear away, thumbs it to the side the way she would flick a cigarette ash. His mother does not enjoy smoking anymore, but then she does not enjoy nostalgia, either. Grief, worry, money concerns; all of those make her cough.

"My question was, do you remember what I told you happened after?"

"You said that, at his death, Father Grigori turned to salt."

Does she know about his plot with Anastasia? She certainly must, this is not a comment she would make a second time. The deep Russian superstition mostly leaves Revekka out. It especially does now, with a dead husband and a son who cannot heal.

She knows then.

Amen, if she is going to accuse him, let it be now. He will draw it out for her, make it vice-squeeze until she gags on it and has to say it. Meanwhile Alexei replies, "That would never happen to a man, not even a magic man."

"My bear, Father Grigori was not magic, or a faith healer. He was a regular man, exactly like papa. But he knew what people needed, maybe because he needed those things himself. He knew if they should have wine, or a trick or a bible verse. He may have become salt afterward, he may not have."

Accepting that she has uncovered the plot with Anastasia, and the details of his business with Natalia, she is not troubled by them. Quite the opposite. Alexei says, "No regular man would die the way you say he died."

"Good sense would have you think so. But it is the contrary. I could, your father could. I have kept this from you for too long. One or both of your parents could die like that."

In the summer of next year, he will mourn not having heard each word of it. He will fight to retrieve this conversation, a fingertip of Catholic water lost in a bath.

He says, "Could? Did you say papa *could die*?"

"I said I could, and that your father could have."

No, her words were clear the first time. She drew no such distinction, and struggles to draw it now.

#

In another day mama tells him of a fight in Petrograd. The city is a mess, it is impossible to know liberal from Bolshevik from loyalist now. She says the soldiers there are merely soldiers, "just like papa." What does she mean by that? To hear her tell it, and quite at once, everyone is just like Alexei's father.

On the first day she and the officer came upon a crowd near the station, it was a sour welcome. The beating had finished moments ago and an angry circle was marching off, perpendicular to mama's approach.

She could not tell which of the men had brawled, or perhaps more than one were involved, but they all had wide forearms, the fists of work.

Their opponent was awake, on his back. Unspeaking, barely moving. Bleeding to death.

The officer said, "Come, Revekka! We can save him. Russia is large but it is only one man, we can save anyone we want!"

They wedged through the onlookers. The victim chattered like a rabbit, which knows no hope or medicine, nor were medical authorities near. If the officer had a method he needed to deliver it now. But they only kneeled at the man's side, some of the blood turning thick.

"We have to act."

The crowd was closed in, and the officer scanned the passersby for something, he did not say. He chose a young boy of seven. Now he took the kerchief from a businessman and her, Revekka's, scarf. He soaked the kerchief in the soldier's blood and held it to the boy's face, for drinking. The child frowned and paced back, but only one step, there was no room for more. The officer said, "No. It tastes good, like health. And it will save the man. When the pavement is clean he will stand up and walk away."

The boy was there alone; either of his parents would have forbidden it but the crowd, an otherwise shocked herd of men, seemed ready to allow it. A voice somewhere encouraged the boy to drink.

The officer repeated, "He will live because of you. If only for that, you will enjoy it."

The boy nodded and bared his teeth, caricature-wide, with, somehow, perfect incisors. The officer wrung the cloth. The boy's twitching mouth filled with blood and the kerchief was ready for soaking again. He swatted the child on the arm and said, "Good! Good." Meanwhile Revekka was struck motionless. He said, "You too! He has no time, go!"

She popped up as if the officer had slapped her face. (Despite it all she would not have hit back.) She fell into action, soaking up the bleeding man's spill with fabric. When the head covering was drenched she coiled it over her mouth, drinking, regretting the taste of ore and unlaundered clothing. She repeated it time and again, the crowd getting hazy. She thought, If you are in the middle of blacking out, *bon voyage*.

"Don't spill a drop, lady! Not one drop."

There was hurry in her side-vision. She did not look that way, but she could trust the others had bent to knees and started wiping blood from the street, drinking at their fabrics when they grew soaked. From then it was only minutes until the man was coming around. A surgeon was here and would tend to the soldier, accompany him to a hospital.

In the end the onlookers applauded those who had helped. It was mostly Revekka, the officer and the boy, and the latter two deferred their celebrity to her. The cheering grew quite raucous before it stopped.

After: the tense visit at Tsarskoye Selo and the slow fare back. On the returning train, the officer heard a conversation between two passengers. Revekka was staring off, through a window across the aisle. The officer said, "Did you hear it? The young man in the fight at Petrograd. We saved him. He is on duty again, ready for action."

"I only assumed."

This pushed the officer's face to one side, a silly look of inquiry. She did not explain, but the reason she knew was the taste of living helix in her throat. She had been belching life all day.

The flavor was full. Stamina, good fortune.

Today she says, "Do you accept what I am telling you? I saved a man by cleaning his blood from the pavement. Nothing more than that. I see that you do not believe me."

Alexei has dismissed all of it but, now that her description is finished, he knows the time is here. He says, "And I saw that you did not believe Anastasia when she told you of the money, from her mother."

"The girl has her reasons. And we can use it, I was not going to turn it away."

"In truth it was a stranger who brought it, not her mother. An aristocrat's wife from Petrograd. I cannot remember her name but I had the sense she would be back."

"Why, Alexei?"

He knows which question she is asking, but will pretend not to know. So far this is exactly what he needed to say, and it is well-performed. No use in deviating from the script with an answer she does not need.

He says, "Because she considers you to be a healer. And me, too, I guess."

"The woman learned my name and address and came before I did? Paid me without meeting me?"

"I suppose."

"Alexei there is one rail line between there and here and my train was stuck on it, while men went through our bags one by one. On the trip west we had to tip half of our rubles, plus any chickens or bread. On the way home, we gave the rest of it away, including some of my clothes. Imagine, a widow, turning over her clothes to revolutionaries."

"She is rich, mama. The rich have their ways."

"Not anymore, Alexei. I've seen it. You haven't seen it and I wouldn't let you. Petrograd is an animal den and the tsar has stepped down. Does a rich man fare any better with an animal than a poor man?"

He does not answer, how could he?

She says, "It frightens me that a woman should visit, and knows more of my business in Petrograd than you did. She is not what you say. We will not let her into our house again."

His mother is right: Natalia Baratova is not what he says. But the woman will come before the end of April. They will not argue the point for long.

Chapter Four

ANASTASIA DOES NOT smell the way she used to.

When she is close Alexei picks up cigarettes. Faint and colorful, but only the darker colors. When she coughs it is more. If she cools his meal with breath it is overcome with tobacco. He wishes she would stop, feels as if it will curdle his food.

Moreover the girl, despite her youth, is always sleepy, smudges her words, stinks of fermentation—the only ether she does not talk about. A countryside girl of 1917 is welcome to drink if not smoke, although it is not like this one to do so. She is hiding it from him, and for once he does not try to bargain. Three months ago he would have compared sins of consuming to sins of the body, but not today. Now, his body is the one consumed, there is no distinguishing sins anymore.

And after two full months in bed the last he wants is to bed her.

She comes today, heavy with nicotine again. She means to kiss him but he looks off, or pretends to. She is hurt by it and makes as if her visit will be brief. She says, "Natalia Baratova saw me on Thursday. She wants to visit again, soon. She is healed, and she has friends who want healing, that is all I needed to say. Can you do it?"

"Mama does not trust her. She is an aristocrat who knows as much as a spy. She travels the countryside free and never gets detained."

"I am surprised you told her, but mama is wise to distrust. I will tell Natalia it is off. That is too bad, though. She was bringing a wagon of grain."

The thought of grasses recalls a fungus in particular and he thinks, *Is that what is going on with her? Is she poisoned by ergot?*

He doubts it but, if so, there is no limit to what she believes. Nor will he turn away the chance for grain. A bushel of wheat would save mama a week of bread lines. He says, "It is not off, of course not. At worst Natalia is another voice for our prayers. As many voices as we can find, no?"

The girl seems to wake somewhat and smiles: "Of course, yes. And forgive my mood. I am not myself. You are always yourself—I should learn from that."

So odd a compliment, *You are always yourself.* As usual he does not explore it and, in time, he will regret that, too.

As it happens she is leaving. She is embarrassed, tired. He is sure it is not the last of her poor energy.

#

For days the boy has dreaded Natalia showing up when mama is here. Yet after the aristocrat has come, introduced herself to Revekka, he is as panicked as ever, all sorts of new things.

In contrary to her promise Natalia does not have wheat.

"My home of healing," she says, without mention of the last trip, the money, their ritual of salt. She takes some of Revekka's hair and lets it fall back in place a strand at a time: "So gorgeous." She turns to Alexei: "You need to take care of this one. Don't let the men take her off, this land agrees with her."

"Silliness." But Revekka is smiling, blushing, every one of her teeth toward the floor.

"Silliness to which?"

"To both. I'll be taking care of Alexei, not him to take care of me." The abashment has moved to her grammar.

Revekka finishes with, "And I could never leave this home." The latter seems to surprise their guest, who moves to Alexei's bed, puts knuckles through his hair, quite roughly.

"How have you been, little one?" Her question is full of time. You could grow old in it, watch children become men and women in it.

She is hoarse, too. Is the nostalgia about to leave her in tears? Alexei says, "Much better."

"Me, too. So much better, thanks to you. Despite Petrograd."

Yes, Alexei thinks. *We should speak of the capital. No more fables or secrets, we will let mama know how you came so far without hassle. If you convince her, she will welcome you.*

But Natalia's news is the opposite from that. She says, "They treat Nicholas with unmercy. They kick at his feet, curse him, say things about the grand duchesses, especially Tatiana."

Her report gives him that sense of true horror again. For the garrisons to dog the Romanovs this way means they are as callous as animals. As cruel to their countrymen as they are to the landowners, and perhaps to their fellow Bolsheviks, just like animals.

Beasts dressed as soldiers instead of men dressed as soldiers. It is hardly a new fear but, at the least, it is a reintroduced one, for the boy to weigh with the rest.

Revekka says, "Those could be rumors. I spent a day in Tsarskoye Selo and never saw the imperials, or the insignia."

"But there is a reenactment of it. Every day, the same time of day, exactly where it happened. The ghosts of Nicholas and of five mutineers, awful people. Walking from Alexander Palace to—"

Mama cannot help but interrupt: "Ghosts? Excuse me, you're saying ghosts? The ghost of Tsar Nicholas II?"

Yes, it is the second time Natalia has said it. He had only just forgotten the first, that lousy spoof about

Tatiana's aggressors turning to lamp oil. For several nights he lit them in his thoughts and they never burned. They only pushed forward, attacking. Meanwhile, the Tatiana he dreamt was lovelier than even her portraits. All the peasant boys used to dream of Alix but that is because they were told to. Tatiana, they dreamt because they could not help it.

The guest says, "I am saying Alix and Nicholas are alive, and the garrisons are alive. But it is a ghost, his ghost. I know the man well, he has the face of his uncle."

"Yes, I have heard of you. The maiden of court, who can travel at will as the Romanovs are under arrest."

Natalia smiles twice, a fragile look. The first of the expressions, Alexei thinks, is her lingering glimpse of the empress. The second is admiration for this noble widow, her persistent doubt. The woman says, "I suppose they trust me still. One does not make the other impossible, you know? The trust of the defected soldiers and the trust of a loyalist."

"I am loyal to *him*, only him." Mama points a hand, two fingers, at Alexei. Natalia turns, looks at the boy, puts fingers through his hair again. His scalp is wet and aching. She says, "Yes. I am loyal to him, too."

"You were saying about ghosts?"

"Never mind them, it is too horrible to say. And ghosts is the wrong word. Nicholas is alive for now. Dear Alix is alive, and the girls are safe."

"That is a relief."

Alexei is sure she means it and, what's more, his mother's voice is the voice of an aunt, one who has just learned her sick nieces are recovering. A relief indeed, and for that he knows mama is keeping something back, yet again.

Natalia says, "I should mention, just being here has cured me. I am a wretch, always. My chest closes in, my teeth chatter. My pupils get this big," she puts fists in front of her eyes, like a fighter. "My husband used to say if he stared too long he would fall in."

Mama laughs louder than she needs to. "Men talk about falling into our eyes. But if they did, where would they land?"

"In my case, my stomach. Everything lands in my stomach." The women continue to laugh and to prove her point Natalia slaps at her hips which, despite her height and the market prices of wheat, are nourished.

Revekka says, "I think they mean some other realm than that."

Now, a drought in the conversation, which a Russian ought to handle well. But Natalia has come too far to leave without treatment. Alexei sends his mother away with, "Some tea and bread for our guest?"

Mama steps out of the room, returns with pears instead, which are no longer for his father. Jarring the fruit has made it soft and your teeth go right through. Meanwhile, Anastasia's salt mix is under his bed, and he gestures there. Natalia bends to retrieve it.

"Thank you, dear heart. I am so improved, you might not believe. Even affairs with my husband are better." She does not pinch at the salt but rather fills the palm of one hand, takes it into her mouth like river water. Eating that much of the spice is like a jab to her mouth, causes her eyes to go moist. She paws at the nose with a sleeve. A peasant's gesture.

Natalia repeats her thanks and says, "Next I will bring a Moscow woman, a Scandinavian. Awful neuralgia. Much too young for such pain, and in both legs. I tell you, bearing a child is a miracle, but some miracles burn like fire."

Revekka shows her eyebrows, sisters in burden. She says, "In our case the fire took both of us. It took my bones and Alexei's blood."

Natalia had expected tea and stirs at the pears instead, reluctant to eat.

Revekka says, "Do you not like fruit from jars?"

"On the contrary, I do, very much."

#

Should they worry about the dogs, too? It feels as if they must, because those are nearer and nearer, always more. The child is gnawed-on with concern as it is, always checking the time, the day, the time again, restless. He has been checking the windows, too, and these feral dogs, perhaps even rabid dogs, are keen to stay on papa's land.

A dog has come inside once, yet only briefly. It was a wild shepherd, eight years ago. The thing was underfed, perilously skinny, with sharp hipbones. Revekka had left the door open and the stud wandered in, confronted papa in the main room. Karl tried shouting it out but it was muddy, with a thick, coarse hide and nowhere to den. It was a terrible racket, the dog howling, the man swearing in an infantry voice. Papa braced himself on a table and kicked wildly, aiming for the throat. He missed, and that was somehow the end. The shepherd was gone by the time Karl rose to his feet again.

When, last year, the autumn turned, there was only one dog, a frightful terrier which had partially claimed the boy's path on his return from school. After a long standoff it seemed the terrier became bored, that is until Alexei ran by and pointed, making a loud vow. The animal chased and the boy had to sprint, scaling a pile of lumber that helped him up to the entry gable. He nearly fainted from the effort and knew that would be the end, waking a minute later to the dog eating his raw innards.

By February, around the time of his fall, there were three. These days there are at least seven, "Seven or more," Revekka says about all groups, especially groups of dogs. "There are no pack members any more, only a pack."

That applies to men, too.

There is a beating in his neighborhood and the rumors are first. You hear it was a man loyal to the tsar, overcome in a brawl by a liberal. The story changes: the same man again, beaten for sport by a group. Bolsheviks perhaps, or defected soldiers. Later still, the numbers are reversed: one liberal, facing a group of Romanov sympathizers, was taken.

Alexei has never seen a nation's unraveling before but this has to be a clear sign of it. Rumor herself is becoming unstable.

He dreads how unrest is spreading from cities to countryside, and has to ask if they are learning about one fight or many. Revekka leaves for a while, a shawl around her neck, carrying other shawls in a pack. He rejects her story from the Petrograd street but she is convinced of it, intends to help, means to drink blood through fabric again. At the least it will mean calories.

She returns in two hours and, shortly from then, Anastasia comes, openly drunk. She admits it this time, and waves at their questions with contempt. "It was a fistfight. Two young men, one girl, nothing mysterious. You see now why I won't lift up my skirt?"

"Anastasia, glory to God!" Her tone is shock but she ought to be pleased, it is a young girl's chastity pledge. When mama turns away Alexei watches her face. Yes, her grin is different than her voice.

"I am sorry, Revekka." Anastasia has never called his mother that before. The short distance from ear to chin gives her face a flattened-out effect. When she yawns—whiskey and disdain—it seems as though her throat swallows her jaw in whole. Both Alexei and his mother notice it and Revekka pours the girl a water without being asked.

Staying wet does nothing for Anastasia's condition and, when she falls asleep on one of the chairs, her legs are mostly bared. Alexei thinks, *Only an hour has gone by and you're lifting your skirt again.*

In the morning his friend is embarrassed, begs pardon and messiahs. In well-fed times Revekka would bring her around with hot breakfast and tea, but there is only tea. It doesn't matter: no meal, no matter the taste, would keep Anastasia from leaving. As a goodbye she tickles the bottoms of Alexei's feet.

He insists that he can get up, walk her out but she waves. "I'll show myself the door. I deserve it."

That she is in such a hurry makes the scene rather weird. Revekka and Alexei trade eyebrows and, when the door slams, neither of them believe it. His mother checks, returns: "She's gone, if that was the question. She's half the way down the path."

Alexei gets up to follow.

He and mama have spoken of walks together, to get blood in muscle again, to rid his joints of the last of the swelling. Why? The country is mad and starved — the town is mad. Army enlistment is down, nearly critical. The war relies on very young men, teenagers. Waiting, being stuck in a bed, these are privileges boys do not have any more.

He may not keep Anastasia's pace and stamina but he will go as far as he can. To stop him Revekka would have to push him to the ground. That would injure him, so she would never do it. She only says, "Stubborn, just like your papa. Always picking the farthest war, not happy unless the way home is more fighting."

Like her best insults it has many halls, and room for echo.

They have not yet traveled a border verst, the length of their property, when they notice a soldier wandering up. Because her admonition still rings in his ears, because mama's eyes turn watery as she sees the man—because of the clouds, poor eyesight and their finest superstitions—he lets himself think it is Karl Shafirov.

Revekka knows better. She rushes ahead, but not the same way the boy would. Alexci notices the barrow, a shape inside. The boy tries to hurry, too.

His mother is crying, but in the aloof, dignified way of the peasant. When Alexei reaches them they are touching at shoulders, bowing, putting hands to cheeks. The soldier is striking in terms that Alexei is too young to get: an irregular beard that does not cover the face, strong shoulders that slump away from the neck. Their visitor's eyes are sad, if only the way animals are sad. He is a man of defeat, yet whom few could overcome in a fight.

It raises questions: why the limp? Why is he not still at war?

Revekka collects herself and says, "Alexei. This is Little Sergei." The boy knows to take a long, attentive look.

\#

She pours boiling water into a cup. She and her son look on to see if Little Sergei's hands are trembling. Good, they are still, although his calm may be professional.

"What will you do now?"

No matter which one has said it, it would have been fair to ask. In front of the man is a plain widow, her hair styled by vermin. Around her is dead land and a resurrected child. No bread, no salary. Sergei does not know about Konstantin, but it is clear she must go somewhere. Nor is it running away if a pantry is bare.

Yet here, to Revekka, is a soldier caught between three armies, more if you count those under new flags. He is handsome in a pouting, artisan way, with a face she cannot otherwise describe. War-efficient, built for a helmet. An infantryman not with a rifle but with parts of a rifle, glued here and there into the shape of a companion, whom he has named. No gunpowder, only sadness brought in close.

It is Sergei who has asked and mama says, "What do you mean? Exactly now? These coming days?"

"Yes, these coming days. About the land seizures and food."

He could say more if he wanted to, about the fall of the Romanovs, Russia, Europe. The reduction of war to industry. That he does not go on leaves Revekka with one answer: "There is nothing of this land to seize. My late husband was going to work the soil when he came home, if there was ever an end."

They watch as she chooses between unwanted gestures, now decides not to gesture at all. She says, "He used to say that farmland is where the gods come to play, but a moorland is where the gods—you get the idea."

Alexei is not so sure the man does. He says, "A moorland is where the gods come to piss," causing Revekka to chide him from under Sergei's laughter: "Little bear, please!"

"Yes, little bear. Please. Tell us more about the gods pissing on your farm." The soldier laughs again, produces a sack of tobacco, starts a roll-up.

Mama says, "But as for the anarchists coveting our land, it has not happened and I do not think it will. It cannot be as prevalent as you hear."

Alexei has not told her of the first round of intimidations, the talkative beauty and the high, silent peasant brawler. Never mind that, those men will be back before two weeks are up. They will come with another man, asking that Revekka's guest return their hair.

Little Sergei says, "You may believe the talk or not, but it is happening all around. That it has not come here is a miracle."

"From what I understand, the Bolsheviks do not believe in miracles."

"But you do." His remark is vague enough to make her look off, as does the way his hands make a cigarette from mere resources.

Revekka says, "What of you, then? The front is the other way."

"I'm not going to the front. I'm thinking of Finland. We have family there."

"Finland is the other way, too." The man smiles around his tobacco, which lends him a rather birdlike appearance and makes Alexei giggle.

This is where their will dries up. Revekka will not say outright that the man can stay, while Sergei will not offer for the two to come along. There is always Freyja, which their visitor claims will slow him down: "Unless it is acceptable that I leave her here."

Mama's disappointment is clear and she says, "You should not leave until the morning. You may of course leave Freyja here, but if you do, she belongs to Alexei."

"Morning? This knee, if I could trouble you for two days of rest, I will pay with two days of work. I could help out around here and in the land." Because she does not speak or let on that she has heard, Sergei can only finish with, "Helping out the way a man can help."

"The way a man can help? Alexei has been the man of the house for two months—he was in bed for all that time. And the years before that, more than I can count, Karl was away at war or getting ready for war. If not that he was getting other men ready for war. I do not know about how men can help. I am not familiar with it and, to be blunt, there is nothing that comes to mind."

Very well, Little Sergei will go when he wakes. He suggests putting Freyja in the footlocker near the door. Removing four of the bolts at her waist will allow her to bend in half, for easy storage.

Mama refuses that, too. She is always refusing now. It takes her days to recover when her moods are like this. She will deny what winds do to seed, disclaim that clouds ever turn to rain. She says, "Don't leave it in the army case. That one is full. We will find a place for your sculpture."

"Not a sculpture, a golem. And be careful about leaving her for too long. They do things. This is why I built her but she is weighing me down."

Do things? For example move, work, speak? Ridiculous! And Alexei believes that mama emptied the footlocker, too. His father's old boots and uniform are elsewhere, all over the home.

They agree to leave Freyja standing in a corner of Alexei's room, with a cloth on her face: "Even if you don't believe what I say, it will help you sleep."

So be it, when Little Sergei leaves he will simply remove it. It is absurd to talk of these assemblies waking up, even waking hungry, chewing on vegetables for the sake of chewing. Afterwards, cleaning the mash from their hollows, removing the steel plates from the bottom of their boots.

As to the second claim, that Freyja's face will cause him nightmares, the truth is the opposite. Her wire-mesh eyes, exposed gears and rivet patterns are stunning. When the boy touches the casing his hands are greasy, and for hours after that he thumbs at slippery palms, puts a nose to fingertips, the stink of rust.

When Alexei has time by himself he lifts at a handle, at one end of the footlocker. It is so heavy a grown, healthy man would struggle to raise one side. But in his state, underfed, bedridden for weeks, it will not budge.

Empty? Hell, the thing is so full it is going to split. He does not imagine rocks would weigh as much. As if there were solid concrete inside, or a slab of marble cut to the exact dimensions, then a footlocker built around it.

If Alexei tires of the golem he will put it in the lake, marked with new questions: —Is it less a sin to lie to a child? Why does so much wheat produce so little flour?

Yes! that is exactly what he will do, and the details make him laugh. Freyja will stand in neck-deep water and answer each question in time, a gurgling voice.

But Little Sergei is not going to leave in the morning. Instead, a tornado will strike at first sun and they will spend most of the day cowering, watching the horizons. In the afternoon they will start to clean up, inspect the house for damage. The last tornado here was

13 years ago; this will be the first recorded so close to the Volga River. In itself, the odd and improbable frighten him. Yet he is more frightened that there are too many for him to doubt any longer.

Chapter Five

IT COMES NOT from rain or wind, but absolute calm.

Mama is up. Making tea, wandering around for breakfast. Alexei is awake in a sort of twilight way, ready for good smells, sugar, plenty of wheat. Their guest is asleep, his foot up, knee straight, just as he asked. The man snores without embarrassment. It is a loud, healthy sound that will have mother and son cracking up if they find each other looking. The proud oaf, his smelly intrusion.

Today, a new rite. Alexei limps out of bed, taps Freyja with one knuckle, smiles at the music of steel and cavity. He could almost spell the tone, *kee!*, but there is no way to write what happens as the note tapers off. It starts as a brief consonant and lives, fades as an unmistakable vowel.

(For this, and because the golem warns him by being still, he knows he should keep it far from the breathy sounds. No vowels, no life. A lesson the Romanovs should bear in mind if they return, somehow, to 1894. They could deplete chosen words by decree, stripping them of their breath and volume: *drght, strvtn, Blshvks, Rsptn.*)

Revekka is shrieking.

Has she burned herself, cut a hand? Are there rats in the kitchen, birds in the laundry? Alexei is up in a moment, jolts his ankles by racing in. She is howling about the ditch, about everyone to the ditch and that—if their guest sleeps any longer—she will bolt him indoors, on the wrong side of the wall from the ditch.

Ditch? And does she also mention a tornado? Alexei takes a look, although he knows that is unwise. Yes, it is a funnel cloud, and so close!, sucking the night out of the sky and drilling it into the ground, leaving behind a fledgling, unsteady morning. The land speed is slower than you would think, and the cone is untidy, both in silhouette and posture, leaning perilously to the side, past its center of gravity. Do they topple like clumsy children and, if they do, is that the end of it? Revekka screams once more, for good. She and Alexei begin to run, despite that they are bad at it.

They could have been at Konstantin's home already, where grandfather has a full basement. They should have sold the old place, made the trip to Moscow. They would only have suffered an old man's storms, the lesser ones.

Sergei is up and looks like he will ignore her outright, wander in the direction of the twister. A good soldier, loyal to the imperials, knows to stand in the dervish and let it take him up, if those are the orders. But no, he is walking there because he is mostly asleep.

Revekka pulls Sergei through the doorway, never mind his weight. It is a sort of unmatrimony, a reversal of the man lifting his bride at the threshold. She says, "You're mad, Sergeevich. Just mad."

They find the arroyo by taking the boardwalk stairs down, otherwise unsure from the blowing dirt. It was daylight a moment ago. Momentum keeps them chins-forward with strong hands on the rail.

The world is tiny, obscured. Also quiet, even without the barometric marbles in their ears. If those recall any one thing, it is the joint ache that dogs Alexei after an injury. It is the sense of blood pooling around the ligaments, but made small, pushed up and to the sides of the head.

For this, mama and Little Sergei do not recognize it. The boy does, his body on loan from the last fall. He pulls at both ears at once and says, "It's coming." Near-deafness turns the sound inward, strips it of treble. An echo for one. It is terrifying, and not only because it reminds him of February.

In this storm, even the topography is at risk. He cannot tell if the hills are flat, or flattened by dark. Mama's eyes are turning to paprika again: such grief, knowing her house will be lost. She holds Alexei's arm not in a steady grip but in pulses, grabbing and releasing with the right hand and pinpricking him with the fingernails of the left. She would never do that otherwise, risk cutting his skin with soily keratin.

She says, "Holy Mary, his salt."

"What?" Is she talking about Anastasia's bag of salt, the counterfeit strannik salt, their faked remains of Grigori Novykh? If she is, that cost would be trivial to replace, no need for a gamble.

She says, "The footlocker, your father." Now his mother is gone, swept off not by wind but duty.

When the tornado strikes the sound is of hail, louder than wind. Yet there is no ice, only pieces of the house coming free, striking others, freeform signal. On the color spectrum of noise it falls far from white, but it is as frightening as white, the same kind of burden to hear.

He says, "My home."

Then, because no one blames the weather for loss, Alexei cries out toward her back, "You're mad, too—" Rock-on-rock pumices his voice away.

Boards and furniture come apart without weight but now the pipes, the load-bearing things answer in low moaning. Not devastation, which means rubble, clues. The wall is only swept off, deposited somewhere. As for Revekka, wherever she is, she is wailing, with no inhale. Alexei is grateful for the sound. It is his only news of her, as dark as it is.

He whispers above the din again, "My home."

Remarkable how little time until it is over. One minute, less. If it happens again he will put a watch to it. He and Sergei let another full minute go by, now look uphill. The soldier offers a palm and Alexei is surprised to take it. His legs are weak again.

Save for finding Revekka they will not go inside. The beams, unstable. Instead of masonry along the back of the house they find a jagged mouth. Debris is scattered within like chewed food on the tongue. If they went in, they might be eaten by falling roof, rafters giving way.

But mama is right here, bawling over the footlocker as she swore she would. Alexei holds her a few fingers at a time.

Her wrist is oven-hot and soaked with mucus, sweat. She says, "Don't make me look," but there are few things left to see. The sightline runs unhindered across fields to another ruined house a half-mile up. The second level, the floor of papa's old study, slumps forward, with no wall or window as support. It clouds the top of the vision like swelling in the eye and Alexei paws at his brow to be sure.

The path of stirred earth runs to the west, an uninterrupted view across a half-dozen farms. No buildings, crops, agricultural equipment. Only angry land, which cold-boils like a photograph of soup.

Revekka says, because she is always saying, "What do I do? What do we do?"

#

At last, a name for the assault victim. It is Boris Ivanovich Buirimov, who lived a mile from here and died at his home. Minutes before the storm, minutes after, no one is sure.

#

Of the missing wall, even the rubble is gone. Little Sergei thinks the large pieces were swept into the lake; if he can recover enough to build columns, it will keep the place from falling in. (Mama whispers that some of Freyja's gears are missing, too, and that this is the reason he will dredge. But that she only mentions it to Alexei is proof that she has no proof.)

The soldier is quick to strip to his cottons, and the hosts, mother and son alike, are quick to take him in, in the wet slip. The man's skin partitions neatly into sunburned and pale, with the exception of his olive-scoured knees, which look impossible to get clean.

Where his body is firm it is positively granite, with kerf marks and veins showing through. Where it is soft it merrily bounces in time with his step. And behind his triceps, where his chest, arms and back all adjoin, is skin over bare ligament.

Alexei's take? It is an honest body, strong from war preparations, well-fed in victory. If the man is lazy with so many choices for defecting, his physique does not show it.

Sergei says, from knee-deep water, "Not much in here. But I didn't think of the slate rocks." Revekka and Alexei share a brief look, now stand in a single act.

"Show me, Alexander. Not all of those are for just anything."

"I understand. But some of them are. We could stack them like this, this, this."

He is making a repeated gesture with his hands, although neither of his hosts is paying attention. Revekka says, "What I should have said was that some are important to my son and husband." But of the eight to ten slates which their guest brings up, none of them are written on. Alexei checks all of them, both sides of each. They are blank, including the piece that is approximately the shape of Russia, which he is sure is the one from before. Not a mark on any of them.

Tonight, when Little Sergei and his mother are puzzling over the rest, he will take two slates and ask the question again, two different ways: Will we lose our farm?

Also: Is the rest of it true?

The mere quantity of superstitions—a few of which are his—cannot all be bunk: the scream pots at Port Arthur, the elevator car at Grand Duke Paul's estate. The poetry, the hen egg. Mama saving the Petrograd man by taking blood into her stomach.

The rumors of golems that wake, take up arms, protect. Metal things that stir to life if you do not keep them shrouded. Also, the shroud. The roof ghosts. They are not all false, no nation tells only lies.

At Saturday's funeral he will learn of another one: that the tornado was the ghost of Boris Buirimov, the man from the fistfight two days ago, who passed in the first moments of the storm.

Throughout the afternoon, into morning, neighbors come, bringing what they can. Little Sergei hauls certain things to the Kabanov estate, including the beds. The woman of the house, Vetta, is the one who brought the beets during the first week of Alexei's injury.

The boy suggested instead they put the beds outside and sleep under the fine weather but mama would not hear it. Their guest, used to worse sleeping conditions than this, would have agreed to either.

#

By the second day Mamontov has built three slate columns, and the leaning house is sound for now. There is something in the engineering which Alexei does not trust. Those slates were meant for asking.

They begin to replace the masonry and, by late afternoon, Anastasia is here. She cries into each of their chests, the soldier's included, and she steals boy and mother away, for conspiring. She says the nervous woman, the one whom Alexei healed in March, has arranged for that shipment of wheat again. She hopes to bring her friend, the mother with neuralgia. Mama will not hear it and, when Anastasia mentions the funeral, Revekka is convinced. "We have too much to do already, and now there will be services? You see that our house is in stones?"

"Did you not hear? They will bring wheat. Bread for months. Enough time for the shops to stock up again. Don't be proud, mama. You might never stand in a bread line again and there is pride in that."

Such a voice! *Did you not hear…there is pride in that.* If Anastasia had lit one of her cigarettes the exhale would have enshrouded mama's face. Next time she should do that. What's more, every angry suggestion ought to be with a puff of nicotine.

Revekka's answer is more tobacco: "I am not proud, girl, I am occupied. The country has gone crazy and the weather has turned against me. I have a sick child, a sick house, and only after this, you tell me of a funeral."

"Yes, and in the midst of so much nuisance is trying to eat, waiting in lines—"

"Not once have I said caring for Alexei is nuisance. It is my honor to watch him, and bring him to health."

—Nonsense!

He does not say it but he should, she deserves to hear it. That is his answer to the idea of a Buirimov storm: nonsense. It is his answer to the second, coming revolution. To everyone bickering, always. So many arguments in which both parties are wrong.

More than those, Revekka's claim of honor is nonsense. Her husband is a dead soldier, and this other soldier will not state his reason for coming. When, for example, Revekka wiped feces from Alexei's legs, it was only because he could not stand. Nothing to do with honor; she should not speak to him of honor.

For now he only says, "There has been a storm. Natalia and her friend are not expecting a palace. You want to be proud? We will treat the woman with neuralgia and she will walk again as God meant her to. Be proud that you are part of that."

From here the afternoon is tense, too long. Anastasia leaves because of sheer worry and Sergei has found his way out of a shirt again. His chest is still, seems unbothered by lifting, hauling, raising stones. The man's tree-branch shoulders, which Alexei already knew through the uniform, are dry, despite the hard work.

Vetta Kabanova says, "Nice to see you have some help."

"Yes, you've all been wonderful. Your family in especial."

"I mean your friend, the young man from Omsk."

Little Sergei is from Omsk?

Revekka says, "Yes, nice to have him." She hurries her stare elsewhere, but goes on: "I doubt we will for long. That one likes to wander. He only came to give Alexei the golem before he went to Finland."

Alexei thinks, *No, mama. If he came here for clay-molding, it was nothing to do with me.*

"Finland!" But Vetta's surprise is too much. The border was a mere 250 kilometers from Sergei's hospital. Barely a day by rail, even with normal delays. Yes, the man has come out of his way for a visit, to a barren place in the grasslands. But Finland is close. A defecting soldier's first pick.

Or maybe Vetta means that he should remain, to fight. But against whom? The tsar's cousin to the west? The tsar himself, at Alexander Palace? The Bolsheviks, the loyalists, the strikers, the mutineers?

It is too much for Alexei to grasp. No doubt his is a child's view, but is that not exactly what the pamphlets have been saying? That the reign of one man makes subjects of us all? That our loss of sovereignty keeps us as children?

This was one of his parents' common disputes. Papa, always faithful to law, made constant mention of it, that self-ownership is a lie. He told Revekka that our bodies and our hearts are God's, and, until the end, are entrusted to God through a tsar, who was born to serve in this way. The tsar was told from youth how to renounce whims and fashions of political thought, and deliver us according to scripture.

But mama said Nicholas II was just as we are, prone to whimsy. "Exactly as you and I are, you should know better."

"I am not talking about this tsar, I am talking about all tsars. I mean what a tsar is, why there is such a thing as a tsar."

His answers never satisfied Revekka, and only pushed her on. Neither of them convinced Alexei, who did not think they were bickering in earnest, but doing it for his benefit. Once his mother told Karl, "This is why you are her favorite. You take all of it to heart. You should have been tsar. Alix hates it, you know?" Just what was she getting at?

Lately mama has offered her same criticism of the Bolsheviks, who make subjects of the people by checking luggage with their fists, letting devils out of prisons and taking farms for personal gain. Instead of one king there are many, but it is still autocracy.

#

Natalia hauls in as much wheat as she said. A groom with a horse pulls a delivery dray, the bed of which bows from the weight.

A second one escorts Hella Jensen.

Natalia's voice is as husky as ever. Is that from the long, dusty travel? She has a tight embrace for Alexei and his mother. Revekka offers tea, but the guest waves it off. "You have plenty on your hands. I know my way around the kitchen if I need."

The kitchen or a kitchen? If she means the wreckage of the house, their home is improved from before, yet has plenty of cleaning and rebuilding to do. Little Sergei's draftees are finished with the rear wall, but they left the funny mouth at the top. Bad teeth, a huge overbite. An illiterate greeting stuck on the bottom lip.

The sight of it makes Alexei want to mock: — Quick, cover it with cloth before it comes to life!

Revekka tells Natalia, "There was a storm. Four days ago."

"We heard."

During the maze of introductions, Alexei cannot help but correct his mother. Three days have passed, not four. And it is impossible that news of the tornado would outpace the trains.

When Natalia introduces Alexei to Hella, the new guest brings him in with both arms. He suspects her as a fraud but now, if he is to doubt, he will have to do it from up close. The embrace blinds him with clothes and smell.

The woman comes off as brave, moist with sweat. Happy but not content. If she is faking the leg pain her acting is terrific.

"Sweet child, you are just as she said you were." Alexei hates it when someone tells him that.

Natalia is pretending to glare, or pretending not to glare at Little Sergei. When he is too far to hear she says, "I don't remember him from around."

"A loyal from Omsk. Wounded at the front."

Natalia has to respond despite that she would rather not. She settles for a curt remark: "Today, to say you are loyal is to fly the Bolshevik flag, which is mayhem. And Mamontov is a strange name for a Mongol."

Alexei thinks, *Yes, that is it!* That is what struck him about Sergei's face, or was it Freyja's face, with its lean geology, the scrumptious shape to the eyes? What we do not see in men, we at least see it in what they make. Little Sergei is not from Omsk, he is from the east.

If Natalia wants a future visit, her timing will have to be better: Vetta and her husband are here and listening. Also, there are the two seething peasants again, the ones who spoke of farm seizure. Word of so much grain will reach them, too.

While the grooms lead Hella indoors, Revekka blurts out news of the funeral.

Natalia says, "A local man?"

"There was a fight, and then of course the storm. A young man, Boris Buirimov."

Natalia breathes in hard. The way her arms fold up, hands clap to the face, you think she has sucked them up, like broth from a ladle. She tries to say, "Boris? I knew him, I know all about him," but she is sobbing already. Her response is so quick you believe she is fooling, but no, look at the red face, tears all the way to the collar.

Revekka touches at her shoulder, "How did you know?"

"He was a boy. Easy to upset but a charming little boy."

"I suppose you're right. He was prone to moods." They have lowered the sound and pitch of their voices and, fitting that, they are making the observations of men.

"I cannot miss the funeral. If I could attend as your guest." That is two nights and two mornings from now. So many guests in need of rooms: three to five, depending. It seems mama should start with the bread.

Or is that one of her pretexts for spending time away? Her reasons for waiting hours at markets for basic foodstuffs? Time alone, no matter how many wait with her.

#

He would rather treat Hella when Anastasia is here. But the girl was hard to find before, and now that she is drinking she is erratic, her every disposition brief. Because the guests will stay for two nights there should be no cause for hurry, but by evening all conversation is done. Alexei finds everyone staring.

He gulps at a first response and offers a new one, which he did not expect. He says, "Shall we pray?"

"That would be lovely, my bird. Such an exhausting week. Really, an exhausting year until now."

It is decided. But he has only two articles of faith and neither are where he left them. The pouch of yearner's salt and the Bible, were they blown outside by the storm? The good book shredded page by page, a psalm at every neighbor's door?

Hella seems to understand. She produces a Norwegian Bible and Natalia brings a cup of salt, a sheepish look. Alexei leafs through the book: Hella's written language is as built from consonants as French is from vowels. This way, instead of a breathing Genesis 1, it is a stammered, choking thing that seems more like panic than faith.

Quite fitting, he thinks.

But he should not assume. From the cover, you do not know if it is Old or New Testament. Heavy print bleeds through the page and the clutter of unfamiliar tongue, with its wound-shaped lettering, does not help. *I begynnelsen skapte Gud himmelen og jorden.*

The names grow familiar as he looks—Samuels, Jobs, Jeremiahs—but whether or not he has found his Philippians chapter, Filippenserne 1, he can only suppose:

"For mig er livet Kristus—" Hella ought to be chuckling at his treatment of Norwegian but instead her eyes are wide, with home.

Mama asks, "What does it say?" and his reply, "I cannot even guess," is supposed to bring more laughter than it does. He should add, —What it does not say is that the mineral we use to cure pork will heal those who cannot walk.

He speaks the passages he knows, which are few. Now he offers verses from what he believes to be Romans, Psalms, Chronicles. At least the labored study, somewhere between certainty and random, satisfies everyone. Anastasia has an odd way of storing her books spine-in. Doing that lends her shelf a uniform appearance: one edition, the full width of a shelf. The same story told by dozens of authors.

More than that, if she wants to read she must identify works by content, not title. He has long admired it of her and now, in her absence, he is healing their patients the same way.

He says, "Are you ready?"

Natalia answers, "Both of us are ready."

Hella is first, slow to reach his side, quick to take the cure from his hand. Mama has taken away most of it, only a precious quantity remains. Alexei would have thought that—even in imperial, now post-imperial Russia—the stuff was priced as a commodity.

As always, what does she know? And what is she not telling him?

There is too little for ceremony. Hella makes sure to grab Alexei by the wrist and touch her mouth to his fingers. If she is acting, it is an untoward detail.

Natalia comes after, with a cute grin. She does not let him feed her but instead dusts the grains to her palm, now licks and licks.

Sometimes when Alexei is bored he will put tongue to hand that way. In his sexual years he will know it as an erotic act, but for now it is just a different way to glimpse himself, nothing else. A look at his salt-nature.

Soon only one of his palms will have that.

Natalia is fully smiling, her mouth huge, doubling her features. She punches the boy in the middle leg: a jab to only the thigh muscle, safe from the joints. Yet the blunt shot makes him gasp and she frowns with the middle of her brow, another of her masculine things. When Alexei smirks back, he longs in secret for Konstantin.

He would return to the scriptures were it not for Hella's interruption. She says, "I know this is impossible, but I can feel it working."

Natalia says, "Nothing is impossible. This is Russia, we have the means. Better yet, it is the kingdom of the means."

Alexei thinks the woman will never make up her mind, but Hella says, "You are right, right as always."

"Is it warming?" Natalia reaches over, a bold gesture, at least with others in the room. She leans in on Hella's leg with one hand, her arm straight. You would think the weight would hurt, or that, at least, it was too close. But Hella says, "It's not warm, it's cold. Any more warmth and I would just leave my legs here."

"When it works on me I feel heat. It warms me all over."

Alexei thinks, *This is it. They are not only fooling me, they are mocking me, too.*

Chapter Six

AT LEAST ONE of the rumors is true. The path of wrecked earth that ends with mama's property begins with Buirimov's. Alexei did not recognize the place when looking east to west, but from here, at the site of the funeral, he does not doubt, it is their land at the end of the wreckage. He can discern their lifeless pond, no question.

And here is the elderly widow, Sophie Buirimov, mother of the dead man, busying herself with two veiled guests. Each are reluctant to sit with the other. It is rare for Alexei to notice, but Sophie fusses at length over the point. Both of the visitors are spire-tall, the same height as Revekka, and seem to have broad faces, not meant for balance.

One has a defiant voice that borders on havoc — Alexei hears her words but can only make out a few of them. The only clear one so far is the people's word for *rapt*, which she offers in a serpentine lisp. —I am *rapt* by your dress, Sophie. The late Boris *rapt* me with his ways. My daughter could not make it but this would have *rapt* her. Who knows what the woman is saying?

Her companion is slightly shorter and more accustomed to work. She has taut, red arms and more agrarian shoulders. The clothes add bulk to her shape, conceal her neck.

Alexei leans in and asks Natalia from the side, "Who are they?"

"I would say they were sisters. Charlotte and Matilde de Morny, if I remember. They call themselves de Morny."

The names hint at the familiar, a story he heard once. Or maybe it is the way she tongues at the words Charlotte and Matilde, which reminds him of so many things.

More than all else the boy notes the past tense and says, "They were?"

"Too long ago. I can't say for sure."

For a woman close to the victim, in tears over his death, Natalia spends much of the ceremony introducing herself, struggling to explain. Mostly she claims to be friends of Karl Vasilievich Shafirov, Alexei's father. The boy wants to doubt it, doubt everything she says, but it is hard to be sure. Papa seems to have known everyone, and why would Natalia lie, right in front of the boy, if it were not true?

He attempts a scene by sitting apart from the aristocrat, far from her scams and masculine breath. But no one mentions it as he moves farther off. In the end he is close to the estranged women, whom Sophie has put in adjacent seats, otherwise they are welcome to leave. Together either way.

It takes only minutes for the de Morny sisters to argue, if discreetly. "I see you have stayed well-fed. You smell like her onions, exactly like them."

"And you smell like me. I'm hardly insulted."

"No insults. Not today. Not in front of—" The shorter woman nods forward, to the survivors, the body, the book.

The priest begins, "Lo, truly, all my days in vanity wasted are—" and each woman looks to the other. The first, the stout one, says, "You should listen."

"I should listen? You are the one talking."

"I have heard prayers before. Remember?"

"Of course I do. I was the one to say them."

When the congregation files out it is through the back, where a pile of vegetables and grain draws flies to the stables. The produce is not for horses. There is bean, corn, some precious meat from a rooster. All left out to rot, Alexei supposes, because of the fear of foul water inside.

Neither the widow nor the de Morny sisters turn from the casket. Nor will Natalia, who fills her chest wide, empties it in a low groan. The ridiculous Norwegian is walking all around, has condolences for Sophie, the widow, the abandoned sister. She speaks a few words to Revekka, who is also veiled. At last she embraces Natalia on her opposite side.

Alexei can recognize a sham even if he cannot describe it in detail.

He will tell Anastasia he is finished with them; if the girl refuses he will be finished with her, too. Mama will probably have them at grandfather's house anyway. Little Sergei's arrival may have pushed that back some, but he, too, will want to come along.

The hell with them. Let him go in spite of it all, get to know his grandfather before the man starts forgetting. Mama swears that Konstantin was affectionate as a young father, no matter that her specifics are few. The man's shirt reeked of sweat and wind, she says, and his forearms were rigid, like Karl's.

In a few days Alexei regrets the thoughts, fears they have conjured something beyond that, past this extended family of Revekka and her guest. Past his patients.

Why? Because men have come for the Kabanov place.

It is not sure at first, because all Sergei can say is there are new horses. For the afternoon, a thudding quiet lies over both properties, until a rifle shot wakes them all. Vetta Kabanova is shouting—you can hear that much from here—and Revekka is praying at the window, picking at her fingertips, doing that mess with her hair and hands again. "They're killing her, they've killed him. Help them, Sergei, we have to help." Yes, their pet soldier has a firearm, but there are four horses there, three with saddles. Alexei visits Freyja, which is leaning into a corner near his bed. He removes the shroud in one, loathing stroke of the arm, knowing it will never help.

It does not wake. The golem of components only stands, mute and lovely, rusting in ways we don't see.

Revekka takes Little Sergei's rifle and says, "They are my neighbors, not yours. If you go over with a gun there will be a war."

She has changed her mind from a second before, and it is an absurd remark anyway, so much she is barely able to finish it. One wounded soldier, finished with a bullet? Hardly a war. And so what if it was, when is this country not at war somewhere? When the days are long, dusk on the country's European edge is dawn on her Pacific shore. A nation with no darkness or rest—plenty of chance for fighting.

"Scheisse," his mother is looking at the Kabanov place again, speaking in fluent enemy German. The boy can only guess as to why. How about this? It is her way of speaking in the most profane way.

Now, with a rhythm that is downright musical, she says, "Scheisse scheisse scheisse."

After the maledictions they agree to approach without arms. For Little Sergei, ever the soldier, it is no less a paradox than making campfires without sticks.

Mama is repeating herself again. She has made Alexei stay back but he can hear her all these yards away, across the lame farm: "Not ready, love. Not ready for it, not ready, never going to be ready for it." Her singsong grief is rather lovely and if, by the end, he has to laugh, it is not because he cares any less.

\#

Before they left Alexei had made her tell the truth about something. The question only vexed her and there was no reason he should know at once, right now, while they had business with the peasant intruders. But he was urgent about it, she would stay until he had an answer: "What was between those two women at the funeral? The sisters; Natalia said their names were Charlotte and Matilde."

Revekka said, "I always swear not to lie to you, but you will never believe it."

"Tell me then."

"There was an accident, with Charlotte and their mother. Matilde was able to deliver her sister again, but not their mother."

Alexei was not sure how to reply but Sergei was curious, "Will they come together again?"

Revekka said, "You see? You men and mockery. I'll be damned if we talk about it anymore."

When the door shut it was a loud, complicated thing, and it is a long hour until they are home again. When they are, Alexei asks, "Then where is Cheraw?"

Revekka says, "Cheraw? You mean Cherkesk?"

He overheard the de Morny women speaking of it, a blunt English word amid casual Russian. No, he does not mean Cherkesk and neither did they. He says, "Maybe somewhere in The New World?"

Mama thinks by narrowing an eye. This is why her responses are sniper-fire, not buckshot. She says, "I suppose it is in one of the mountain chains. Did you hear this from Charlotte, at the funeral?"

So be it, her answer is both rifle and scattergun. How did she know?

Revekka says, "Those women are always talking about California. Alaska, Wyoming. I can only say this, some Russians come to our town for the farming. Some like the colder weather, I suppose. But a few come for the dead lakes. And when they leave, it is for another dead lake. In a place without so many neighbors."

Now it is the boy's turn to wonder: does she mean Cheraw, or Cherkesk? In time Anastasia will research it and find that it is a new, tiny population in Colorado. She will tell him more of the state: her mystical peaks, the capital city exactly one mile in the sky. The air you breathe is half-ether.

#

Vetta and her husband are here. They carry day luggage and their pockets swing with contraband, likely food. The peasants have the Kabanov home.

Sergei has been talking at length: "—12 men, we can guess a few rifles each. Some of the wives look as ready to fight as the men. Add to them the sons that can shoot, you have two dozen, against those three."

The simpleton, is he numbering the men who helped rebuild? Or those who attended the funeral? If

Sergei believes the odds are 24 against three he is wrong. All of Russia wants to own a farm and there is only so much land to be had. Soon the three men will face a score of their own and one day, those 20 will side against thousands.

Vetta does not need Alexei to say it. She shakes the idea of fighting from the head, a vigorous left-right you think will make her ill. While her husband talks of razing their house the woman says, "What of your clay outside, near the pond? We could send Andrei and Alexander to the Yanovsky place, to pray for gin."

By Alexander she means Little Sergei, although Alexei takes the order to heart, never mind that the woman points her finger away from him. He wants to go, does not care if he slows them down, which would be unlikely. They would take horses and make frequent stops as they squabbled over directions. All Alexei would have to do is keep up.

He will not voice his doubts—he and mama are indebted for the beets—but what she wants with the clay is silly. She is to offer the peasants gin, same as a Trojan horse. That would put the intruders in a heavy sleep, delirious with river air. Dozing in their boots. Meanwhile Revekka and Vetta Kabanova would make jars from the earth. During the small hours, Sergei and Andrei would sneak in, cut hair from the men to leave in the pots. They would cure the lids in place with grout.

One day, two days, and it would be time. In a private ceremony they would smash the ceramics apart.

Three screams, one pot each, and any man who wished the Kabanovs bad luck would be dead. If any of the three peasants lived, it was because they were ready to negotiate.

Scream pots: Alexei has read they are the origin of the clay golem. Instead of keeping the victim's essence in an inert container, why not give the ceramic legs, a voice, will? Why not let it walk our cities before you shatter its head? It was a more public spectacle that way, and the shame was tastier. Yet a problem arose, the golem manifested its creator, not the wretch who had given up hair.

It was a special sort of rabbi who could murder a terracotta rabbi, his own duplicate.

Go beg for alcohol, or collect mud for sham magic? For Alexei there is no question, yet Revekka will not hear of him making the trip. It is too dangerous for a boy, a sick boy. It is too much a risk for any of them, except that Andrei has property at stake and Mamontov is a soldier.

She says, "One townsman is dead already and a farm, mind you the very next farm from here, it's almost taken."

Look at her, too blind, or daft, to recognize when done is done. It is painful to see in your mother but she chose the words on purpose, *almost taken*. Come now, the men next door are wearing Andrei's clothes. They have opened every cupboard door. They cannot take the Kabanov property any more than they have. There are no degrees of taken.

Yet again, there are things he has kept from her, too. It is not fair to blame her for being ignorant. It is no more dangerous on the road than it is right here, at her table. When he does not answer her Revekka says, "I can see it in your eyes, Alexei. What is it?"

"It is nothing, mama."

"Whatever it is, you do not think it is nothing."

He did not tell her of the March incident because it would worry her, make her act without reason. But it is too late to avoid that, she is at it with both of those. He says, "The peasants have already been here. Stood at my bedside this close, to Anastasia, too. That I am here at all means it is not that dangerous."

She is Freyja-still and now says, "Who came? You mean they were inside?"

Of the two intruders he only remembers the speaking one, strangely delicate, the sketch of a beard. Alexei cannot resist his own lie. Everyone near to him is doing that: scream pots, metal girls, souls that cannot rest. Chastity, the book of Matthew. Why should he be the only one left who tells the truth, an unwell child with his one truth left? He says, "There were five."

What, now? Hemophilia, a truth? Yes, is that not what a hereditary illness is? The vaporous pal who comforts you in odd ways, reminds you to be better than you are?

He repeats it, "There were five men."

Where did he get the count? Three from the Kabanov property and one extra, to exaggerate the point. Everyone does that, but it would add up to four.

Four men, and between now and the day of his shattered arm, there are four excursions. The last will be the reason he is maimed.

Vetta shrieks, molding one hand with the other as if both were made of clay. It was silent a moment ago, but now sounds are popping like hailstones. Rifle fire.

Before Sergei reaches the window, they hear a terrier yelp.

It is not an assault, only peasants managing their new property, although dogs firing on dogs is hardly a comfort. And with every poached animal the intruders perfect their aim.

At least he remembers now why the surname de Morny is familiar. Something with the scene, everyone rushing to look, has taken away all doubt. His mother uses the name at times when men come, asking about the Shafirovs. When she is frightened she will introduce herself as Matilde de Morny, and claim that Alexei, Revekka, Karl left the region years ago.

On days like that, Alexei will watch the men leave. Every time they are tall, like papa, and have papa's rather martial walk, hands in near-fists at their sides. It has happened at least once since the telegram.

#

For the first of the operations, the men go out for spirits. Alexei thinks, *Yes, let everyone here do something about their moods.*

Their sense of magic-justice has left them rash, and a little crude. Andrei belches openly and the smell is of malnourishment. When Little Sergei wanders off to piss he does not go far enough. Alexei can see him clearly, and wonders about the soldier's mostly bald pelvis.

That makes him remember a fear, yet another of his obsoleted fears. This one, at 12 years, was his worry that, when hormones came, they would give body hair to everyone but him. And now that the hair has come, he is afraid it is too wiry, too filthy-looking and overgrown. No one should see, Anastasia most of all.

For their second mission—Sergei is treating them as military objectives now—both couples present gin to the Kabanov occupants, a goodwill visit. Afterwards, the women bounce legs as they might with fussy children on the knee. They stare, but at nothing.

Very late that night is a rushed third assault. Little Sergei calls it off for reasons mama will not say, but at last, they repeat it in the stale hours, two nights later.

Each of these takes longer than it should and between them, the harrowing act of waiting. The adults are still bickering about government things, never letting up. They argue the divine rights of tsars and the influence of monks. They squabble over the three great plagues of typhus, famine, illiteracy. They ponder the ethics of the strike, the seizure of trains, assassinations.

Every time, without fail, there is a stalemate over the goddamn means to production.

If their economics is to be believed, there is a Russian way, a Bavarian way. The French, Pacific Islands, New World and savages all have a way. Their talk of other lands, or perhaps something more fundamental, has left the women in tears again.

That kind of sadness, Alexei thinks, is rather like the power from a mill. Part of their grief is deliberate, well-engineered. Yet the installation would not move were it not for the water, which is timeless and from all around. Water from the mountains, sky, waves, condensation, and from inside the body. The mill by itself is inert but the water is innumerable.

Anastasia might credit him with fine poetry but she would chide him for the essay.

This is how the girl understands her sadness-books: when we are born we are ignorant to the line between self and others, we fail to see the divisions between infant, adult, plant, animal, mineral. We mistake our mother's heartbeat for our own. When we are close to her chest the two pulses sound like one pulse. This is our only true happiness; it is gone within months. Every tic, every nervous act, even in adulthood, is that search for her heart again, for the sound of a mother's blood.

For practical reasons we start to distinguish ourselves from our surroundings, discern our id as unique from that of mother, sister. We cut ourselves away from those we hate and then, from those we do not hate. From roughly Alexei's age until early adulthood, we become experts at it.

It is a survival urge as much as a prideful one, yet it is the pride that breaks our hearts. We further distinguish ourselves with lines of race, gender, voice. The separations become terrifying yet our distractions—art and literature, music and religion—separate us further. It is a biological thing that will in time leave us for dead and then, as infirm old men, we realize we have taken it too far.

We are the naked diversions, who do not know what makes us content. Our rocks are both treasure and gutter coping.

It makes him smirk: like everyone, he needs a distraction, always and now. But by no means will he join Vetta in her dark clay arts. Our hobbies should, at best, never lie to us. He will thresh wheat instead, sift and grind it. The winds are high today, good for winnowing. But if the women mention Isaiah, Ezekiel, Romans, so help him he will dump all the new flour into a lake.

He nearly says as much. When he begins he announces: "I'm taking a stick, not a staff."

"Take whatever makes you happy, Alexei." Mama always uses his forename when he speaks like that.

He has not been raised to produce. He has no threshing talent at all, and they suffer an early scare. A splinter of wood comes away in his hand, a pure-white pain running from palm to forearm. Yet when he stops and watches, no blood.

As he gloves himself and starts again, their moods lift. The farm seizures, the imprisonment of Nicholas II, the terrible state of Russia, all of it starts to cool, obscure. Perhaps it is better said: the fog settles in.

He enjoys swinging at wheat. He likes the hiss of air around the stick and the muffled impact. He offers thanks after every blow, a holdover from Orthodox mass, continued thanks. A song for only him, until Little Sergei comes and slaps him on the shoulder, calls him a miller.

Alexei would like to say, "There are no millers anymore, just the wheat barons," but if Sergei would challenge him on the point it would be all he has, a slogan and a pile of chaff.

On the third morning there is an apparent sign of victory.

Alexei wakes after sunrise. The threshing left him exhausted all the way to the eyes. Vetta, still unconvincing as a witch, has chosen pots for each of the three locks. The containers are ugly and squat, look more like wrists. He will reject that distinction soon.

Yesterday mama tried to fire six pots and six lids in the oven. Before, Little Sergei had joked of smearing terracotta across his golem's face, to keep Freyja from being cast out by the others. But the soldier's accidental curse of mud over metal extended to kitchens, too, and the wreck that Revekka made of her oven is distressing.

Who knows? With fear of capture she may have done it on purpose, ruining the place before the peasants could come and ruin.

One of the six pots did not set up and Vetta has broken another carrying it there to here. Of the four remaining, she has hair for all but one. She sets the lids in place, seals them tight, leaves them to cure. The remaining empty pot is back indoors. A revolver built for one bullet, unloaded, laid somewhere.

The boy is urged to put another slate in the lake.

It takes a while until his yard is clear of visitors and, when it is, he does not have much time to think. It should be an enduring question and what he opts for is, —Is this the better way?

He hopes his mother does not hear the splash, because if she does, she will know right off.

"How long do you suppose we—?" Vetta does not know how to ask, nor does she want to.

Revekka says, "I cannot guess. We could ask my daughter-in-law, the little mystic."

Does she mean Anastasia? Little Sergei and Andrei point grins at Alexei, and that confirms it. He resents her for implying it and ought to point out, the girl is more devout than any of them.

Alexei only says, "Years, probably. Years and years."

"Years! Holiness, no. Your mother will not put us up for years."

What was it the girl said about the war for the ports? That the tsar assigned Grand Duke Kirill to the Petropavlovsk in early February, and that ship sank in April? Two months, then? He thinks, *Forget how long mama will put you up. I will evict you myself if it takes two months.*

No matter, two of the pots are to be smashed before that, as the grout is still drying. Before they fill with screams, not that they would. And the third jar will be lost in disorder.

The peasants are here again.

Each has a telling dent in his hair, which is filthy. Thick.

The shortest, the talkative one, may be the pretty interrogator from March, but if so his beard has filled in. His teeth and fingernails are caked with grit. His sleeves are cut short, for farm work.

Alexei cannot say if the voice is familiar or not: "Making flour, we see?" The men are aiming their rifles toward the sky, in the unmistakable way of the revolution.

Chapter Seven

"THE FARM is a barren place, you say. You look and there is wheat for as far as the sky, but forget that. This farm is special. A soldier bought the place because the land is dead, the water is dead. Good price for a soldier."

On mornings such as this, the first to panic is the first to speak, and the answer comes before any better sense. Today it is Little Sergei, from whom, more than any other, Alexei would have expected gunshot, not words. A mouth turned to discharge. He says, "The wheat is a gift from a friend. She was concerned for us. We are hungry just like you, and tired of waiting in lines."

"Waiting, you say waiting?"

If Alexei knows anything from watching men fight, it is that an aggressor repeating the other's words is the last thing before violence. He has wondered about it at length, if from afar. With time he has dismissed all other explanations and today only one is left: a repeated word is the word that does the most harm.

The peasant says, "Two nights ago you waited. We saw you come with your scissors and torches, thought you wanted to tailor our clothes."

Vetta shields him from the scream pots with a wide crouch. She is sitting near two of the curing jars, and the third is inside. The man lifts a side of his mustache, a deceptive grin. He says, "Oskar wanted to let you in, a nice gesture, he thought. Other two wanted to kill you."

At last, one of them is named. Too bad it is the tall, apparently stupid one, who never speaks. The peasant concludes, "In dark times the hags tailor the clothes. They fit better at first but at night, stitch by stitch, the fabric chokes you dead. You go in your sleep, killed by clothes. Hags are free to do it again and again."

Because Alexei spent the early spring denying faith, superstition, faith healing, he admires the visitor's rather practical way. There is a certain trust in this man. It is a contradiction but he cannot help it; a ridiculous yarn about strangling men with their own shirts might be true, the only kind of fable he would believe.

Then again, what next? Piano notes rise up and strangle the composer? The clay seizes the blade from the sculptor and cuts him with it?

Revekka comes forward, arms flared out in vain protection of everyone. She says, "We are no hags, and there are no darker times than this."

"Not hags?" He, too, steps in and scratches a temple. The absurd gap in his hair seems to itch. You hold out hope that the man will not nudge Vetta to the side, expose her scream pots, yet that is all he intends to do. He notes Little Sergei's rifle and does not treat the woman unkindly. He only crowds her away.

The ceramic is in sight and he grins, no doubt knew about it all along. He shatters one of the jars, a moist-sounding *klink,* which Alexei has to struggle to hear.

The man repeats it: "Not hags? Not a living farm? A bottle of gin is an offer to trust? The father is counting your lies and even us, new neighbors, we can tell him about three lies."

The soldier and inventor says, "If you touch her, you can tell him in person."

The peasant grins: it was an elegant threat he did not anticipate. "No, sailor. I will not harm the girls. I see you men, even you, little boy-witch. Coiled so tight about the girls. I will not hurt them, and they are not our kind either. Are you, my carnation?" He draws a finger under Revekka's chin and she swats it away, an unwanted bird.

At last Oskar speaks: "Your gun, sailor."

"My gun?"

"We have three, you are one. You have your training, but we shoot wolfhounds to keep them from chickens, just your size." Oskar's voice is like new milk, hot and buttery, and he leaves the grammar vague on purpose. Is Little Sergei the wolfhound or the chicken? Is the remark patronizing or a threat?

The soldier half-agrees by unloading the cartridges: two in the magazine and one in the chamber. Capacity for four shots, but ammunition for three. Alexei feels cold in his stomach. It was a sniper's gamble.

The shorter one turns to Andrei and says, "And you, white?" Andrei's clothes are all uncolored, except for the dusty appearance and clay stains at the knees. "Are you shooting with bullets today? Or only gin?"

"Neither."

"Neither." Andrei's response has inflamed the man somehow and he approaches Alexei, repeating the word again, reaching for Oskar's weapon. "Neither?"

The boy does his best to stand tall but what he wants most to do is kneel and shit, to break into a run just after. If the university students ever came back it would be a good study for them, the twin urges of dignity and foul groveling, among those set to be executed.

That would be a difficult grant, no question. A brief research window, all subjects under duress.

"You say neither? Here is a neither. You neither visit us up close nor visit far away. You will forget about your land and your—" He has grunted with the word *land*, heaving the rifle butt at Alexei's head, not quite finishing the demand. The boy raises a forearm in defense, crying out as the wood strikes him below the elbow. He falls back and the peasant is mostly on top of him, with Little Sergei's breath in both of their ears. The soldier has tackled the peasant and, in that, tackled both of them.

It seems all of them are shouting, Revekka more than the others, and for the long minute it takes to happen Alexei can only free a leg. Now the gunshot, the terrible wood chopping sound of fist on jaw, fist on forehead. The handsome peasant curses in his otherwise level throat, with no apparent need for breath. Also, Little Sergei's blind rage and profanity, every curse a mention of hell, whores, fellatio.

Strange how, in the realm of the profane, the mother of the trinity, the mother of the enemy and the harlot all are the same mother.

As for the gun fire, Vetta is bawling. Andrei is speaking with a weak voice.

It is a gray sound, like the gray of an old man's skin. Was Andrei shot? If so, the bullet has not only killed but aged him. Alexei sacrifices a boot to the fistfight and tumbles sideways to his feet.

It is as he feared: Andrei's chest and clothes are torn as a single garment. Vetta is kneeling over his head and no doubt her inverted face makes her husband seasick. The third peasant has been trying to pull the soldier from his companion and now, with an instructive crack, Oskar finishes it: a rifle handle to Mamontov's eyesight.

The short one has to kick at Little Sergei to free himself. The man is too handsome to fight so well. It is a frightening riddle.

The peasant stands and pants, tells Revekka, "As for you. You and the boy can stay. Keep muddy land and your muddy house. Catch fish in this ghost pond. But if you go further than that, I kill the boy."

Lastly, to Sergei: "You will go."

The soldier will need to wake before he can answer. Better yet, the defiant bends in ankle and neck are response enough.

#

"Your brother and his sons are in Khabarovsk. You should go." Andrei whispers this as he would a promise and Vetta, speaking as the jilted lover, shakes her head with disbelief. She begs him, with knees in dirt. When the intruders left Revekka hurried inside, but seems to have forgotten what sent her there.

Little Sergei whimpers in his sleep. It is an unflattering animal noise, which Alexei and the new widow will keep to themselves.

As for the boy, his joints are filling again. The handle-shot to his elbow is bad enough, a warm stone sheathed in numbness. But his knees, which overextended when Sergei and the peasant dumped on top of him, are doing something to his nerves. Turning them sick, lousy in color.

At last mama is back, shrugging at the sight of Andrei, commemorating his ground with something dusty and white. She helps Alexei to his bed while the soldier comes around.

The neighbor has time alone to choose if her husband is dead. His body, ever gradual.

#

At dawn Mama offers her land for a burial but Vetta does not care to wait. Sergei is in no condition to dig and Father Rauf would need days to put on a funeral. Meanwhile the widow is earshot from her husband's murderers, her seized home. She only wants to go.

Will she leave for Khabarovsk, Moscow, her childhood place of Listvyanka? No, she will not hear of any of those and seems intent on only wandering. When Revekka finds Alexei making a private face she says, "Leave her to it, bear. There is no improper way to grieve."

Their neighbor opts to burn the remains instead and, despite the need for lumber, Sergei erects a pyre of two meters. He is unhappy about it yet Revekka hands over the last of the coal. A better fire still.

This is how she reasons it: the nights are getting warm and they do not expect to stay until winter. Mother and son will head to Moscow. Little Sergei will make his way to Finland. The peasants in Vetta's home will come, chop Karl's place into cords, use walls and beams for firewood. Revekka will be damned if she leaves one more stick behind. It would only help the vermin endure. The coal alone is worth a winter.

At last, an argument to which the boy is receptive. But Alexei prefers they tie rocks to the dead man, let him become bones in the lake. Better than that, hang a slate from every one of his limbs. A question for each, an eternity to work them out.

Sergei has built the pyre across the water from here, some 80 meters away, but he did not account for the wind. While Alexei lies and waits the scent drifts over, a difficult smell for him to reconcile. The women howl above the sound of burning.

It is a magical night, but not the sort he would have liked. Magic should do violence to our encyclopedias, tear the covers away and let pages flow like rivers, all contributors at once. Everything is possible.

Instead this kind seems to decide everything, declare the current page to be the last, only page.

Revekka is first to come back, checking on the boy with a palm on every joint. The scrape along his middle arm will keep bleeding, yet it is the leg they are watching. Instead of disrobing him mama tore his pants from ankle to mid-thigh, breaking the seam apart. By evening his veins are dark and, after an hour of those dreams again, he wakes to pain. There is all manner of color under the skin.

During his February injury the lake was ice-rimmed, lethal at long exposures. Perfect for inflammation and regulating his panic. Now, the May waters tend toward cool, but not enough to heal. By noon the third day he is desperate. So much fidgety unrest dumps him from bed onto his bad arm, and he crawls just to crawl, his mother and her guests behind him in a slow, preposterous chase.

Pain and fever cause him brief seizures—at least mama and Sergei think they are seizures. He is blacking out over and again, forgetful, confusing names, oblivious to that papa is dead. He paws around on the floor for something to grab, eat. For several minutes he finds comfort as Sergei holds his legs, wagon-style, a meter above the floor. It has to be a ridiculous sight and the boy would giggle if he were able. Instead, he has a long piss, and Revekka puts a towel to the mess, cutting away what is left from his pants. Stripping him in front of the guests comes off as a reprimand, but he is too pain-mad to care.

Her choices for treatment are few: does she offer the boy whiskey, some gin? Today will be an awful day already. Long, hungry, claustrophobic, nor is alcohol a wise treatment for hemophilia. But the boy is ranting from ache, swimming in it. Look here: the fall has caused more injury to the rifle-butt wound. Pink blood runs the length of his forearm, the same veiny direction as a river.

At last mama feeds him scotch, the more expensive of the two, for which Little Sergei traded a box of cigarettes. The boy gulps at it like water, returns with an empty cup and a panting mouth. Maybe with the exception of *vonko*—Austrian?—there is no word for the first of four stages of drinking: the warmth and calm after the night's first sip, especially after a sip of wine.

There are plenty of words for the other three stages: *pompette, borracho, ossified.*

No matter the term, the boy finds it uproarious how they share one expression: Sergei's concern looks the same as Revekka's outrage, and mostly like Alexei's pained fire-breathing, which he catches in a mirror. He chuckles low, promises he will sip at his next and last scotch, despite that he means to gulp it down again.

She sneers and says, "Very well, thirsty little fox."

"I am as always your servant," but when she hands him the glass, the last of the bottle, he empties it like a wino. He says, "To yours," and laughs about their faces a second time.

As it happens, the boy is not a happy drunk, but a surly one, like his grandfather.

When he pleads for Anastasia it is late, the third day. Like after the February tumble, he will be bedridden for weeks, although the pain is worse this time. Mama says, "Sergei went for her earlier, you had nodded off. She is not well either. Fever, and pain all over."

"Send him again."

"What about Father Rauf?"

Will they sing from this page every time he is laid up? Does Alexei of Petrograd have the same talk with the empress over and over? Revekka notes the mean look and says, "No? Then what if I prayed with you instead?"

"If someone is dying right before you, you should send them off without fables."

"Little bear, you're not dying."

"Another fable."

A spring rain is here. The sound is like caring applause, all over the house. His short, painful life has won him an ovation.

#

When he wakes Vetta is gone. From here it is a more regular morning, the kind they were supposed to have when Karl bought the house: soldier, mother, son. The grounds have a thick, unrested look and the dead lake is full past the banks, an unwanted metaphor.

There are two or three dozen acres between mama's house and the Kabanov place. A lone squirrel occupies all of that now, eating, running off, now stopping to eat again.

It is clear mama and Little Sergei whisper because of him, if not about him. She is saying, "Put it in the sculpture, then? In your sculpture?"

"I can't believe you would. Who knows what would happen?"

"No one would think to look there. And she would be twice as heavy, too much to carry off."

"She would be 10 times as heavy, with no way to predict what she would do."

"Sergei."

But you know by the short word that both of them have decided.

There is no sound beyond that. Only the temperate calm he is scared to address by name.

#

Revekka has asked them to keep the rituals, if not the word of the scriptures.

The rites calm her, which calms her son, brings healing. Neither Alexei nor Sergei could deny her that and soon, after so much prayer, and another day of keeping his feet up, the knee is better. Still the large skin, the discolor and failure to clot, but the acceleration of pain has stopped.

His elbow is worse.

Every one of the boy's wraps has bled through and he is doing something with his hands, clawing them toward the wrists, which Revekka writes off as anxiety. But no, he is losing feeling there, and in his ankles, too. After a day of this she ought to cry out, —Which is it, Alexei-bear? Pain or numbness?

The way he imagines panic, his chest would be huge with air. Instead his breath is quick, incomplete, as if the volume of his ribs were sand. The boy is dying.

In his arm, the first signs of rigor mortis. Revekka asks their guest for a surgeon but, to Alexei, a priest would be better, which is rare for him to admit.

Mamontov says, "Vetta's father was a surgeon. She would know the trade."

"She left, and who knows in what direction."

"But we know, my gold. We know her direction and that she cannot have made it far."

Perhaps Sergei is still dizzy from the fistfight, and Oskar's rifle-punch to the head. At times the man seems to wake during mid-sentence, wander away to piss, smoke. He loads his gun with difficulty and aims it at the floor, exactly between his boots. Alexei thinks, *This is a soldier who does not trust himself with a gun.*

There must be a name for that at the front and, more likely than not, the name is cadaver.

There are no beets this time. No citrus, bread, pears. Alexei's flour preparation waits outside, half-finished, left behind for the mice. Revekka sighs again and again, the only noise in the room. Between her breaths, Alexei's room hisses in damaged quiet.

When she leaves she does not say what she will do, but Alexei knows the sound exactly, it is the impact of a stick across chaff.

Her wheat threshing is more rhythmic than his, and after several measures of his mother's strike, exhale, strike, exhale, he eases into something of a nap. He dreams of kings, but not Romanovs. Dreams of socialists, not Bolsheviks.

In each of these they are too few to feed so many.

#

She calls him back not only from sleep but from an awful gravity. It keeps part of him there.

"Alexei? Alexei?"

"What is it, what?"

She said it three times and he answered three times. Or is it one time, or none at all? He turns his head side to side and that makes him alert, but he senses that, whatever this is, they will talk about it again. What she wanted him to hear was, "You're making a dreadful sound."

"Sorry, mama."

"Alexei?"

"Yes?"

She considers it and says, "Later, I think."

You have to be deliberate in it, to die thinking exactly what you want to think. Fatigue keeps hurrying the better, more vivid thoughts away: Anastasia's smell, mama's hot breakfasts, papa's jaw. Even when Karl had just shaved his face was like sandpaper, which the boy used for an itch almost anywhere. That, or the bottom of his father's calloused feet, which might as well have been boots.

Yet these thoughts keep sinking underneath the paler ones. Those sad and denser things that, in health, we needed to write down or else we'd forget: science, doctrine, literature, history. Yes, history, more than the others, which is a surprise to him.

Mama speaks of a certain magic in waking, the hour unknown, and hearing a dog moving around. Awake but silent, as if it was being courteous. The animal is bathing or just listening. After a shared time, however brief, you are back at rest.

Because they do not have a dog (an hour ago there were geese), Alexei listens to Revekka. She is not a good substitute.

#

She says, Alexei? Your inflammation is worse. Would you try Galilee one more time?

Not tonight, mama.

I understand. Not tonight, little bear.

It is full sun now.

#

He is feverish on the lips. Inside, along the gums, the roof of the mouth. Dying is hours away at best and he will spend most of those hours asleep. Nor is it good sleep when you sense yourself licking at a hot, sick mouth.

#

It has taken two days but a surgeon is here.

Mama has done something to the walls. Or rather, it is morning, and the walls have turned to light on their own. When things were still Alexei struggled with the blankets but despite the wool, cold came in from all sides. Then, the sensation of his mother's fingers in his hair, spreading, tickling his scalp, despite that she was asleep.

The doctor looks strong and beautiful, ready to tell a happy joke. Or is he a regular fellow and anyone would look like that now? Alexei is hiding his crotch with his good hand, but the man inspects that elbow first, leaving the child exposed, grimacing with effort, trying to do something from the opposite side. All he can sense of the wounded arm is a cold, large thing taking up space, pulling at the side of his chest, pressing into his ribs, too soft to be stone.

Revekka says, "Sir? The injury—the other arm."

"You know we farmers can't tell left from right." When she does not laugh as he intends the man says, "It's just for comparison. You don't want me moving the bad arm this way."

Revekka snickers, looks down, does the thing with Alexei's neck and hair, maybe for the last time.

Little Sergei says, "The men next door put a rifle butt at his head. He raised his arm and it hit him here."

"You've told me."

"When we fell on him it was the knee. But that much is better. He turned out of his bed from pain and landed on the elbow again."

The man is frowning at the leg, a touch over every joint. It is a gentle exam, but Alexei takes in air through the teeth. It is a sound without a name, sort of the reverse of a snarl.

"We've given him gin for the pain."

No, they have given him scotch for the pain. The gin was for the peasants, for Vetta's witchcraft. But

Kabanova's only lasting spells were Andrei's death and a curt disappearance.

The physician appears to lose his strength: "Alcohol, for hemophilia?"

"Not for hemophilia, for the pain. We were not sure he would make it through the first night."

The surgeon has crossed the foot of the bed, now bends over to sniff at the injured arm. "Spirits are not my field, but I'll wager you made his condition worse."

"We won't serve it again, sir."

The man shakes his head, breathes unhappily. What is the difference? Fermentation in the glass, or in this visitor's awful breath? "With all candor, we might be administering it again, in only an hour or so."

"Sir?"

"We cannot save the arm."

Chapter Eight

LITTLE SERGEI and Igor spend precious time looking for chloroform. Fever keeps changing the doctor's name to Ivan, Iosef, Immanuil, but every nap changes it back. Best then to only sleep.

Awake or not, the boy hears all of the voices, and he has made up some of them: Ilia, Ignat, the rest. Sounds are multiplied by mama's floor, made louder by walls.

His options are few: amputation while drunk, amputation while sedated, which is unlikely. But scotch lends him a manic, observer's feeling and he would rather not take bone cutting in that state.

Why do they not just smear clay on the damaged part and be through with it? The world has been eons like that, is he wrong? A core of blood-hot marrow with a veneer of ice and mud? It is easy for us to forget because we are trapped in our middle temperatures in the form of lukewarm, fragile protein. But it seems to Alexei to be the only fix.

By the sound of him, Little Sergei understands better than the physician does. Alexei hears the guest sniffling, speaking in a new pitch. Also, the bass-clef rhythm of mama thumping him on the back with a hand. It is a satisfying drum line, but born in Revekka's preference for inward passion. She would have hated any of the previous eras and it is astonishing that she knows the Bible at all.

"He will be well, Captain. If nothing else, we still have my husband."

So many errors in this, including Sergei's rank. Is she as mad with worry as she sounds? Could be, but the man's hysteria has rather wedged mama to the side, leaving room for only strength. The boy would guess marriage works the same way, everything decided by limited space: who will cook, which one sleeps late, who tells the jokes. If he survives his youth, and if Anastasia ever shows up again, they will work through each of those together.

Another temblor in his upper arm, geothermal pain in the shoulder, ribs. The hurt does not wake him nor does he recognize it at this scale. Instead he dreams of an embrace from Grand Duke Paul, who cites the magic of economists, Revelations.

Is it true? Alexei is returning to the New Testament? If he is, then suffering is exactly as the textbooks promise it to be, the death-blow to reason.

In time he dreams of Grand Duchess Olga. She is the plain one in life, but here she is as lustful as a swimmer. Revekka has been shoving at the boy and now he wakes, reluctant to leave the girl half-dreamt.

Mama says, "Take this. They're here, and Doctor Igor has a fire going. Take it."

She pushes a spilling handful of salt at him, holds a spilling cup of water in her other hand. The uncontrolled nerves extend from her palm to cup to drink, and the surface pops the same as their lake does in heavy rain.

His mother has turned to downpour, their first confirmed miracle.

Alexei waves the salt and water away, too tired for rites anymore. Moreover, when he searched around on the floor two days ago he came to Anastasia's bag of salt, which was missing since the tornado. He ate some then.

Revekka persists; he swats her hand away and she swats back. "Take it. Nothing else will save us and you need to be ready. When they cauterize your arm I will smear another handful at the end."

The end. She could not have meant it like that or perhaps she meant it exactly that way. The end of your arm is the end.

The boy makes as if his refusal is for good; as if, when he stares off, he will not look back or answer anymore. But he is too bedridden to state much of anything. As for mama, she only stands and spills. Something in that is chilling to him but he cannot place it. For only this reason he gives up. He gestures in disgust, swallows most of the grains, discards the rest by sweeping his hands together.

"Alexei! That's valuable!"

"Valuable?"

"It's all we have—" but she leaves the last few words in the ether. It is all we have, what? To eat? To sell? To slaughter our fields full of hog, then store the bacon?

But his reply, too, cuts off in its place. Natalia has spoken of warmth and Hella Jensen told them of a delicious cooling, yet his response to the healing salt is neither. Instead he is aware of a certain ampleness: the sense of muscles, lungs, bones all filling out at proper density. When mama lets vegetables go to waste, which is rare, he has seen a distinct wilting before they fully spoil. Losing volume. Moisture and air returning to the air. The mechanics at work here are the opposite of that.

Alexei feels his shape returning, his posture rigid again. His voice is back and, despite so many wry words, his mouth is drenched.

His pulse gallops like horses, from fear and restoring health. He says, "Cut it now."

Revekka calls out, if only to persuade herself: "Doctor Igor, Doctor Igor! The boy is ready."

Sergei and the physician have been cleaning the saw teeth, tending the fire, watching the horizons for newcomers. Sergei runs his palm a full circle across Alexei's face—ear to chin to ear—and says, "You say you're ready? None of us are ready. But you're a brave old bird."

Speaking of newcomers, only his mother is supposed to call Alexei bird.

The doctor comes in and calculates. This is too much time dithering around while the patient is trying to be still, trying not to pulse his hands to fists and back. He is bouncing each ankle, waving with his feet. At last the boy thinks, *Get on with it, you son of a whore!*

It would have been his first spoken curse. What's more, their guest seems to have heard. Igor jolts the way any man would, if he were electrocuted by a motor. He says, "Don't be in a hurry for us to start. This will be horrible, truly."

"I know."

"Do you know? We are going to move you to the floor and our best hope is that you black out soon, poor bastard."

Despite his rising strength it takes only two hands to lower him from the bed: Igor's left, Sergei's right. He is no heavier than the curtains and, when the soldier places his body over the length of Alexei's body, it is time.

The soldier is crying again, and Revekka is set to join him. Sergei tries to say, "You ought to go." But no, mama is holding Alexei by his living wrist, and her palm is as cold as his dead palm. Above him a huge, blubbering man is speaking of revenge, murder, the bodily torture of another man. It is an embrace by warfare itself, which bawls more than you would think.

To his side, a mother's hopeless charity. She says, "Please, doctor."

"My heart bursts for you. Maybe if it is truly numb."

"Cut it off before it kills me."

"Christ and Mary, forgive."

Igor cocks his arm back and Alexei looks away. The first cut is through skin, which wakes the cold tissue, sends lightning to Alexei's shoulder. The limb is his again and he jerks it free without knowing. Mama cries out as if the pain were hers. Or was that Alexei's voice?

The surgeon has to correct his stance for the next cut; he weighs the boy's upper arm with a knee and holds the wrist far away with his free hand. He says, "That was the worst of it; the inner tissues are not the same as the outer ones."

It is openly a lie, although Igor means well. Of the circular amputation, that first, tentative slice was a 20-degree tear. There are still muscles, ligaments, major veins and arteries to slice through. That is to say nothing of bone, or of the sewage that spills from the hollows, the act of the body poisoning itself in defiance. The man has to cut away the rest of the furious skin, too. More than 300 degrees' worth.

No, that was not the worst of it.

Then again, Alexei's pain is awful. Not remarkable, mind you, only awful.

When the physician saws again the boy's length and breadth turn to magma. It is blind, all over, neither oscillating nor steady. Alexei knows he will vomit yet he howls instead, causing his rectum to swell up, strain. The boy fouls his back, the backs of his legs. He can only answer it with piss; the warming streams on his pelvis exactly like those on his prone elbow, pissing himself from bladder and vein.

Every sense is umbrage. The body's inner smells are set loose, and numbness does not obscure the sick tugging at his underarm. He cannot choose whether the floor is too hot or too cold.

Between Revekka and Sergei—or is it both of them?—there is a rather songful wailing that sea captains ought to use. And if the boy is not mistaken the surgeon's voice is close to breaking.

—Stop where we are, he can tell the guest. —My arm is healed. We feared it was dead but every nerve is alive. Look how my senses are working again, I can tell your breath from Sergei's breath by the way they land differently on my skin.

But that is wedged in his throat, locked behind the pressure in his jaw, molars on molars. His veins are taut from forehead to throat, lost somewhere near the chest. His gripping teeth are causing injury all over, deep inside, no matter where. You have to remind yourself that the house is not burning.

Igor pushes the saw out, draws it back, each of those running high voltage from elbow to shoulder, hertz down to the cavities. Revekka stands to go. Probably too much carpentry noise for her, and no woman could watch a son's face twist into something so meaningless.

The boy knows that but still calls out. He sends every curse he can remember, blame and spit. He faults Revekka for the hemophilia, Little Sergei for the peasants, Igor for the imminent death.

More than those, he blames Anastasia for her chastity, for reading all the science and philosophy books aloud and then claiming the human struggle is rubbish. She is overjoyed with magic then *tsks* him when he speaks of oddities.

No, he blames papa the most. Always at war, murdered on the lines every time he was deployed and, at last, murdered on the lines for good.

But look, a sign of blacking out! There is a catch in his breath that muddles him, dulls the blades all over: Igor's saw blades as well as the blades of pain, panic, digestion. He defecates a second time but that is only from momentum, and the act dulls him further. His vision turns to sound, the brightness of the room is white noise.

"Sleep, friend. Sleep until you're well." But the saw has reached muscle and Alexei howls again, the combustion has returned, his respiration as high as ever. An erratic seizing in his arm causes spasms from bicep to shoulder to upper back. If he were in a standing position the cramps alone would drop him. Mama is here and pushes the saw away, applying salt to the shower of blood and dropping shawls all around him, a blizzard of linen. Anything left of the salt she presses in his mouth and he swallows it, tries to drown in it.

The minerals ought to sting the open gash on his arm, or parch his mouth, already drying. But in both of those ways he is too overcome to notice.

Even now the pain, however cruel, is quantifiable. The heat, awful, but not otherworldly. The fear, no different than he has felt before, so many times. Ask him one day about the scorpion in his shoe. He is enduring.

No child should have to and, by point of fact, he is surviving better than any child would. He repeats that, if with only an inward voice: —A man is cutting my arm off and I am enduring.

Revekka says, "Drink it. Drink, idiot!" She is pushing blood-soaked towels at Sergei and has the face to say her guest is the idiot? The soldier opens his mouth, squeezes the blood into his ugly gruel of spit, mucus. The physician returns his saw and slices once more, up and back. Alexei has another minute of pain, muscle tremor and panic until, finally, the early moments of anesthesia.

Did she find the chloroform and administer it without him knowing? Is he blacking out at last? No, he watches as they collect and drink, collect and drink. The explosive heat in his arm lessens to a simmer. The operation, now an irksome tugging. After a time, full bodily calm. The shapes of the pools of blood make Alexei wonder about the shapes of islands.

Within another minute he is asleep, despite that Igor still cuts into marrow. Alexei knows that flavor well: so many nights eating seared chops, digging his fork into the savory part.

#

He wakes to a low burning in the high arm. The stump is nearly cozy in its wrap, swaddled in cloth. He is on a bed again and the brown curls at his neck are drenched to black. Still the odd strength and defiant thoughts. He is not bleeding anymore and, while the inflammation in his knee concerns him, what remains of the arm is improved. The procedure, a likely success.

The men are outside and mama is quiet, wrapping something in bloody towels. She works with her back to him: a forced, often redundant act that means she is hiding something. He knows the answer but will ask, just to hear her say it: "I'm going to live?"

"You will, son. I promise. It was a miracle. Doctor Igor cut and cut and we did it, Little Sergei and I saved you. When I drank up your blood I could feel you coming back to life."

Normally after a remark like that she would kiss him, come over to hold him, sob. But she presses on, collecting the last of the towels and rushing the bundle away, a bomb she hadn't intended to make. It is his lower arm.

The ice-blue claw is forged into its last shape. The plum-stained fingers are meant to hold a plum, which is nowhere around. The elbow, once swollen, has collapsed like a fat man's shirt. There are two inches or so of meat above the hinge, and that much slaps around freely above the joint. Further up, the fraught amputation wound: muscle, skin, jagged things. Full descriptions need the words of vultures now.

Knowing mama she will ask Little Sergei to bury the arm. The soldier will agree but only if the hole is to funeral specifications. It would take him a week to dig and Revekka would check on him time and again, cursing his slow progress. She might say, —It's only one goddamn arm, Mamontov.

If Alexei were blunt, he would tell mama that her story of the beating at Petrograd was a lie. That she invented every detail: the man bleeding on pavement, the cleansing of a stranger's blood with clothes. The drinking, the applause. They were not exaggerations or tricks of the eye, but whole inventions. Time has fooled her into believing it, improved the lighting and added details. But it began with fiction.

It was the salt that healed him, not her ugly ritual. The mineral calmed him, restored his strength before the cut and sedated him during it. It slowed the bleeding, cauterized the wound afterward.

He figures the salt is still at work, muting his pain, keeping him groggy. When mama returns he says, "That was not the yearner's salt you gave me?"

"No, little bear. It was your father's."

"Father—you mean the monk?"

She laughs and laughs, comes from opposite the room to tickle a rib. "Funny boy. Your father was Karl Vasilievich Shafirov, in the imperial army."

"I know his name. But you said Father Grigori may have died like that."

"I didn't say he would be the only one."

"One day, will you?"

"Probably. But that means you will have my salt, too."

She has answered the wrong question. He meant to say, —Will you admit he was the only one? Instead she has offered that she is a being of salt, just like Karl. Why, then, isn't Alexei?

She says, "It will protect you, keep you well." He suffers a hateful thought: If that is true we will need your remains soon. We will have emptied papa's footlocker in no time.

Emptying it might be a blessing. As medications go this one is crushing in its weight, a burden for a large ox.

#

Tonight he will work on the questions of his mother and girlfriend. Their scriptures, fables, medicine. What is left to solve when he nods off he will try to figure in his sleep.

The first is easy: Karl Shafirov died in battle, just as the officer and Prince Vladimir said. Perhaps he spilled the way Father Grigori did and yes, perhaps those are the minerals Revekka fed him. And let us suppose they worked.

But if so, Karl Vasilievich Shafirov is not his father and Alexei need not refer to himself as Karlovich again. Mama had the boy's discarded arm in whole, with a wad of towels. If both mother and father are gifted that way, Alexei would be, too. His arm would have turned when Igor removed it. Better yet, it would have spilled at the moment the tissue was dead, still in place, a shower of grains down one sleeve.

If Alexei was like them, when Revekka cut his hair the clippings would turn to coarse. (Or is *coarse* a yearner's insult and he should use the more agreeable French *sel* in its place?) She was always discreet when she groomed her husband, both hair and beard, and she rarely trimmed her own hair. Or if she did, Alexei never saw. Now that Alexei is considering it the man shaved near the dead water. His clippings, if that is the term, gently dusted the bank of the pond.

In the end, the officer must have delivered Karl's remains in the footlocker, hence mama's silence about the contents, and her reaction when she opened it.

The next problems are more difficult: what else has mama refused to tell him? What has Anastasia kept to herself? Did the two of them discuss it without him? The way he understands it the girl's idea of tricking Natalia Baratova was itself a trick. If the aristocrat was healed, Revekka and Anastasia must have conspired. Yet they seem always in disagreement, fussing at each other, because of each other.

The last problem, and the one that will perplex him for months, is why mama hid such an effective treatment for as long as she did. She administered tiny doses to Natalia and Hella. She prayed bedside through Alexei's two critical injuries. He lost his arm because of her indecision. There is a chance he will still expire.

He can dismiss two of the quick answers: that she means to kill him and that she is trying to more carefully portion out the remedy. A woman intending to do him in needed only to wait, the dead arm alone would have finished him. Listen to her in there snoring, exhausted at last. No woman guilty of that would snore like she is.

And, although Revekka was stingy with her treatment of Baratova and Jensen, when it was sure that Alexei was passing away she threw handfuls of treatment at the boy.

This is what he will realize, before he dreams of contenting things: Mama has not spoken of the side effects yet. Natalia appears well after several tastes of the salt and Hella seems improved after one. But with years of use, their patients might regret it, become dependent on it, or their bodies might turn to salt, in composition. Or something else.

Alexei does not hurry through these riddles in a night. The coma is long, poorly timed. When he wakes again there will have been a second revolution and, this time, his dear Russia will be all Bolshevik. Mama and Sergei will have spent half a year selling things, finishing and selling Freyja, cooking new salts and offering their own counterfeit salves to the rich.

One of the better rumors will say that Alexei continued the practice in his sleep, and his mother would never contradict that.

Never mind his doubt. When this child, her persistently skeptical child wakes, it will be both infantry and the fable which tend to him.

Chapter Nine
Kholmogory – August 1744

THE WOMAN from Oridinnes, Chehreh Qajar, was shivering, wagon-sick. The men who brought her were quiet but their fighting clothes, their gear, were noisy. It was dark, and it seemed to have been dark for a while, maybe for a full day. A wide river, which she could hear but not see, leveled the terrain to flat and brown. The landscape was odd enough to frighten you.

The Russians had found her in Mount Paul, across the mountains from Oridinnes City, in the forests near the border with Ethiopia.

They had questions, and she answered some without evading. One of the men, Vasili Mirovich, was gentle, with a healthy appetite, a heavy musk in his clothes. He spoke a few words of French, she trusted him. He built a wooden crate as she had asked, each dimension roughly the length of an arm. He dug a hole, putting aside whatever dirt he produced in the first hour. From that depth, he filled the box with earth, hammered the lid shut.

One of the other men said, "Is it for devilry?"

Those were the years of ugly magic, in some company it was impolite to discuss at all. Chehreh heard of corpses that rose if you shrieked in their ears, but only the most loud and vile shouts. After a time the revenant would stink again, would lie on the earth again, and was harder to wake the next time. After a few rounds of this it became deaf, nothing would work, fully dead at last. Not the kind of magic she would discuss with a stranger.

She had heard of tinkerers who used piss for alchemy. Also: buildings where a violent man would rise from the echo of your feet. In those places you had to walk barefoot and slow, or you would be killed in the hall.

She said, "Not devilry. Just silly folklore. I should not have asked." But she had fussed over that cargo, a crate of soil, more than she did her clothes. Anyway her garments were plain, and she had no need for fashion at home, where it was hot, moist, always work to be done. She was ravishing, with gentle bones and a frank, steady gaze. Men and her mother said it was a loss to cover that up. She had scars from age 17, but that was the only reason for full dress.

It took days to convince her and two more days to prepare. After that time, about a week, they set out from the squawking trees of Mount Paul, found silence in the dunes, ate scorpions raw, or maybe the horrible things were already cooked by moonlight, still living but a ready meal, black all the way through. You needed only to catch them and cut away the stings.

As the weeks gathered for months they, she and Vasili, sensed a loneliness in each other. Chehreh missed her country of secrets which she otherwise claimed to hate. Vasili wished again for his hungry, unstable, devout country. Russia was too big to know, even to long for, yet somehow he longed for it.

The man was rough with her at first, but her ground covering would take care of that. "A little, Vasili. Eat only a little." He nodded off while still chewing. His eyes blinked shut and he snored in funny puffs of breath.

When she bathed he swore to kill every man who did not look away.

The trip was seven months in all; in that time she fed Vasili her whole quantity of herb, only Vasili. She could have murdered all of them with it, with only half that much, but he begged for it, compared it to brandy, and she rather liked when he was happy. Some nights she would tickle his chest, had to quiet her breath when he reached over. Now, tonight, the trip was finally done, and she realized the man had spent too much time drunk on flora.

There had been three seasons, four thousand miles, to tell her about Kholmogory, but he never did, not quite.

They had promised a fortress with thick, stone floors, infantry guards, a lifetime of safety. Yet she knew a prison when she saw it. Even in the middle of the night you could tell the place was gray, built entirely of rectangles, few windows.

She said, "Will I be an inmate?"

"No, we told you. The boy is the inmate."

"But the boy and I will share a cell? Am I free to come and go?" She turned to Vasili, but he would not look at her.

"What am I here to do?"

"You will tell him of his life. You and he are the same, are you not?" She nodded. That was one of her first lies.

There was a sandstone courtyard in the detention wing, another rectangle. Chehreh asked Vasili to remove enough paving slabs to plant the dirt they had brought in. They had lied to each other, made love, then continued to lie, and he was in no place to refuse. Indeed he preferred it like this. He would not be the one to close her into the cell.

The boy, the prisoner, was asleep when she came, and his renowned stutter was sleeping, too. His voice was meditative but stupid. He spoke in the same front-of-mouth French as Vasili.

He said, "Are you here to be another Anna?"

The Russians had told her the boy was four but he looked smaller than that. And no woman had seen a child so white, with such sad gestures.

Chehreh said, "Do you know me? The jailers believe you do."

"I do not, but you know me. I am the *souverain*."

#

By morning the child was awake, waiting, holding his Bible. Her vision was improved but only somewhat. A glow came over, through windows she could not see, light bent once and again until it warmed the room, like irrigated water.

The boy was frightful to look at. Thin, filthy, too short, with a complicated expression and large forehead. He handed her the book, which was handwritten in thick letters spaced far apart, split into long, narrow columns, about one thousand pages. She guessed the language to be Greek but no matter which, the alphabet was not familiar. She would even have struggled with French, but this was gibberish, as much diagonal scribble as calligraphy. Meaningless dots, symbols, sketches.

The boy said, "My—favorite—book is Haggai." He was stammering this time, popping his lips to finish sentences: *mon, livre, préféré*. With so much time and struggle between words, every one of his statements sounded like a lie.

"Is that why I'm here? To read a Bible to a vulture?" The term only came to her at the last moment, she barely meant to say it. But yes, that was exactly the bird she meant, an unflying, sickly-pale vulture, always starved and waiting, cawing about the dead, a safe distance from the living. If any beasts were the doorway from one realm to the other, earth and afterlife, they were vultures, and this strange boy.

He said, "A minute, only one—minute. Of Haggai."

He was used to begging, that was past all doubt. The one who begs is the one who is used to receiving. But who shared a cell with him before? His mother, likely, but then why was he alone? Famine, sickness? Vasili and his wagon mates came without introduction, asking questions about Chehreh's beating in 1740, they knew the date better than she did. They spoke of her connection to a youngster in Russia, born on the same day that she was slain, or nearly slain.

No man was closed off to her, especially then, in her first life. She sensed the answers they had hoped for, what promises they were authorized to make. They said, "Do you have any thoughts of him now? Do you see his family? Are you content to remain here, or would you accept the hand of the empress?"

The boy seemed to have expected her, even called for her. She knew better than to deny him something as reasonable as this, a quick lesson from the scriptures. If she held out he would only rant about it until she changed her mind. She would have plenty of time to concede, she might as well concede now.

She said, "A minute or two of Haggai."

"Yes. Thank you—yes."

She was familiar with it, guessed it was some 800 pages in. She flipped toward the end of the book, pretended to leaf back once or twice, and recited from memory. At home, she had spent most of her Bible hours reading opening verses, where the names were new, not ready to disappoint. Haggai 1:1, Luke 1:1. 1 and 2 each of Corinthians 1:1.

She was more familiar with the gospels than the rest, but this illiterate child would not know the difference. She said:

"In the second year of the king came the word of God from the prophet Haggai, the head priest, and it said: The time has come for the Lord's house to be built."

She stopped, and the child jumped. He was busy at her robe, his attention on her right breast. Vasili, her lovers, the husbands of Mount Paul had agreed on this, if on nothing else: hers was the chest of a man, placed high on her torso, commonplace. Yet it was taut, lovely in its own way. This one was too young for a sexual appetite, nor could he distinguish the curves of her body through so many clothes. Was he looking to nurse?

Chehreh said, "*Souverain*?"

"I am—hungry—hungry. Too much."

"There will be bread soon, I can smell it. I hear the place waking up around us."

"What does it say?"

It was a fair question: what did the building tell her? For the boy, their unnamed convict, it was the same, dull cell as yesterday. In his experience the prison's walls were quiet, the same secrets already told. But this Oridinnes woman was a new arrival. She could unfreeze it, if not the stones, the voice of the place. Of a body's many rivers the voice is the warmest, ready to thaw, spill forth, flood a room with its currents.

"What is—it saying?"

She pretended to listen, which is the same as listening. She said, "The place says we will not be here long. And we certainly will not be here long before we eat."

She began to read again, improvising the second, third verses of Haggai, for as many as the boy would listen.

#

The food, considering everything, was not bad, not like she had feared. She counted six inmate voices in this hall, which faced the mountains, mostly opposite from the hated river. If there were eight such halls per floor, with three floors, and say every cell was occupied, the population was fewer than 200. With support personnel and wardens, she guessed it was 200 exactly.

Yet there was enough bread for these dozens of prisoners, many of whom worked in the sandstone haul. Over the first weeks she smelled tobacco, tea, perhaps a bite of pheasant. No village in Russia dined as well as these condemned few.

(The meals came through double grates, four feet apart. The second grate, the one on the prisoner-side, opened with a lock and pulley from the warden-side. It was a device for feeding animals, not for a woman who looked after a boy.)

After a fortnight she could not keep the wonder to herself. Once, while the child napped, a member of the Russian infantry passed the cell door. Chehreh said, "Who is he, sir? He has enough food for a grown man, and before me he had a breast for milk. He has a new Bible, and calls himself sovereign."

She had not learned much Russian from Vasili, despite their months together; only enough to cause offense. The infantryman kicked the gate and spoke quickly, mostly in echoes, and she could not distinguish voice from iron. He said: "Only God is sovereign. The rest of us are subjects, even the heathens, who do not know better. Subjects!"

"Your tsars are no subjects."

The man leaned in close and all she noticed was his beard.

He said, "I am to kill anyone who speaks of him as a Romanov. I am to throw his coins into the bay. I am to burn his prayers. The boy, too. If you say it again I will set both of you on fire."

It was the first she heard of the name, even in French, English or Oridinnes periodicals. Romanov, a son of Rome, where the oldest Christian church was born. Chehreh was not Catholic but she loved the mass, with so many voices in unison. A place for food and wine, a place for wanderers to sleep.

Nor did she misunderstand the guard's oath to burn prayers. Words, which she assumes to be ether, would only boil from the heat and scald him, blasphemy becomes injury.

When the boy woke she said, "Tell me your name, *souverain*. Your real name."

"Salzdahlum, I think. Yes, it is Salzdahlum."

"No, that is a place. At least it sounds like a place. What else did your mother call you?"

"She called me—tomcat, Haggai, Anton, squirrel."

"She called you Haggai? I have been reading Haggai to you."

"I know. But she—I know."

"And herself? Do you remember what she called herself? Was she a Romanov?"

"Mama said—Mama said she was a—Carlovna. It is—everyone else who called her a Romanova."

The floor was hard and cold, and soon Chehreh could not tell stone from elbow, hip, buttock. Pains in her shoulders inched from her biceps to forearms, wrists. She was used to sleeping on packed earth in Mount Paul, but today's rock foundation was unbearable. She and the child recited prayers of tyrants, hunger, jail cells. With every few sentences she paused for the stammering boy to catch up: "Rescue my soul. From this prison. For I anoint your name. The right ones. Will be with me when you are good to me."

In time she tried reading the Russian as Russian, not just as a street map for remembered verses. But the

Oriental languages, even their holy words, were closed off to her.

It was a lousy idea, besides. She might have erred only by one page and built a deluded second tongue, her every syllable wrong. A tower of nonsense, every floor more misled than the last.

#

It was spring before Vasili saw her again. He was lean, even more than before, with awful hollows under the eyes and so much unused pants fabric. Chehreh did not know what had become of him, but what she hoped was that shame had eaten him from the insides, underneath his clothes.

She nodded. Yes, that had to be it. No man will disrobe when he is ashamed.

He said, "The dirt you brought in from the Oridinnes. It is still in the courtyard. It has grown over, with sprouts all across. You must tell me if those are the same from the transfer here."

"I am sure they are. Enjoy it, I would rather go without."

"But the preparation, and the dosage?"

"You could eat it all as a single meal, raw. It would be quite an intoxicant but you would be well. I exaggerated the risk to be stingy."

Quite an intoxicant, indeed. That much would kill him, and everyone here. They would be dead before they were drunk. In lesser doses the leaf was a stimulant, similar to the khat of Ethiopia, but more sudden, quieting the speech. The toxic levels of the plant were hidden by myth, often silly myth. Overdose was impossible to research, more feared than understood. Yet the amount she was suggesting, she knew it to be murder.

Would Vasili be her test subject? Likely not, the man seemed to know what she was up to. He said, "You are being casual hoping I will eat it, share it around. I know the men here, they will finish it in one night. The place would die around you."

"And I would starve, and this one would die from worry. And no one outside would see any difference."

She knew he would plead, and it came to her at once. She said, "Yet we are freezing, even now. I will not last another winter. I am surprised the boy has made it this long."

The prisoner said, "And there is no light, for reading. I am a prince of the Russias, I should be reading."

"The two of you have books?"

"He has a Bible, and he is right. We have to strain our eyes to see."

Vasili nodded. There would be skins for warmth and a lantern for the dark. She would ask for more food, too, even companionship. He was ready for those; he knew she was going to ask before he came.

She was not careful with the years and damn it, they began slipping away from her, and scattering like vermin. Or rather a lovely, rare sort of vermin you had intended to keep.

#

She rather enjoyed the boy's company. Too bad, then, that by his fifteenth year, Chehreh knew that he would never leave a cell, and that she had to assassinate him.

She would have brought him along if they were freed. If she were living in Oridinnes again, in her home town of Mount Paul, she would take the boy in. Yet the men, even Vasili, had decided that she was the child's lifelong steward. It was simple, the steward only needed to take the boy's life.

How would she accomplish it? Malnourishment and restricted movement had wasted her body. They were about the same size and he was uncivilized, the mass and temperament of a dog. It would have been difficult with a weapon, and she was unarmed. She started calling for Vasili again, and one day he came:

"I need some of the leaf. I need the ground covering." She had taught him how to dry it, remove the roots and corolla, save the seeds for planting.

"There is so little left. And it sickened the men. What do you plan for it? One of our men has died and another is almost gone, he does not speak at all. He has not moved in weeks. There will be an investigation. I cannot risk the leaf in your hands, or any hands."

She believed him, every word. In recent months there had been an administrative shift: infantry hurrying past, meals that took too long or never came, stale bread. Wardens cursing at each other instead of at the prisoners.

"If I can heal him, you will let me into the halls. You will let me into the courtyard, too, so I can tend to the crop."

"You know of a cure?" Vasili was reaching into the cell, tender again. But she pulled away with one shoulder, not tender, but with such stealth you could have mistaken it for that. It was the stealth of a lover whose beau was asleep, and she had an arm under his neck.

Vasili said, "You must tell me. I will procure everything, before dark today. I will start to heal him tomorrow."

"No. I am wasting away here, look at my legs." Her knees were complex now, with joints and ligaments showing through. "You will bring the man to me and I will fix him. Then it will be as I said. I will stay as a prisoner but will have free use of the grounds, and the kitchen."

"I have told you over and over you are not a prisoner."

"Does a free woman look like this? Does a free woman beg to take a walk or wash her blankets?"

When they brought the patient it was as she expected. The man had a warm chest, cold limbs, his jaw was loose. He was about 25, the perfect age for this sort of cure. He had a sharp beard and, in happier times, an intoxicating stare: the perfect patient, too.

Too bad for his pretty wife—at least Chehreh guessed the boy was married, and that the girl was as lovely as he was. He might not be married after the treatment.

"What is his name? I will not heal him without it. A woman has to know."

"Anatoly Fedorovich. But if he gives up the ghost, you must give up the name."

"Then I am sure I will keep it."

Vasili and his brother-guard were reluctant to leave, and the boy, whose name was Ivan Antonovich, was reluctant to turn around. But Chehreh insisted. She said, "No matter what you hear, you must face the wall until I am finished. This is not for a boy to see."

"I am not a—boy anymore."

The men had brought a few ounces of whiskey, as she had suggested. She decanted half of the drink into Fedorovich's mouth, and the stricken man coughed twice. The sound was a great distance away.

Part Two

March 1917:   A provisional government forms
April 1917:   King George V denies asylum for
                        the Romanovs
May 1917:   Army desertions continue; chaos
                        within the provisional
                        government results in high-level
                        military resignations
June 1917:   The Petrograd Soviet seizes the
                        Kronstadt naval base
July 1917:   Uprising in Petrograd causes the
                        liberal coalition to fall apart;
September 1917:   700,000 railway workers are on
                        strike; Leon Trotsky is elected
                        chairman of the Petrograd Soviet
October 1917:   The Petrograd Soviet creates the
                        Military Revolutionary
                        Committee

Chapter Ten
October 1917

IS LITTLE SERGEI conducting drills outside? Mostly they are shouts, or just one constant shout. Dust, urgency, a man without his wits.

Revekka, civilian or not, runs a drill of her own: "Son, now! You can't sleep, there was plenty of that!"

She is hollering as if the boy recovered days ago. The way he remembers it he woke only twice. Is she not telling him to dress for the first time?

She looks in again, "Alexei!"

"I am, mama. At my best." No, he was listening to himself snore, leaving air at the top of the throat until it dumped out on its own.

She sits, and seems to know she does not have time for it. She is dressed for cold, and action. That same wool coat from before, with her fox-hide cap. Two scarves. When Igor came for Alexei's elbow it was spring. Today the trees are fingery again and wind has done something with the leaves. How long was he out? He does not want to ask but he is exhausted, no chance of doing the arithmetic on his own.

Revekka says, "I'll tell you again. I want you to listen this time. The government fell while you were asleep. There are more men at the Kabanov place—"

"That was before. That was February, remember? My fall."

"Yes, and it happened again. The first time the tsar abdicated to the Duma. This time was only some days ago. The Duma abdicated to the soviets, you could say."

His breath levels out, he is at risk of sleeping, even now. Mama becomes impatient and says, "And I just said there are more men at the Kabanov property. It is not safe. We waited as you tried to get up and we saw the place turning to hell. We waited and famished."

Yes, if there is something different with them it is that their faces are haggard, sad with skin. Mama in especial has a new face. If you told Alexei it was someone else he would believe.

"The men have not come back since?"

She may think he has clipped the sentence in half but he has not. The object of the question, that is to say the time the peasants killed Andrei and broke Alexei's arm, is always here, needs no mention. Almost the way old languages do not speak the name of God because it is forbidden and understood.

She says, "No, but they will."

"What happened to my arm, mama?"

She breathes in well, thinks of looking around the room but there is nothing to see, only him, his interrogative face. She seems to think, Fine, then. It is not as if losing a few minutes will bring anything back.

She says, "This question, and no more? I answer and we catch our train?"

"This question and you tell me what happened to Anastasia. I was awake for it, for something."

"No, Alexei. This question and you can ask Anastasia what happened to Anastasia."

The terms are unfair, he will likely never see the girl again. Yet he has no choice but to accept. He nods, and she bawls because of it, her voice turning to falsetto. Seen that way, you can only wonder if all singers are singers because of revolts.

#

What she said about Grigori Novykh was a lie. The man was a fraud, however intuitive, and he used the tsesarevich's illness for recognition. She told the boy about salt in the river, hinted that it belonged to Novykh, while she knew there was none.

The murder was brutal but unmagical. There were reports of a Petrograd sinkhole the next morning but Revekka has seen the photographs. The monk's face was beaten, his unmistakable hair a tangle. On his forehead, a likely gunshot wound. Father Grigori was beaten and drowned, exactly as Yusupov had confessed it. The dissolute healer was extinguished, and not in the way of a yearner. Good riddance to him.

Revekka knew what she said of the strannik was impossible, yet she wanted to prepare her son for the nature of Karl's death. She had endured that once already but never guessed it would come soon again.

Then days afterward, a bullet struck Karl in the abdomen and his ghost was slow to give. While Vasilievich died, he confessed the plot to Prince Bey, a story that began with an African woman, perhaps from Sudan, born before Empress Catherine was born. The woman spoke of herself as a purveyor, although some men used cruel, other terms.

Instead of an army cot Karl's deathbed was a sheet, near an empty footlocker. Despite the cold he took off boots, socks, anything with pockets. When he passed, Bey only had to sift the clothes out, pour the salt from sheet to luggage.

Karl's dying hope: Bey would deliver the footlocker to Revekka in prompt time. But the prince was injured, too, and could only notify her with telegrams, and a message from the Petrograd officer, whom Karl had recommended. Mama opened the suitcase that first night. Alexei heard her do it. She had thought the boy was asleep.

Revekka does not know all of it, either. When Anastasia and Alexei first put the yearner's mix together, he was bedridden. It is likely the girl found Karl's salt, added it to the blend. How else would it have healed Natalia? Or, less likely, Karl had sold his minerals to vendors and it stayed in markets all that time. When the girl went asking around for exotic salts, the result was a terrible coincidence.

Or there might be others like Karl in the market.

Not all are dead, either. Some could hawk what spills from their hair.

When Alexei was caught in the brawl between Mamontov and the peasant, she fed him a dose of cure from the footlocker. During the procedure, as the wound gushed onto the floor, she fed him more, smeared it on his amputation. His body needed a coma to fully heal but every month or so, perhaps four times in all, he woke. She quieted him again with another mouthful of salt.

"Look. It has fully grown over. Not even a scar, just skin. It is as if you were born this way."

Yes, the stump is in full health, such as it is. Smooth, a bit too pale, with no hair. An elbow of muscle, which is a thought that makes him shake his head.

She has hinted at all of this already, and what was left to guess, he already guessed. As confessions go it is a lame one; she is mostly repeating what she blurted out six months ago.

He says, "What else are you keeping from me? Why do you offer it to Natalia a pinch at a time, but when you gave it to me it was in heaps? Why did you wait so long? Is there a chance it will kill us?"

"No, not you. In the end you only took a little. Natalia, I suppose so, if she keeps at it."

"Why do you suppose that?"

"Alexei, for the last few days we thought you were waking up. Now, with the revolution and what is happening at the Kabanov farm, we have to go."

"Maybe. But will you stop referring to it as the Kabanov farm?"

Which of the last two terms does he dispute? He owes this strictness of speech to the girl, who, if he would be blunt, owes him some carelessness, especially now.

#

Of his recollections from the last six months, Anastasia is the earlier of two. Alexei tried to write the day off as a coma dream but the details never changed, and for that reason it has to be real, a true incident.

The girl was in shrieking pain, although he could not discern why. The taste of cigarettes and alcohol was all over. Then the vows and pleading, the sound of chairs or women toppling. Clothing being ripped off.

He remembers searching for her by calling a name.

After a muddled bit, mama put the girl out, saying, "And you. I ask for you in vain for a year, and this is how you come? Drunk as a cow and wearing only bedding? My bedding?"

Alexei did not recognize the third, female voice, "You know how these things are. They have befallen you, too."

"Things are this way in your house, maybe, but this is my house. Cover yourself and go."

Alexei looked briefly around, saw a naked woman, no older than 21. The stranger covered her brown stomach with a sheet. She said, "You can apologize later. I need to rest."

"On that, we agree."

It seemed that Anastasia came naked, too. Revekka said, "Girl, I will find you something to wear for the walk home. This one, she can go the way she is and no, you are not borrowing my things."

"So sorry, Revekka. Sorry as always."

From then he must have turned over, briefly woken again. Mama became a dawn-window, and he could not decide if that meant good luck or bad.

The second memory was no less raucous than the first. Yet for this one, little about it was in question. Revekka was rhythmic and out of breath. After a minute, Little Sergei sounded that way, too. A few minutes of effort and then whispers.

So be it; Alexei had a new father, anointed while he slept.

#

They leave so much. All of Karl's clothes, including his civilian ones, which makes Revekka scowl. From today the woman will look like outrage, no grief anymore. And has Little Sergei borrowed some of papa's old things, tailored them to fit? It is difficult to say. His plain, shapeless trousers could belong to any man, Karl included.

They leave most of the books, texts for school, history books. The boy tries to avoid any wit that begins with *How fitting—*, or, *Very telling—*. Also: the boy's miniature trains, soldiers, plush toys will stay behind.

They leave their sketches, his notebooks, anything on paper. He finds a destroyed garment that smells of Anastasia. He does not want to ask mama about it and tosses it in a corner. Nor will the girl come, by chance, for a goodbye, and he does not want her to.

They leave the shovels, gardening tools. During heavy rains Alexei and Karl would rush outside, start digging holes, barely able to wait for a mud fight. Or better, they only did that once and the boy has turned the memory into more than it was.

They leave the flour and, by all means, the wheat. Has Natalia brought more? It seems so, and Alexei will have to ask of her once they are settled on the train.

They leave Freyja, wherever she is. Mama has put only a few things in day packs—one for each—and in the footlocker, which Sergei will carry in a wagon. The soldier has fashioned a metal replacement for the boy's lower arm. Why? Is it because he longs for the golem already?

Never mind the rail haul to Moscow, Alexei dreads their hunger and fatigue on the way to the station.

Only a dozen steps past the threshold and she turns, looks at the Kabanov house. She says, "May we only see you again in hell." But in a few hours she will have to visit the place.

#

The car is empty, save for them. There are so few trains in the stations, yet no one is traveling? It can only mean, as papa used to say, there is a needle in the bag.

As they wait for the sound of steam, a man and woman come. It is difficult to tell their ages: she is dressed for extreme winter and does not remove her hood. The man is ruddy from work, with broad agricultural shoulders and pants that fit tightly all through. Despite his impressive body there is a frailty that Alexei cannot place. Sadness, cold, prolonged illness, it could be anything.

Another couple is here, with a young girl, maybe 10 or 12. The ages of peasant children are difficult to guess; so many are underfed, shorter than they are supposed to be. The girl has untaut skin around the mouth, with lips curled back into a macabre smile.

The child stares and Alexei thinks he is standing in the way. He begs pardon, allows her to pass but she does not move, only stares some more.

He repeats it, "Sorry," and does his best to ignore her.

There is one more pair, two elderly sisters settling in, and this is when the uniforms arrive.

Whether they are rail authority, military, soviet, they do not announce it. Their guns are enough, as are the ill-fitting belts that mean hunger, unbalanced accounts.

"Tickets?" They have stopped at the front-most passengers, the frail man and his cold wife. It is the darker-haired of the two who speaks. His partner, for now, is drunk-quiet.

The passenger is taken aback by mention of fare. He says, "We showed tickets to the conductor. He punched them at the time. I can show you, too, but they are punched."

The authority says, "Conductor checks for boarding train. These seats, premium seats. If you have coach tickets you can buy premium tickets."

"Which seats are coach? We can move."

"No need to fuss. It is cold, the price is not much." Something has convinced the man, or did his wife put a slight touch on the arm?

The passenger says, "Very well, what is the price?"

The one in uniform bends forward and writes, fingertip to palm. A spectral number, but in flesh, too. The perfect number. It makes the passenger flinch and he says, "Take your time with the others on board. When you have come back we will have decided."

There is nothing for them to decide. The man is stalling, nor is he good at it. The fairer of the two agents, quiet until now, has a sideways bend to his spectacles: "With others on board. Yes, civilian, we will let you decide. Take as much time as you want thinking about coach." His heavy emphasis on the last three words smears them in sound and meaning. Next time he should only use the words he intended: *thinking about removal, thinking about consequences.*

The men approach the old sisters and ask again. Now it is a farce in the truest sense. Scripted absurdity, the same unreceptive audience night after night. The drunk one says, "Tickets?"

"No need for games, young man. State your amount."

"You are oldest here. I think you need more help with things, ask a lot of questions. Ten rubles, maybe."

"Ten! Does the train take us to Amsterdam?"

The men chuckle. It is a deep, lapping sound that reminds Alexei of water after a storm, which should be comfort and nostalgia, not threats. The boy cannot guess if Amsterdam is far or near and can only echolocate based on their response. But it seems the agents do not know either, and have answered this way only for the edge in the old woman's voice.

The sisters are collecting their things and the men put palms out, urge them to sit again. "No, no. Ten for both, five for one. It is good service, the premium seats. Very worth the price."

The women were not going to negotiate in the first place, and one says, "Fine, then. Five for each, for our souls and our persons."

"You say there is difference?"

"Do you?"

Outside the wind does something to the coupling and Alexei sees that he can look far out, well into the horizon where lines of buildings, utilities, silos become a layer of fur. Normally mama would give him an elbow for being inattentive, but she is looking at the same thing. Too terrified to glance forward.

The first authority says, "We come to terms, but nothing in your bags of state interest? No German marks or gold?"

"If we were taking gold to Moscow would that be a violation?"

"German marks, bad for you. French money, Finnish money."

"It is clear you intend to search our bags and look, they are right here. We have no German or French or Finnish notes and we have no gold. But you did not answer my question. If we move gold, or any commodity from the country to the city, will a soviet intervene?"

Revekka leans in to Sergei and Alexei. She says something with her mouth, beneath whispering. Alexei only sees her teeth, no words, and shakes his head. Little Sergei is as deaf to the thing as the boy is and he stares, no answer.

Mama tries again, her words a light mist. She says, "If they are searching the bags." The moisture of her lips is as loud as the question, if it is a question at all.

Everyone here—that is, the frail man's family, the parents of the young girl and Revekka—are watching the interrogation. They are murmuring, checking the windows. In order from front to back, Sergei is next, and he shares a row with the footlocker. Revekka and Alexei are just behind. If the men discover papa's salt, the best you can hope for is confiscation. Mama and Little Sergei have not discussed it yet but at least they should keep some as treatment. A handful for Alexei's health, some for selling to others.

At worst, they will be charged with some kind of fable-crime, suffer the same as the empress who, for years, humored the strannik and put his buffoons in high ranks. The trial would be long, or perhaps lethal in brevity.

The uniformed man says, "We check bags, like you say. We find something, we talk. Who knows what we find, we will not argue about the laws of every little thing."

He lifts the first suitcase onto an adjacent seat and his partner takes a second one. Yes, the women have mostly brought clothes but the authorities choose to make a spectacle out of looking. They say, "What is this, what is this," with violent sweeps of the hand through the length, width, depth of the bags. Alexei can only compare it to school, for instance when a headmaster checks a satchel for tobacco. By the end of a search like this you are sure the contraband is there, despite that you packed the case yourself, only hours before, and have never owned tobacco.

One of them says, "And this?" The agent is holding something at the woman's eye level, out of view.

"My mother's pendant. She passed and it is worthless to you."

The man nods, says, "Good. Five rubles each."

"All of that for the same price as before?"

"Civilian, it is a long day. If we negotiate again it is bad for you."

The woman nods, they transact.

Revekka's hands are like ice and her fingernails jab at Alexei's palms again, harmless ice picks. They have come to Sergei, and the footlocker.

The soldier greets the authorities with a full introduction, no chance for them to cut in: "Comrades? I am Alexander Sergeevich Mamontov. I fought at Tulcea under General Lesh, during the reign of Tsar Nicholas. My father fought against the Japanese in the ocean war and I will take this soldier's widow to her childhood home. One train, no further than Moscow."

By appearances the men want to believe. "The imperial army. Bad treatment for you. Years of cold. But your uniform?"

"I was injured and discharged. My knee, in combat." He is standing to lift his pants hem, to expose the scar. But the men sit him down again, in case. "No, Mamontov. You may relax. Your passage is good, part of soldier's pension. But the woman and the boy, each a different fare. And this is your luggage?"

Revekka is praying in exhales and Sergei says, "Yes, but only books. Moldy nasty things, the woman is a sentimental."

"Tell me one that isn't." He lifts the handle at one end, gasps a funny note, true effort and the mockery of effort. He says, "A whole library with you. Tell us what books weigh so much?"

"Only trifle, comrade. Novels, the silly kind of novels."

"May I see? So much weight in here. A labor for you, carrying around trifle novels, like you say."

Revekka's hands coil around Alexei's wrist like snakes. She says please three times, not clear whom she is asking.

The boy whispers, "We will get there."

The second one opens the crate. Across the top are Revekka's books, Anastasia's books, including the Bible and Oscar Wilde. It is like a full layer of fat over broth, which is fitting, because this salt used to be meat and the man would stay alive by reading.

"Only novels you say? That is funny, soldier. Or maybe not funny. Every soldier knows the Bible is a novel."

"At Tulcea, I came to know."

The man opens *Melancholy* and says, "This is French?"

"It seems."

He takes the book out of place. Alexei holds his breath but sees the second layer of covers. Not sure how many strata are left; that is to say, if the books are mostly salt-cured or the salt is mostly book-cured. The man holds the pages up for Revekka to translate but she is not able. Alexei does, but he skips the first paragraph in entire, any mention of Heliogabalus and Sardanapalus, or the pope. He says, "Today calmer and no less ardent, but knowing life, and that we must bend. I had to restrain my beautiful madness."

To be fair he skipped the mention of dreams, too, it is not the proper audience for that. Not the men in uniform, not mama, not Little Sergei. Yet one or both of the old sisters would have enjoyed it.

The other passengers are whispering to each other, at least pretending not to hear.

One of the agents says, "The goddamn French, no?" The man laughs, turns to his drunk partner, insists the other one laugh with him. He repeats it, "The goddamn French." Their reaction to poetry is no less rustic than that of Alexei's classmates, and all of those are 14 years old, the most violent and nationalist of all possible ages.

Alexei meets eyes with the authority and looks away, looks down. He sees that the second layer of books is dusted with white grains. *E voilà*, if the men ask to see one more novel they will discover the contents of the luggage. Alexei reaches for mama's wrist this time; it surprises him that he has a free hand at all.

"Much to protect here, so much nonsense. Difficult to protect nonsense. Bags full of almsgiving and we are asking almost nothing. You have money left to buy things for God at Moscow."

His companion is more direct: "Like I say, the soldier is welcome in my car, you ride for free. The boy, his beautiful madness, three rubles. The woman, everything breakable, her breakable soul, six rubles. One ruble for help when we unload, 10 in all."

Revekka has been trying to interrupt: "Three rubles, six!" Now that the man has stopped talking she can say it for them to hear: "Ten rubles!"

Alexei grabs hard; every time she speaks a number the man will add that price to her debt. More than this, the timbre of her voice gives away that they do not have much. If she cannot pay the negotiations are done and they will lose their seats, any seats. Mention of coach is the agent's way of threatening eviction.

He says, "It is fair, good train. Fast, not any stops."

"Sir, I have taken this train before. I do not dispute that it is worth the fare. But I doubt it is worth the threats and coercion after I have paid my fare."

"Threats and coercion. You forget yourself, civilian. I did not seat you here, you did yourself." His mood deliberately turns hostile. Alexei fears men like this the most, those who can light their outrage at will, and with the most unlikely sparks. The man shouts: "Stupid whore, every hurt soldier can carry bags for you, you still respect us! Ten rubles or you can lick the honey from our eggs." The way he voices the threat makes it sound delicious.

"I apologize."

"This? You read this before you answer? You need wisdom?" He has unpacked the Bible and dropped it at her hands. She fumbles it, drops it, whimpers at the thud when it strikes the floor.

Alexei sees the rectangle of salt in its place. It is a small window, somewhat the opposite of stained glass, but a new architectural detail for the next time a church builds in Russia. A window to death itself, beyond all known value.

Little Sergei has noticed, too, and slams the lid closed. The report is loud, quick, like that of a rifle. One of the sisters gasps and Mamontov has only a moment to explain himself. He says, "Woman, please," and barely has to feign his anger.

Mama picks the Bible from the floor. "I spoke unwisely, gentlemen. I agree with you about that. But 10 rubles, we cannot afford it. It is a month's salary and my husband has been dead since February."

"This is a problem. We have three families here and only one is paid."

One of the sisters has stepped into the aisle and says, "Friends? They can have our fare."

"No, lady, that is not necessary."

"I insist. A terrible time for us to visit Moscow, we just realized."

The agents ignore most of it but one of them says, "February?" It is the drunk one again, and he has made a connection that is not there. His indignation is just like the other's: lit, extinguished, lit again on command. In sudden anger he punches the footlocker exterior.

He repeats, "You are widowed from February? Where was his station? Tsarskoye Selo?"

"Her husband fell at Tulcea, where I was hurt. The records are clear. It would be impossible to prove before the train departs but I will bring them to you, brother to brother."

"No, Mamontov. I see how you treat brothers. You say you fell together but you are here, carrying his books, reading his poems. How else do you serve your brother, or are you only serving his wife?"

"I would have asked Karl to do the same, if it were me."

"Friends, did you hear? The mother and son can have our fare. We paid you the 10 rubles; that should be enough."

The uniformed men trade stares, no need to speak further. The first one says, "The two of you get off the train?"

At least now the invention of coach is in plain view.

The woman nods and the agent says, "There is the matter of unloading your bags, unloading her books, listening to her disrespect until Moscow."

"We will pay the three rubles for the boy. He is frail and missing an arm. You would not deny him an administrative guardian?"

"The soldier is the guardian. This woman, only annoyance."

"Then six rubles for her. The boy has already paid his fare, and keep in mind he is infirm."

Revekka gestures with her heart and hands. The woman returns it and says, "Those are my terms, friend."

"Sweet woman, I owe you a debt."

"Only we trade in credit and debt, whore. The child will thank her in other ways."

You can only believe the sisters have purchased your escape.

#

Negotiations with the others are brief. Alexei sees that there are three more travelers here, originally booked on the following train, he is sure.

Soon the agents are gone, with no mention of the weak man and his fare. Never has a fault line cut so straight or clear.

The train lurches once, begins to inch ahead with grimy clinking. Revekka has time to say praise but only that. After some 80 meters, the train stops again.

Their first soviet-era ride is over.

The agents are back, with two other men in uniform, and eyes for kindling.

The drunk one pulls the frail man up from the shoulder and lifts him, if not from his feet, past his center of balance. The passenger makes a crude thing of rising seated-to-standing, tumbling over the adjacent bench and dropping to all fours. Along the way he cracks heads with the agent, who curses, leaves a boot in his ribs. The passenger cries out and Little Sergei stands to say, "Please, comrades!"

They do not hear, nor would they have pretended to hear. Revekka shushes him back to his seat and the agent kicks again. The passenger's wife stands but one of the men cocks her neck far back with a palm. She grimaces under his glove, her eyes and cheeks turning to wrinkles. He has the hand of a flatiron but his touch is rather the opposite.

The authority shoves her back like a training dog until she says, "Don't hurt him." The plea confirms it: her husband looks to be strong but something has debilitated him. Hunger perhaps, or the last time they took a train.

The first uniformed man says, "Me hurt him? You are in premium section. Everyone is paid, your games hurt them. The train is delayed now and the next time they ride the price is higher."

"Take it, then. Take what you need."

"Too late to agree, civilian. We wrote you down as disagree."

The authority takes a suitcase, one of the three, and holds it open in a snake-jaw. The woman blurts out something as he lets her clothes tumble all over. Garments are on the seats, the floor, some on the frail man's back. The agent slaps through pashmina and silk, but that is all there is.

He says, "Help me, you pricks."

His companions jump, each grabbing for a bag — only two are left. The last of them helps the first, looking around in fabric. When he tires of that he kicks the man to the floor.

The passenger had been sorting through his clothes, too. The sad hands remind Alexei of an earlier day: once when there was trouble between his friends in the schoolyard. A hopeless affair, like this one.

The man's bass-drum torso reminds him, too.

The passenger says, "Please, friend. You will empty it."

Is he referring to the last of the bags, or to his stomach? Bread-line hunger, sugar-line hunger are shared Russian traits. The new government may not see it that way or better yet, they do not consider themselves Russian anymore. Most likely, they think of themselves as the first Russians.

Either way, that is the last of the boots, and not because the man is pleading. One of the authorities has a find. He says, "Comrade," and every man in the car is ready to answer.

Now: "Comrade, it is here." He bends, holds an impressive bundle of rubles in his palm. He is careful with it, as if he held an exquisite bird, still too young to live out of the nest.

The drunk one is pawing at his brow. He checks the material of his glove, takes the glove off, wipes at his forehead again, checks bare fingertips. For the nuisance he says, "Barely enough, but it will earn you your fare. Up."

The man spits and stands, brushes debris from his jacket-front. He is brewing a curse but knows better.

Anyway, there is no time for it. The drunk agent removes his hat, lets it drop to the floor. He runs a bare hand through hair and checks again.

What is bothering him? Sergei and Revekka share a glance. They shrug: We shall wait and see, the gestures say.

Everyone in the car, at least each of the men, is mindful of his face. Makes sure history will register pride, no matter the conditions.

The first agent says, "This is what negotiations look like. The price is the price. No privilege for aristocrat, friend of Romanovs. You want privilege, you go to London and tell them you are a grand duke. No problem for you, everyone is a grand duke."

He laughs, happy with the beginning of his remarks, although the effort has made his hair wet. Like the drunk man did, he puts the hat aside and draws a long sleeve across the forehead, checks the sleeve.

He says, "But here, this train serves everyone. Farmer, landowner, old, sick. Favors for one are injury to the rest. There will be no more—" Whether he is mostly finished or only setting out, hard to know. He looks straight up, seems to inspect the car interior. But the ceiling above him is as plain as cotton.

"Goddamn elevator lifts, grease all over."

Alexei wants to say, —Elevators?

The agent is swiping at his head and yes, there is a distinct sheen to his hair, the dark color turning black. The frail man has stood, grabs for his wife, backing away from two of the agents, who are an oily mess. Yet the car ceiling is until now bare, and there is nothing on the walls. Only the authorities and the train floor are in question. The sickly passenger looks toward the rear of the car and shouts, "Tsesarevich, careful now!"

Tsesarevich? Until February, this was a title for only one child, the apparent tsar, the most loved and dangerous Russian. Today, without an imperial line, the word is meaningless. One of the old words. But the man seems to keep the lame honorific for Alexei.

The agents are staring at their palms, fussing over their clothes, bending at the shoulders and neck as fluid comes trickling down.

"Serves you right, you whore." It is the frail man's wife who has said it, and she steps forward with a bold right-hand, snapping the drunk agent's face to the side, spraying not blood, but oil. The punch was light but glanced across the nose, which causes the man to sneeze—more combustible.

You do not accept that Karl's salt is secure until you accept that the agents are dying, one by one, and are about to put the car in flames. Everyone here will burn but it is a victory even so. To hell with them or, if that is not the right way to describe it, to them with hell, the devil can come here and end it.

"Mama, now!"

The authority strikes the woman back, a grunting blow to the midsection that takes her height away. She plunges straight through, as if the floor has opened up. The train has myths of all kinds.

Sergei is the first to act, swinging the footlocker to his right and now metronome-pitching it to the left. It breaks lengthwise through one of the starboard windows, both a skilled and lucky toss. The rest of the train is havoc, while the frail man and one of the dying agents are trying to box, and another uniformed man drops to the knees, howls with fear. Every one of their movements, every arc of the hand dots the inside of the train with more kerosene.

The two recruited agents come rushing at Sergei, each doubling the other's threats. Alexei cannot help but think, *One day Freyja's voice will sound like this.*

Little Sergei points toward the opposite door. "Go!"

Revekka hauls Alexei by one arm. No grip is sure now, with so much oil, and they have to follow the couple and daughter toward the rear exit. But as Sergei reaches for the door the handle slips out of his grip—oil again—and more agents step him back. They are rushing, shouting; it has nothing to do with graft.

"Comrades, the elevators!" Their shirts are soaked, hats slipping to the back, ready to fall.

When the first agent spoke of grease from a lift, Alexei did not question it. But now, despite the fisticuffs, he remembers. Cargo does not stack above the passenger cars. The industrial freight is overhead, but several couplings back.

It is not grease spilling in through the seams in the roof, it is as Natalia said. The men are splashing.

The boy turns to watch it happen.

The frail passenger has overcome the second agent, pushing him down and away. It is hardly an accomplishment: the soviet is mostly clothes, and he shouts with a loud gurgle that terrifies the others. The last boarded passenger is engaged with a third, leaving only one mobilized for duty.

It is the first, the most indignant. The one who offered Sergei a pension for his service.

He says, "Cut them down!" But the drunk one is on fire. So, too, is the agent who lost his height. The forward-most couple is in flames. The woman shrieks as her husband takes off a coat, beats her with it, now cringes from the fire on his arm.

"Tsesarevich, please!"

Sergei is bellowing for Revekka and Alexei to follow, despite that there is no exit. An authority in the rear of the car has gone up. They are trapped between two fires, which are reaching far across, meeting in the aisle, a handshake of combustion. Alexei senses wild heat on his skin, his forehead is dry at once. He fears even a brush across the metal prosthesis.

Without speaking Revekka and Sergei lift Alexei, aim him feet-first and stomach-down at the busted window. "Wait, wait—," Revekka is breaking the larger glass shards with her hand, whimpering from the cuts.

They inch him through, wrists last. He kicks at the side of the train, shoulders rolling into angles. Sergei releases first and, absent a more proper send-off, mama waves to Alexei by losing her grip on his fingers.

After February, he does not enjoy the moment of falling anymore.

The straight-leg touchdown ignites both of his hips; for that moment he thinks the fire has spread from the authorities to his trouser material. He rolls—at best the maneuver is a sloppy guess—and checks the embossed palms for blood.

Agents are running up from the vokzal. Whether to assist him, arrest, or look in on the fire, Alexei is not going to know. Half the distance between the station and the burning passenger car is the freight. The most visible of loads there is a shipment of elevators, loaded top-up, the doors taken off for shipping.

He leans into a sprint, his boots pinching at the tops of his feet. Such delicious joint health, he has never felt it like this. Was treatment always that simple? To cure his hemophilia he only needed a footrace? And if so, does Alexei Romanov know?

He has never tested his speed and he is not especially good at running. The boy's chin is well past his axis, and he wonders if his gallop is becoming a fall. But look here, a hand is at his shirt, lifting him upright. Not in urgency, not in anything can you mistake a mother's touch.

The sounds of her feet were underneath his own but it is certain, Revekka has escaped the fire. The boy does not need to turn around to know.

The station men have halved again their distance to the freight cars. The boy is sure, the authorities will try and intercept him. So much cluttered hollering is impossible to make out but now Sergei is here, racing to the car, along with a fourth passenger. The better numbers mean they will make it through. Alexei celebrates with a rather breathy sob, but has to swallow it whole to keep running.

When they reach the last coupling he tries to jump ground-to-bolt and misses. The first step abrades his shin, despite the pant leg and heavy sock. He answers with a silent profane word.

"Up, young man! Up, up!" It is the frail one, a widower from only moments ago. Considering that, his voice is clear. There is too much fluid in the hollows when Alexei is afraid, which is all the time. His throat drowns with mucus, every one of his demands is washed down to a plea. Not this one, an emergency has made the weak man strong.

The boy lifts his foot again and slips again, another scrape to the shin. This time he cries out, no curse, although everything around their escape is cursed.

"Alexei-bear, please!" Now an unsaid miracle: the group of men coming from the station only runs past. Good, that will give them one more minute, but Revekka knows better.

She says, "My God, the salt," and turns around, chasing after the men, running toward the footlocker. For now Sergei ignores her and their new companion does not feign interest.

Alexei attempts the step a third time and secures his footing, a boot on the coupling, enough to lift himself to the platform. From here, it is an easy climb into the elevator.

Moscow is inside the car, now all around him.

He offers a prayer to the dead agents: You were right, the trip took only an instant. Just like you said, the premium seats were worth it.

Their lamp oil had a faint amber hue. If you drank it, and you were benevolent, would you always be warm and well lit? No one here will try, he will have to get around to that with Konstantin.

He waits for Sergei and the frail man, whose name is Nikita. As he stares through to the hectic train station, he knows he will wait a great while for Revekka.

Photographs of Moscow are always gray, but behind him the city is vivid, just as he thought.

Chapter Eleven

ALEXEI HAS BEEN hungry since he can remember. Tonight, sitting at grandfather's table, it is finally the opposite.

He chews until he is acidic, belchy. Nikita and Little Sergei, too. None of them have eaten so much in years.

Finding the place was not an effort. The elevator car led them to the state university; from there it was a short walk along the river. Grandson and grandfather always took that path when Alexei was young; today he led the men not by memory but rote. His companions did not question. Their grief was subdued by following.

Alexei had never considered it before, the numbing act of turning yourself over to someone else in whole.

From the river, the walk was about 10 minutes. The old man was sobbing already, hurrying across the grounds to Alexei, lifting the boy to his chest. Mama rarely answered Konstantin's letters in good times, and since the February revolution he only heard news once, in July. Her envelope had been opened and approved by officials, an early censoring.

The man did not know of Karl's death and when the boy told him, Konstantin dog-cried on the lawn, fingers in the grass. A man who feared he had lost the rest of his daughter this time.

A brief drink—everyone's hands were shaking—then dinner. Grandfather served chicken, potato, beet. Bread with butter, apples for dessert. Alexei never turns food away and had to follow Sergei's lead. Their new friend, too, was slow to refuse. In mourning everything is slow.

At last they have finished eating and clearing plates, at almost midnight. On a normal day it would be the old man to retire first, ask to finish speaking in the morning. Tonight it is the opposite; the younger men nod at everything, and Nikita catches one yawn after the next. It is rude to do so and he tries squeezing them in tight, right there in front of his mouth, like cigars.

Grandfather says, "Now tell me of Revekka."

Alexei and Sergei look at the same blemish in the wall. Nikita, who does not know of the host's temper, says, "There was a fire on the train." The man lurches forward, but the guest puts out a hand to reassure. "My wife was consumed. Your daughter survived. This one lowered Revekka and the tsesarevich to the ground."

"I am in debt, Mamontov."

"Decide that when I find her again."

The old man turns to Nikita and that one says, "We were running toward the vokzal, which was at the rear of the train. Rail workers were coming from inside—I suppose they meant to help out. Help their comrades, maybe. Your daughter knew we would meet at the freight cars. There were elevators there."

"Elevators for taking up?"

The boy is prey-still; he hopes the guest will be careful. Nikita has three times referred to him, Alexei Shafirov, as the tsesarevich, and is about to tell the old man that Grand Duke Paul's doors were loaded for hauling out of the sticks.

Nikita says, "No. Elevators for walking through. Moscow was only a footstep through."

"Ridiculous, sir. I suggest you catch your breath and explain it differently."

"It's true. We waited for her but she was following the rail workers. Something about her luggage."

"Careless. Careless! That dumb girl. Probably seeds she found, or some book with lambs in it." That Konstantin sounds so much like the train authorities means all of them are right, or wildly wrong. The man drops a fist onto the table, a garden of sounds.

He says, "Now you have lost her or left her to be arrested. Or she's trying to walk here."

The men do not dare correct him, lest the matter of Karl's salts comes up and they never get to sleep.

Sergei claims he needs only short rest and will set out for Revekka in the morning. Nikita makes no such claim; the burning death of his wife has closed him off. Also, he is staring at Alexei with an uncanny bluntness. Not that his glance is in any way menacing. No, the boy's parents used to look at him like that too, looking straight on the same as, say, the walls of a room.

The old man says, "In that case, Mamontov and Alexei will take my bed. I do not sleep at these hours. Son, I will ask you for a favor for when you wake, it does not matter what time."

As Sergei protests the host tells Nikita, "And you may stay in Revekka's old room. She was a stranger to you and it will haunt you less than it would these two."

Here is the favor: the man keeps a room in the basement. There is a steel door with a small portal, a rusted latch. On the floor, a field skillet, recently burned. Grandfather has brought a pile of dried sticks and says, "For the morning, and this is not urgent. Any time will do."

He makes as if he is lighting the sticks and putting them in the skillet, leading the fire into the speakeasy. Yes, there are burn marks around, under the top side of the portal. Someone has done it before.

Konstantin says, "Use this for fire. Enough for smoke, not too much. Make sure the smoke is in this direction." He points into the room, nothing much for Alexei to see, although there is expensive furniture inside, it looks cozy.

"Do you normally do it?"

"No, never. I can't."

"You're unable?"

"Alexei, enough. You open my house to strangers. In return you will do this for me, without question. Are we finished?"

The boy fears Konstantin's temper and unsteady hands. Whether one or the other he could ignite the house, raze it down, burn them to death while they sleep. Weeks from now, when Revekka comes, dragging papa's 200 pounds of salt by the handle, she will find ash, four more containers' worth to haul around. With that in mind, finished is exactly the word.

But more than this, he fears insulting his grandfather. He says, "I will."

"Good boy. Do it quickly and be gone, do not wait near the door. If you do not see me after an hour from that, do it again. We should be off now."

The man whistles and strokes Alexei's head as he would that of a pet. It is good to be subdued again.

#

Little Sergei is jittery tonight, despite their fatigue. Alexei senses it without knowing too much, that the man would be a terrible fit for Revekka. Papa slept well, could doze off because of anything: a breeze, a good noise, others who slept. He spoke of it as the soldier's talent. The sound of a low, scratchy voice made him tired, and he could nap at any time of day, if only for 10 minutes, upright in a chair.

Mama is the opposite. She needs preparation to sleep: the right clothes, bedding, a flow of air through the room. Any lapse in this or, for example, something in the distance she does not like, and she will miss her chance. It is not uncommon for Revekka to be up until the silent hours, or daybreak, when it is too late. Sergei and Revekka would only cause each other to stay awake.

The thought reassures the boy, but then again, is it why Anastasia refused Alexei until the end? Because both are like Karl, they would doze the hours away together, their lives mostly sleep? From there you cannot help your next question, and it is one you have had before: how would Anastasia get along with Little Sergei? He cannot help the idea of her legs, strong from adulthood, with knees cocked at angles and the dumb infantryman in between.

Damn him for the apparition, if no other damning reason, and now they are both awake. Little Sergei, that is to say, the embodied Sergei, is conciliatory: "You'll sleep tomorrow at least. Maybe tonight is for deciding things."

Maybe. And there is little doubt that Nikita is awake, too, deciding on bereavement or action.

What he most expected Sergei to say when they stirred was, "Thinking about her?" It would have been a vague question that made Alexei roast with jealousy, hot all the way to the metal arm. Sergei has, a few times, spoken of Revekka as his little cigarette. It is an odd nickname, but charming if you work it out. My lips surround you, my lungs fill with you, you burn me from the inside.

What, then, would Anastasia call Sergei? My jackal? You devour me, I cry out, you piss near my door so the other dogs know their place?

Throughout all of it—their whispering, banging shins on things, the cold toilets—they do not once hear Konstantin. The host is as quiet as stale air, and there is plenty of that to be had in an old man's home.

#

"Alexei. Alexei?"

It is Nikita. The time is four o'clock, and the boy fell asleep after long hours of shifting around. Mamontov has been snoring, hand to crotch, mostly bare, diagonal to the bed frame. His rustic sexuality has driven the child to a nearby chair, and now it forces him out of the room.

"Christ and his wounds leave him. Let him be."

Alexei is miffed with Nikita for waking him but it shows as annoyance with Sergei, who is only resting the way a man ought to rest.

Nikita limps behind him and finally, at this discreet hour, they can address it at last. The boy says, "Why the limp? You are strong otherwise." He puts his shoulders out like a bird does and makes his forearm big. Here in Moscow there are so many birds you fear they will come together as a group-beast. He says, "Strong?"

"I would like to believe so. You do not know this yet because your guardian died young. And I should say that first, I am sorry for your loss, I cannot imagine. I can only say, you will see him again, I hope it is soon."

"Thank you."

Alexei has heard odd expressions of pity before but it has been a while to hear one like this, and never from a fresh widower. Nor do the condolences answer questions of the limp.

Nikita says, "Not all fathers are dangerous, but their hearts break easily and that makes them dangerous. I suppose I am seeing now that my father's heart was broken." He lifts a tight pants hem, has to peel it upward like fruit. There is a raised and crimson scar there, which you could easily mistake for a vein, cutting from mid-calf to the shoe. It continues around the curve of his heel and stops, you have to think, at the sole of the foot.

Is this the cause of his frailty? Or, after he became sick, was this the thing which urged him to rehabilitate, to be strong again?

Alexei tries again, "What happened?"

But the man will only evade: "No different than what happened to your arm. But worse will come of us if we do not get away."

He is searching Konstantin's home for money, guns, bona fides, anything. He looks under rugs, inside food jars, behind icons, in the folds of chairs. It does not take long for the man to become desperate, and he searches between dinner plates, sifts through rubbish, checks the downspouts outside.

Alexei follows him room to room with, "Is this why you came for me so early? What are you looking for? If it is a small favor, I am sure grandfather would allow it, whatever you need. Why do you not answer?"

Nikita will leave, he has stated as much. It is hard for Alexei to know if he is going with the man, or keeping an eye out to be sure he does not steal, which by all means he intends to.

"We cannot stay, Alexei. We have to go at once." Nikita finds nothing, except this fork in an odd place, with the tines bent out of shape then pressed back. Alexei shakes his head: there is too much to say about it to say only one thing.

"I came so far to get here, after six months in a coma."

"Yet you don't wonder about him? His daughter is missing, his son-in-law is dead. His grandson is maimed, with a rusted arm. The country is starving and overturned. But he feeds us then goes off to bed. He does not wake, or cough one time."

The old man's stingy demeanor has always bothered Alexei; this is a criticism the boy would have made on his own, in the same words. But for Nikita to say it inflames him and he returns with, "Then what? You would rather he fix all of it from Moscow? Himself and in a single night, a silly old man? The strain on his heart, it is lucky I did not kill him when I told him anything."

"No Alexei. I know these men and their metal rooms. They were all over Petrograd. You do not worry about killing them that way."

Nikita checks outside again, but for what? Rubles nailed to the castle walls like pamphlets? When the man leads the boy inside, neither of them remember to close the door.

"Then in what way do you kill them?"

"Believe me, Alexei. That was not my point."

"The question stands, why do I trust you at all? We only met yesterday, you followed me out of a fire."

Nikita says, "And then I lifted you up onto the freight car."

"And then you called me tsesarevich."

The question has chewed at him all night. It would have been sedition nine months ago, to use Alexei Nikolaevich's title with a common orphan. Today that younger Alexei is locked away in house arrest. The two Alexeis share forenames and a bleeding condition, but there is no mistaking them.

Our Alexei, that is, Alexei Shafirov, has seen photographs of the tsar's son. What with the expensive clothes, scheming grin, only a stooge would get it wrong.

Yet this man is not stupid and that is why the boy is so disarmed by it.

Nikita says, "They explained it to me a little bit at a time, over time. I have not visited the clinic in seven years. You must forgive me, some of your people are dog quiet, but others talk just to keep themselves awake.

It is too much sometimes. And no one has said a word since Sarov."

"Sarov? The baths?"

"We will discuss it on the road. I am not sure if you are toying with me and this is not the place."

"If I was the tsesarevich I never once met Nicholas or Alexandra."

"I do not know how it works and it seems you do not either."

I do not know how it works. The man speaks of it as he would a rare camera. Where is the lens, how do I feed the film? It is too absurd for Alexei to state it: I am Shafirov, he is Romanov; we are separate. Separate the way river and bank are.

"I will stay. You can tell me now."

"Alexei, by the time I recognized you on the train it was too late. Those animals were hassling you, everyone. I did not want to make it worse. I should have said it to you somehow. But we are going to Petrograd. We can bring the soldier if you need."

"Petrograd!"

"I saw what you did to the men on the train, with only your arm. You can save the Romanovs from outside the village gate. We do not even need inside. You can free Russia. I will not sit here and eat lotus again, not with your grandfather. There is too much at stake, and we still have time to right the country."

Alexei ignores mention of lotus and says, "Those men combusted, there was elevator grease throughout the car."

The boy does not believe that, nor does Nikita accept it. The man takes him by the fleshy arm and pulls down hard, all the way. "Listen to me. They may have beaten us again or killed us when we arrived, or killed me along the way. They might have killed other passengers tomorrow, next week. You stopped them and I owe you for it. But for all you knew they were finished with us. You set them on fire and it took my wife. It nearly took your friend and who knows who else died for that. You are coming with me."

There it is, the man is insane with grief. Should the boy call out for help? No, he will handle it by himself. Nikita's madness alone is stifling, the mere act of clearing a throat could mean discipline. Also, Konstantin has not settled things for leaving Revekka at the station. There is danger no matter with whom.

And of the three unwanted men only one has demanded the boy come along. Also, there is Alexei's surging resentment of Mamontov, the pinyin who takes what he should not deserve.

The boy pulls his elbow free—always the concern for his joints—but tells Nikita he will go along as ordered. Nothing beyond that; he will not accept talk of alchemy, express sorrow for killing a woman he did not kill.

Nikita says, "You burned them because you wanted to. Only the tsesarevich could have done what you did."

"You are wrong, twice wrong. Maybe more than that."

And because they are talking without listening Nikita says, "I guess the man keeps his money and valuables in there with him. I would, right there in the metal room."

"The man, my grandfather?" Alexei has lost his patience and glory to God, look at his hand! In anger his knuckles have swollen to the size of a brick, he could knock Nikita out with only a hook. No, that is not possible, it is a trick of the eye, a matter of rage. But is this how fights begin? One looks to his hands and says, Yes, they are just the size for striking.

"It will be like he said. Wait for me, and if I do not come in a short time, light the kindling and put the pan in, through the slot. If I still do not come, light some more."

That is not quite what grandfather said but close enough. Moreover, it confirms that Nikita was listening in. When Konstantin showed Alexei the room, their strange visitor went out of his way to overhear.

They walk downstairs. At last, there is no more arguing.

It ought to be a simple matter, letting themselves in the door, looting the place for money, travel papers. But while Alexei is preparing a match, Nikita gasps, flinches. He swears with words and body: "I knew it! A lotus hive. Are you ready to believe me?"

"You're stung? There are bees?"

"Listen to it. Christ the Almighty this is warm." Nikita leans in toward the partition with one hand and puts fingertips to chest with the other. Mama used to do that with papa, especially after a gin, when papa would talk to her in the voice. It is an erotic, almost feminine touch.

Is the man tipsy?

Alexei joins him, an ear to the hinge, the dark room just past. He hears an elemental whoosh of bees, an enormous colony. He puts a hand to the door and Nikita swats it back, saying, "What? Do you not hear?"

Of course he does. Even through metal walls the noise is intoxicating, never mind the stings. Our towns would sound better this way. He says, "Is it not too late for bees?"

"Late! Young man, a hive is always awake." The boy had meant late in the season, too cold, although that question, too, is wrong. One winter he was surveying the land with papa and they came to a fallen tree, with a comb attached. Bees, which he believed to be dead, filled every cell, visible from the posterior ends, a funny sight with stingers and thoraxes.

He pocketed the comb for honey. It was dry, stank of weather. He figured there was none to be had but he wanted to keep it anyway.

Later, near the hearth, the comb roused from sleep. Mama swatted at the air and at the revenant drones. "Out, out!"

Nikita curses again, but it is a slow curse, not so easy to finish. He puts his back to the adjacent wall, slides down by bending his knees, nearly toppling forward. "The smoke, Alexei."

"The sticks? Do I light the sticks?"

"They'll bury all three of us, yes!" Now, because he has invoked his wife, he says, "Poor Dina, poor Dina." His hand is vaguely over his face, he bawls through it like a lifelong drunk.

Did he mean to say the hive would kill them? If the man is intoxicated Alexei will get no real answers until he sleeps it off. He has to take Nikita at his word, now tugs at one elbow.

"Sir, please. You have to stand."

"No, son. The smoke is the only way." Nikita hiccups with pain, another sting.

"Please, just come. We can use the skillet another day."

"Not for food, idiot. For smoke. The smoke puts them out."

No, Nikita is wrong. Alexei has seen it himself. The heat will wake them, send the hive all over the house. He bends low, reaches an arm and a metal arm behind Nikita's waist, tries to lift. But the man is heavy, it is too late. They will stay where they are.

"Damn!" Nikita is stung again and drops to the side, snoring. But it was Alexei who shouted: pain runs from hand to upper arm, an unwanted reminder of his surgery. The flush is immediate. Calm, soft and, as Nikita had said, deliciously warm. It is not unlike your first taste of wine.

The boy has never had more than a taste, he is not sure what to expect.

He rises, leaves a palm on the door for balance, searches the room for matches. It would be easy to write it off, that he will never find them, but he has to go through with it and look. They are not on the speakeasy sill, nowhere on the floor, nor in the hall outside. He checks Nikita's pockets—suffers another sting—and has to admit it, his grandfather forgot to leave the phosphorus.

Any choice from here is reckless. He could look inside the metal room and become peppered with venom. He could attempt a one-handed fire from only the bare sticks. He could wake Sergei, tell him they will leave the older men here, to their fates.

But a third sting runs all through.

Fatigue hangs on his neck like a weight, a shameful one. He sits, cries for Dina, too. And for Karl, Revekka, Freyja, Anastasia, and for all of the salt he is going to leave.

From the sound of it his heart has moved from chest to metal arm. A music box slowing to quiet.

Chapter Twelve

THE MEN RUNNING toward the fire did not run for long. Like their associates on the train they splashed, cried out, burned. Revekka tried to feel horror as she stepped away, so much heat. But if you hate a man enough his death will make you emptier.

By now Alexei, Sergei and the stranger were through the elevator car. Unseen on the opposite end, with no chance of seeing her, either.

Christ the anointed! There were four lifts, which one did they use? Her risk of making the wrong choice was too great, nor could she have lifted the footlocker that high. In time the flames brought onlookers. The men would have to wait for her in Moscow; she would buy tickets for another time.

So be it, the agents were boiling like radio static, but they had survived long enough to split Revekka apart from her son. Her only question, then: what of Karl's salt?

She was able to drag the cargo along the elevated walkway, as the ruined train drew most of the attention. The vokzal was built on a raised foundation, and the rotted lumber skirt surrounded the base of the walls on three sides. The fourth side was bound by the track, and an inevitable hole had formed at the corner, about waist-tall. There was enough space to push the footlocker through, an almost snug fit and, at a glance, the luggage formed a crude patch. It would be safe overnight, but curious boys or railway men would find it soon. She would need help tomorrow, to bring it home.

There were few whom she could ask. She considered everyone and ruled them out, one by one: not Father Rauf, not Alexei's headmaster, not the February officer. It was a sad inward pageant, for which the award was known ahead of time. But she could not bring herself to crown him until the ceremony was finished.

Vetta Kabanova was gone and the poor woman's husband, Andrei, was turning to fingernails. The Yanovksy home was too far and another weird request would only draw attention. Most of the locals were Karl's friends, not hers. She confused their names, did not recognize them in town. But they recognized her, spoke of mundane things while she tried to carry on: "Revekka, Karl's wife! I saw your son and his friends this week. So tall and healthy! With your eyes!" Often she would lie, tell them she was not Revekka, but a de Morny.

What, then, of Matilde and Charlotte? It was best if Revekka did not visit them, or the town would see the three of them together. At least for the Buirimov funeral they had been veiled.

She would never ask the purveyor or her homely daughter, not again. She had solicited their help plenty, nor did they answer with much. So many years had passed, she had yet to see if Vasili agreed to the Oridinnes trick for long life, or because the purveyor was so much to look at. The woman's features were lavish. Soft and Roman.

Anyway, Revekka feared the purveyor's ancient manners would give her away. A stunning woman, a dreadful trap.

Both families, Russian and Oridinnes, knew to keep the children apart, but the purveyor's daughter was a natural. She showed up one day and leaned into the window, staring in at Alexei, talking non-stop, her words silenced by glass. Anastasia did not deserve the boy and at least she knew, ultimately, to refuse him.

She could have sent for Hella Jensen or Natalia, but no. She would need the Baratova woman soon enough, to finish the treatment. She stopped in place to listen to that word again, *soon*, which was rarely appropriate. Days turned to weeks here, especially when things were urgent.

Instead of those she would plead with Oskar and his companions, whoever was still at the Kabanov house. Without Sergei or Karl they would discover the salt in their own time. But if she opted to tell them outright, she might have some negotiating left. And she could let these dumb, shouldered rustics carry the case.

The plan was imperfect. But if it became too much, that was what the lake was for.

#

She passed the first night without sound or candle. It was her first empty home since before she married. Nor did her lover call himself Karl then.

She expected a quick sleep, restorative, an easy morning, but she had become too accustomed to having Alexei here, or Karl, Little Sergei. So the time was long, mostly dread and heat, instead. Sometimes our fevers are from worry, and we can splash our faces with any water, no matter the cold, with no effect.

Yet at two in the morning, she left her bed for the lake anyway. The unmoving thing had come to mean death to her, and the water was too dark to see. She could only find the pond because she knew the path by heart.

She did not sip at it, only put it to her eyes, but she could taste it without drinking. It was a steely flavor, like when you touch fingers to mouth after using a garden tool. If she would have tried drinking the water would have passed through her fingers, turned her reflection to nonsense.

While she was outside she righted an overturned chair. There were points of icicles turned upward, like a row of teeth. Didn't one of Anastasia's poems write of time as ice crystals? Frozen into discernible bits, ready to snap? Didn't others speak of time's open, starving mouth?

She should have just kicked the chair and smashed them all.

In time she dozed. She dreamt she was an angel, then a devil, then a woman and, at last, a child again. Only then did she know she was ready for anything.

In the morning she walked to the Kabanov property.

Oskar greeted her with a drunk and terrible look, stepped out with a backhanded swat, which caused her to whimper, put her hands out. But she did not bleed, or fall. That was an early, good omen.

When she could she said, "The land will be fertile again. I need your help, but when it is ready it is yours."

"The land is dead, you tell me. And the lake, yes? Better than that, it is the reason you bought it, for the dead lake, but it killed the land." He scarcely acknowledged her. He was staring out at the dawn, causing her to turn and stare, too. Bolshevism needs scriptures, she thought, or at least tragic plays. The mythology could be practical, local. Gods with office hours, small administrative staffs.

She said, "The lake will never be alive. Well, you could drain it and remove the deposits, then let rain fill it back over time."

"Woman, it is early. If you are not here for that you are not here, you know?" He was tugging at the front of his pants as a biting dog would. Very well, she knew all men to behave that way. Alexei, with no stimulus at all, no knowledge of lovemaking, would arouse just waking up for the day, thrust his hips in his sleep.

She said, "For as long as my house is upright, men will try to plant on that land. Larger and larger numbers, always more desperate men. Hungry men with guns, like you were. You would never suggest to lay down with them so do not suggest it of me. You will treat me like an associate."

"For as long as the house is upright? It does not need to stand, we could bring it down."

"Only I know how to fix the soil. My father shipped a container to me, the contents will cure anything. Even you."

How did she come to tell this lie? Her father had been dead for half a century. The man never would have believed modern industry, the way distant magic became everyday machinery.

"Cure me? I am ill because of your voice, that is it. Cure me with quiet."

Revekka knew the insult for what it was, a last protest. There was no violence in his words any more, only the dull resentment of a man who knew, from today, that they were bound in contract. Even the feral dogs were keeping a distance from the home, both the Shafirov and Kabanov homes. The animals stood and waited, but so remotely she could not tell one from the other. Nor could she count them anymore.

She said, "The box is not safe where it is and it weighs too much for me to carry. Only I will know of our arrangement, along with my friend Natalia Baratova. You will send for her and help me carry the shipment back here."

"Your soldier will know. And I think you do not tell your son?"

"The soldier took my son to Moscow, to keep him away from you."

The man considered it well, his lips no different than if he were smoking. But because he had no more cigarettes, he agreed: "Good. We see them, we kill them."

"You will not have to do either."

"Your voice. If I tire of your voice, I keep the shipment for myself, plant the seeds myself."

"We do not need to talk if you prefer. But the land will not produce for you. The container is only salt."

Together they shiver in the same way, they kick at the same Russian dirt to warm up again.

#

They will go in the afternoon. She waits long past boredom, resignation. By all means she keeps an eye to the windows and the trees are dead calm again, down to the farthest leaf.

It causes her an odd association. She remembers a childhood dog, one she buried near an oak, and she cries about it. Terriers deserve more than their brief lives, which we forget soon.

If Oskar comes now she will have to chuckle. The dumb farmer woman, a wet mess of tears, drenching her late husband's shirt over a pet.

It is more ridiculous than the peasant could guess. Her Russian credentials set her age at 38 and, to look at her body, she seems that young. But the terrier, whom she called Bruac, died 70 years ago. When she buried the dog she felt she had buried the very idea of friendship. At the time friend was an Arabic word, *sadeeq*, one who tells you the truth and believes you are telling the truth.

Sadly, every dog is like that. What truth, then, does she take from the starving mongrels that confronted her here, in the main room? Or forced her hemophiliac son to take a different route from school? Even those which show up in packs to—deliberately, it seems—be shot?

When Oskar comes he is alone, no barrow. Good, let him exhaust himself by showing off, carrying the footlocker back from the station in the most preening way. Sergei, an infantryman, could barely haul the thing from room to room.

No doubt Oskar means to double-cross his friends. A divided enemy, better for her. He says, "If your mind is the same we do it now. If not I come back with a torch."

"My mind is the same."

"I will bring your container today. Tomorrow I look for Natalia Tatishchev, or who knows what name. Natalia of Petrograd, aristocrat woman, close enough."

"Her name is Baratova. I will send you with an envelope and a letter, with some salt. She will come."

Revekka is relieved, if not surprised, that the footlocker is untouched. Oskar drags it from underneath the station (in the end she convinced him to bring a small wagon). After he loads it they check inside. He exhales hard, seems to bury his disappointment in a cough.

No, that is not it. He would never bury anything for her. He says, "You say salt I hear salt. I think, maybe she is speaking like a woman and salt is something different."

"No, this is something different." She reaches her palm in, ladles the minerals like water and offers it. He refuses. To prove it is safe she pinches some with her opposite hand and now, after so many months, realizes the erotic nature of the act. I am taking my husband's spill into my throat. Here is some for your throat. Perhaps my son and his companion will sell it by weight to others. Strangers taking him into their mouths, at great expense.

It is her first taste of Karl in this medium.

Anastasia's mother was unclear on what would come of it, yearner ingesting yearner. Nor did Revekka think to ask. But a son ingesting it, anything could happen.

The lacerations in her mouth, yesterday's punch, become warm. Not located stinging, as you would expect with salt, but gentle all over.

She nods, a good first taste. She says, "You see, comrade? I keep my word."

He huffs, steals a large pinch and reaches far back into his mouth, as if prodding around for a toothache. He swallows with discomfort, sighs when it is finished and says, "You say comrade when I tell you."

It is a lovely day, considering all of it. The air is warmer than it should be. The sun cuts low across the sky and the shadows are long, everything is key. She grins: the poor sleep is making her thoughtful, but no, she has to resist that. This man does not deserve her best.

"To your house now? Or do you want a train to Moscow? Three days of waiting, two hours of travel."

"To the house."

Will they see anyone she knows? If so, what will come of it? Keeping peasants from starting a war is her first concern, she dreads the thought of an encounter at all. But the villagers they see on their return are all strange to her, and it is a bitter lesson in what she should invoke. A much more pertinent, second concern.

When the house is in view she puts it together, Oskar has been pawing at his left hand with his right. It began minutes after he took the salt; he did it once when they set out, several times along the way and by now, it is constant. At last he stops, drops the wagon handle and rolls up his sleeve. His face curls with inquiry.

"What is it?"

"My burn." He has pushed the arm of the shirt high, past the elbow. If there is an injury here she does not see it. He twists his hand to an almost comical angle, pressing his bottom lip out in concentration. He is not as beautiful in muck as his shorter companion, the one who is first to speak. He is good-looking enough, although the wringing arm and trampy expression make her giggle.

He stares in perfect accusation and she answers directly, "Nothing there. The salt cured you, didn't it? Whatever was there, you have no pain at all." To better punctuate the idea she thumps him on the exposed arm, nor does he flinch.

She says, "Are you still nauseous from the sound of my voice?"

"I did not say nauseous, I said ill. Nauseous is when I take you on a boat to drown you."

"I understand."

"Your salt can fix small burns, I am happy for you. Different question, can it fix 300 acres?"

If the man expects 300 acres of wheat he will have to put his army together again, raid other farms. Raid into or wed into.

While she is thinking of that, just where are their lovers, *prometteurs*, marriage hopefuls? She has seen a few women come in for trysts, transactions, but she thinks an ambitious man should not bother with those. He expends his best energies on leases, not on deeds.

Instead, the men are locking each other away, into land work and cheap romantic purchases. That is why there are no fiancées; none will allow it of the others.

#

In the morning she begins on a patch of ground, marking a square with a knife and weighing a handful of salt on a scale. If she needs, let us say, 50 more pounds for Natalia's cure and hopes to deliver 60 acres of farm to the peasants, she has two to three pounds of salt per acre. If it takes more than that it means a smaller working farm or less mineral for Natalia. Her early measurements need to be precise.

That assumes it will work at all, and that the men do not kill her in the meantime, doubling their quantity of fertilizer. Little wonder that the purveyor kept her allies few, most of them yearners. The others were the most loyal of patients, some of whom she was responsible for making ill.

The math discourages Revekka, but she may have erred in her division. The test ground, some 80 centimeters on each side, calls for at least an ounce of cure. Yet to distribute evenly across the whole farm, she can only spare a fraction of that, one percent of it at best. And some of the land will need enriching more than once.

She will prepare it the best she can and plant only wheat, or another grass, which fills in its bare patches with rhizomes. And of the peasant farmer, Oskar is on his way to the rail station now, presumably to find Baratova. What of his hand gesture earlier, when he saw her with shovel and gardening spade? Could it have been a discreet wave? At times Karl waved briefly like that, when they caught each other walking barn to shed, stable to barn. Quiet lightning, but very high voltage. The fuel of a marriage.

She nodded upward at Oskar but did not return the wave.

She is ready to work but gives up after only minutes. The iron of the blade makes a terrible scraping sound across hard earth. What with the clay and rocks she can barely engage the shovel at all, a thin two inches, not enough for the tool to stand on its own, the visual standard for a farm to produce.

She jabs again and again; wanders from her marked square of land and tries here, over here, closer to the tree. She urges herself on with this idea: one of them will dig through the stratum of rock. Either she will, for planting, or Oskar will, for her grave.

She sticks at the earth near the lake, now crosses to the opposite side of the property, from which the Kabanov home is blocked out of view. No matter where she is the blade finds gluey dirt, a layer of white grit.

Forget the shortage of fertilizer or the promise to Oskar, which she never meant to deliver. It would take her a generation to turn all of the soil. Anastasia's mother would have died again in that time, another footlocker of salt. Charlotte would have died, or is it

Matilde? A third container. Her shortage will be resolved over and over by the time the land is ready for planting.

Back to the small test plot. If it takes all day to dig, so be it. Revekka will have to eat first—she is trembling with weakness, hungry all the way to the throat—but she and Sergei did not leave much food. They meant to abandon the house two days ago.

She makes twitchy work of opening the last jar of pears, nearly vomits before she finds the flour, which she eats from her palm. Between the fruit, wheat and water it should turn her insides into a stucco dessert, filling if not nourishing. She sits, continues to sit, admits that if she does not stand again now she will sleep for the day.

She begins with a slate of chalk, unsure if she is chopping at something that is wide or deep. The best she can think is to slice at it with the knife-edge of the blade. Breaking it up is about 10 minutes of work and it reveals more striations of clay, chalk, sheer rock. If soil is the skin of the country, this is its bone, exposed at the hands. She is filing away at a Russian knuckle and has finally broken it free, only to find more ligaments, bone.

There is no more skin, no matter how deep, only macabre fingers grabbing in.

In practical terms she has to dismiss the thought of digging. Oskar will be here with Natalia soon, his end of their contract delivered in less than a week. He will demand to see progress, and not just treatment for his small burn.

But in symbolic terms she cannot resist the idea. The nation of Russia is not a creature of flesh and hair but a skeletal thing, rising up, sipping dead water. It has a mind to stagger, like all things stagger, toward the ocean. But it is so enormous it does not have to choose which one.

This does not take a week. Oskar is back in two days. He comes without Natalia, and then Sergei comes without Alexei.

The peasant is first. After an evening of scraping and praying, Revekka has opted to farm a different way. The summer tornado bared pieces of slate, limestone, raw ceramic, which they used as columns. Six months later the indentations are still there, and she finds autumn mushrooms growing in some. Fungus means scat, soil and water. She should try planting without the salt.

It might be a ridiculous sight, but no more than she deserves: clumps of wheat pushing through a few, irregular holes in slate. Patches of hair in a man's weathered scalp. The rest is raw, nasty skin, which makes you hope there is no wind.

Her home is not along Oskar's route to the train but he crosses her property nevertheless. He says, "No trains today. Tired of waiting, tired of the walk."

"No trains after what?"

"After what happened what? Yes, if something happens there is a train. If something else happens there is no train. A new something, train again. Your question is stupid, your favor is stupid. One more question and no favor for you."

Idleness has done something to his nerves. Given the impact that adrenaline has on time, you have to wonder which of the two is more accurate, adrenaline or time. She considered it once before, the way a split-second twister turned her house to pebbles.

Yes, those are exactly the comparisons she wants to make: the peasant, the tornado. Their brief releases of energy, in frightful amounts.

He is yelling: "I ask no questions of you, never. My favor is due! You know that, yes? Or do you need to ask another stupid question about it?"

That he struck her before draws an unusual bond between them. His tone becomes penitent and he takes his leave, face to ground: "I try in the morning. I am bad liar, the men think I have boyfriend in the capital."

Is he making a joke, is she supposed to chuckle? She only smiles instead and continues to dig. She does not cringe when he passes. If anything, the opposite is true.

Nor is the Kabanov land swaying with crops, either. There are some, but less than you would expect. If Karl's salt does not work the peasants should bring her on as agriculture consultant. As many times as she has died, she has become a woman of soil.

#

In the morning she visits Charlotte and Matilde, looking for seeds. On purpose she wears a bad hat and poorly-fitting dress, which make her look like anyone.

No surprise that only one of them is here. It is Charlotte, the older of the two, also the younger, depending on how you figure it.

Charlotte is discreet, dressed for sightseeing. Other than that she is sitting, reading, brewing tea. She hurries Revekka inside, urgent to shut the door.

Pleasantries are few, and they share so much already their discussions can be brief: "I never could say, so sorry about Vasili, sorry again."

"Thank you, but it was Karl, we preferred Karl."

"Maybe. But I prefer Vasili. I cannot help but say, there was a man with you at the funeral. A rather handsome one from the east?"

"There was a woman, too. Do you not remember? She knew you by name, even if her face was unfamiliar."

Charlotte nods and frowns. It is an ugly look, which is what she intends. Her voice is pushed back into the throat, an ugly sound, "I understand. I did not consider that. This is taking you a long time. We thought you had doubts. We thought the Mongol boy was your new Karl."

"The woman came to me by accident. My son found her, through the Qajar girl."

"If Anastasia found her it was not an accident."

"Not on her part, no."

"Then you had doubts after all?"

Revekka considers it. A yearner's death is like a slow dream, but with obliterated self. Disoriented, sad, very nearly cruel. Rebirths are mostly the same, except her adult limbs become stuck in the mothering tissues and she pulls hard, sobbing, with vague curses. After each time, a vow that this is her last.

Sometimes, as with the last time, it is lethal to the surrogate.

If she would not put herself through it again why would she put Karl through it? Yet she has to think of Alexei's condition, the injury, the violent men at the Kabanov home. Also: the amputation, the coma, the odd elevator to Moscow.

The answer is yes, she has had doubts, nor will she apologize for them. She says, "You don't?"

"I suppose I had it easy. It is Matilde you should ask, cutting out all of her woman things in case we ever asked her to deliver again." Now she says, "Why have you come, you never come."

"I am planting seeds, any kind of seed, it makes no difference. Wheat, rye, whatever you have."

"We have none, Anna Revekka. You should try the market."

Revekka nods and, after brief salutations, she closes the door. This is the last they will speak, today and for good.

Seventy years is plenty for old alliances to become weak. It is rather like the hinge of a door, meant for use, for bearing loads, but only for a time. No one would expect a door to open and close for a full human life.

#

She is reluctant to do so, but she has to ask the Yanovksys again. That they come through a second time, Revekka does not believe it to be an overstatement: she owes them for her son's life. In addition to seed they offer flour, which she will use for sifting the tiny quantities of salt. Back at the property, she fills the slate-holes until they are fully white: seed and salt, flour as a visual marker, to assure herself that she has even coverage.

Little Sergei gasps when he sees her. Despite that her back is turned she knows he has come alone. She cocks her palm back to strike him and he does not block it. The sound is ringing and hot, and she flushes both sides of his face with it. Now she looks to hit him again and he grabs her wrist.

"He left, Revekka. Or maybe Nikita took him. We spent the night with your father. The next morning they were gone. Nikita, your father and him."

Konstantin is not her father. Not Alexei's grandfather either, but there is no use telling them that. When Revekka's delivery killed his daughter the man took her in.

Part Three

April 1918:	Alix, Nicholas and their children are transferred to the Ipatiev House, in Yekaterinburg
July 1918:	The former imperial family and four others are executed
January 1919:	Compulsory grain requisitions begin

Chapter Thirteen

IN KONSTANTIN'S BASEMENT, after the first few stings, all felt warm and close. Alexei had dreams of sleeping in summer, of young Eros. There were no injuries to think about and Russia was at peace. In his sleep there were no Bolsheviks yet, nor any Romanov titles. In their absence was the end of hunger and war.

He dreamt that his ruined arm was still metal but had skin grown over. Nerves were filled in underneath and his prosthetic fingers could touch like a regular hand.

He woke to a dragging sound. He was being hauled upstairs. A slight whiff of fire.

Now, as his befuddlement lifts he finds Konstantin, Nikita and three cups of tea. Outside there is fresh powder up to the ankles. All is quiet in the snow unless it comes very close.

The younger man looks frail again, keeps his legs together and his elbows brought in. He is pale and the scalding drink puts color to his mouth. Only there and only for a moment. When it passes he is as white as bone again.

Konstantin says, "You were stung doing what I asked you to do?" He turns to Nikita, "Then you came looking for him, and you were stung, too?"

Alexei cannot state the details in time. He looks down, the same fright every boy has when he is forced to lie. Nikita says it in his place. "It is the opposite of that but yes, in a word. I have experience with lotus colonies and I thought it better that I smoke them back instead of Alexei. What child of 13 could follow that kind of instruction?"

Alexei sneers. The man has shouldered the weight of answering, and with an insult, a made-up age. Or is that the tsesarevich's age? If so, starting in July, Alexei Shafirov will always be 13.

Nikita deserves Konstantin's reply: "For what good it did you, all of your experience. I found you twice-wet in the shirt, top and bottom. And I suppose you were snooping around, how else would you know?"

"I was wandering your house in my sleep, and I found myself in the basement. I am sorry."

"Do not worry, friend. Tell me about your colonies, though."

"I exported bees from Jaunpur. I rode with the drays myself when I had to. The widow Ella, then the Grand Duchess Olga."

That much is as Anastasia described. Then again, she and Nikita might have read it from the same anti-Romanov propaganda. The boy will not allow it as proof just yet.

Konstantin says, "Jaunpur?"

"In the east. My wife's parents are from there."

The old man is impatient with the answer and Alexei does not blame him. Any place you can name is in the east, depends only on the time of day. He says, "Everything to the heathens, I suppose."

Nikita says, "Sir, if I may? There are types of bees that do not require smoke. The drones sting for a few hours and then return to the hive."

"Yesterday you spoke of urgent business north, or was it east? You two may finish your tea but, by your own word, you must be on your way after that."

Did Konstantin overhear it? Or did Nikita mention it directly? Alexei cannot remember but they are beyond that now. It is snowing, colder than freezing. No one would put them out in this weather, yet Nikita is about to have them expelled. It must be a bluff, his grandfather would never do that, but the frail man presses on: "Yesterday? You believe we slept for one night?"

"Yes, comrade, we slept for one night." Nikita is pinching at the skin on his forearm and Konstantin says, "What is that? If you think you are winding a watch the bees have made you deranged."

"I have no water under my skin, which does not happen in one night. The day we met it was cold but not freezing, not cold enough for snow. The sky was clear, now it is all clouds."

"Weather can change in a day."

"Sir, I wonder if you know the month and the year. The date is not important." It is an unfair question for whatever elderly man, lotus or not. But to ask one's host, that is difficult to forgive.

Alexei stares into his cup; he has yet to take a sip. If it were empty he would stare.

Konstantin says, "I will not rile you talking about my daughter or politics. Just as you will not question me with riddles or days of the week." He stands for necessities, explains only with a hand at the front of his pants. "Those are my terms. You will leave an old man alone for now or, by the time I have put on my face, you will be off."

When grandfather's footsteps are quiet, Nikita leans in, his head and voice down. "Alexei, we do not know if it is October or January. Look at us. We are parched and starved. We do not know if it is day or night, and we have only been to his basement just once. Think of him—how many days a year is he like this?"

As Konstantin bathes and readies himself Alexei follows Nikita to the university. A vendor with a loudspeaker is there, with yesterday's copy of *Pravda*.

The date is November 1.

As a skeptic Alexei feared the unusual but did not believe it. Now, his skepticism is disproven and he cannot claim the opposite. He both fears and believes.

There is nothing to reassure him anymore. Not doubt, not faith.

Nikita asks the vendor a few different ways: is the dateline correct, is the dateline from yesterday, would the paper ever print an advance date?

Their stings were on October 29, and today is November 2. Four nights of bee toxin, with the narcotic wearing off, the men rousing, being stung again, slipping away again. Nikita says there are devices for letting smoke in after time has passed, but they are costly, not always effective. Princess Ella used to bring an oven into her containment room and slow-cook a hen. Over the hours the bird would heat and dry, finally burn, and smoke would come out of the oven, sending the drones back to the hive. The princess would wake and eat, cutting away any charred bits and serving the meat with wine, dates.

"You know so much about them."

Nikita has bought them coffee but Alexei's was quick to become lukewarm. It reminds him more of cold biscuits than of percolation, and the boy can taste it along the roof of his mouth.

Nikita says, "I told you and Konstantin I was a merchant."

Alexei was speaking of the Romanovs, of the fables that Anastasia would tell. Stories he rejected, but now Nikita, a stranger to her, is confirming them. He says, "We should get back."

"Another moment, I cannot bear the thought yet."

The thought of what? The man is warming both hands around the cup, with a sort of insect brittleness you guess he feels all over. At last, this is the frailty which Alexei saw on the train, the one Nikita explained as an old injury, something to do with his father. The boy was supposed to assume the man was violent, but what Alexei saw was not hurt, but addiction. Nikita's heart is something less than a pump now. More like a beggar's tin with too few coins.

The boy says, "Is there not a way to dispose of the lotus?"

Nikita holds up both arms: they are dressed for blizzards. "Look at us, we could do it now. The sting does not go through heavy material. But that is unfair. He agreed to put us up for a night provided you gave him smoke in the morning. We failed him, and we paid for it. We cannot take his hive away for that." The man thinks and thinks. "Although it would be easy."

Nikita longs for it, even now. Alexei can see in the way he pulses his mouth. The boy says, "How much more do we stay?"

"You say we, how long do we stay? He is your family, not mine. If I am wrong about who you are this is the best place for you. Violence, starvation, your mother is detained probably. Your father."

"Then what man would subject his family to this? That was your question, not my question."

"I will not do it, Alexei. And I am not going help you if you try to do it."

Something is different, and only from the last minute or two. Nikita's face has changed, although his will changed first. It is said that a man stares with his will but that cannot be true.

When they are at Konstantin's house again, they show him the November 1 issue. The older man is unmoved, seems to have accepted it in their absence. He is surprised they came back at all and says, "You think four nights is long? I have a treat for you. My brother Evgeny has a good hive. He bought it from you, from the sound of it."

Konstantin says, "We will stay here for a week and eat. We'll get fat again, then spend the winter with him, in rounds."

Alexei tries to warm himself. After the one time, and it was cruelly brief, the idea of lotus sleep is eating him up. For that alone Nikita ought to get the boy out of here, subject him to wild cities and trains instead of a caring old man.

#

With Little Sergei gone there is a bed for each. But when their host is asleep Alexei visits Nikita again. They cross arms over chests, stare at the paints above, their shoes on.

"What does he mean by rounds?"

"You'll see in a week. We should eat well."

"Is there any danger in it?"

"You saw as well as I did. It was your first hive and we almost slipped away, all of us."

Alexei, staring high, says, "Is there no way to talk you out of it?"

Nikita sips at a brandy. In more normal hours, with a house full of bustle, we miss the sounds of breath on drink, fluid in the throat. Tonight, in the dry and quiet, those noises are loud.

The man returns his glass to a side table and says, "His brother's house is the best place for you. Your enemies will look for you here and at your mother's home, but they know nothing of where we are going. At least your mother will know where to go when she finds no one here."

"Enemies?"

"The ones I told you of."

"All you said last night was we needed to leave at once, for Petrograd. That men would come for me and that we could save Russia from them and from the soviets."

"And you reminded me that Tsesarevich Alexei is some other boy, to other parents."

"And you said they would come no matter which. Something with you is different, now from then."

Alexei has misrepresented the conversation twice and it was five days ago, not one.

Nikita says, "Nothing is different. Only our plans. I am still set to protect you."

He speaks in the language of great sacrifice but he drafts the contract with alcohol, asks for three months of bees as an honorarium.

#

It is not his favorite memory of papa, only one of the clearest. At times alkaline wind blew across their lake, through the bedroom windows. Mama would say it smelled like ocean but Alexei was unsure, despite the trips to Petrograd. He would confuse that musk with others, especially on mornings when Karl was home. He will never sort them out until he comes to know his own musk.

That day he brought his knees to stomach; his parents touched feet at the end of the bed. A cradle of sorts, and he looked at a scar across Karl's abdomen.

"What happened, papa?"

"You mean my cut? This? That was a terrible day, I thought I would die for sure."

"Karl, don't scare the poor boy." But all of them were smiling. One of papa's stories, a rare treat.

"Mama, let him tell me."

The man sat up, said, "I was in the forest, near where I was born. You remember the forest, don't you? It was too wooded for homes, stables, anything like that. You built things miles away then lifted them up at the edge of the woods. You skimmed the house across the tops of trees and then left them in place. You remember?"

"I do, I remember." And in the way of a child, this was true.

Karl said, "Over the years when the trees died one by one the house would work its way to the ground, eventually, but it was still closed in. Sometimes a branch would get in the way of doors or windows, but at least you had firewood. You would just burn the leaves around you and they all went up. It would keep you warm until spring, when the rains came."

"They never burned all out?"

"No, and that's the story. A man came once, an ugly, skinny man with two teeth here and one tooth here"—Karl pulled his lips back for this part—"and he said, if you stop lighting the fires I will heal your scar. I told him no, we will all freeze but he said the trees could only take so many fires. One more and the whole forest is gone. So we stopped, and the snows nearly buried us. But when we dug ourselves out we saw that we were on the top of a glacier. We put blades on our shoes and skated all the way to the ocean."

"What is out there?"

"What do you think is there?"

Even as a boy Alexei could sense the problems with the story: the origin of the scar was unsure, the sorcerer did not live up to his promise and the revelation was up to the audience, not the storyteller.

The moral, if papa intended a moral, did not apply to him.

Tonight he wakes to Nikita's forearm across the face. That one, too, has fallen asleep, yet continues to fight. The man's snore has a rather seagull caw to it; you cannot help but count the ways luck has turned against you. An old vow, coming home.

#

Alexei does not think much of Evgeny, who is manic and gassy. He forgets both of the new names and talks only of colonies. To avoid premature stings he wraps himself in bandages to the nose, with an aviator's cap and goggles, full trousers, a shirt with sleeves. He and Konstantin fuss over the hive for an hour; by the time they have finished Evgeny has gotten too hot and removed the clothes, but not the bandages or pilot gear. The effect is of a great albino lizard and you find your mind running off, to where the man can catch flies from the air with his tongue. It is everything Alexei can do to keep from laughing.

They are tidying the place up—Nikita, too—as if before a very long trip.

"Alexei Karlovich, be a friend and fetch my brother's mask." So formal, and Konstantin's house is 10 minutes by foot from here. The boy hopes to convince Nikita to come along, for a last appeal. But Nikita is fully wrapped, too, staring at patterns in the comb.

He needs fewer than 30 minutes round trip; his only concern is finding the way back. Alexei lifts a pack of Evgeny's cigarettes—not for the tobacco, but on the other hand he will try that if his mood changes. For now he means only to leave clues in the snow at various places, the mouth-end aimed in the direction of every turn. The air is calm but a wind could follow behind and mock the effort. Spinning, burying or removing the cigarettes, sending him anywhere.

He has not read Frank Baum's book but knows the idea is a remix of Dorothy Gale's ballad, however slight.

And best if the wizard was not a sham this time, one who could unravel some of the spells against him, reinforce others.

The cigarette plot adds five minutes to the walk and he is at Konstantin's house for an hour. Not all of that is for looking. It takes little to find the aviator goggles, but not until he slices his hand on a bare nail in the master closet. He is gathering clothes for a look in the speakeasy, does not see a removed shelf, or the steel point exposed. He reaches, shouts, pulls back, ripping the outside of his hand a second time. Already the stream of blood down his wrist and a few brown droplets on the floor.

Devil! Goddamn Evgeny! He will die now and for what? A forgetful old man, his foul dependency? Without thinking Alexei brings the metal hand to the fleshy one. There is no comfort to be had.

You try to recall how moments like these are defining, but instead he is bent on running around the house in panic.

Mama was clear on what to do: wrap the cut, lie flat, raise the hand high. Do not look under the bloody cloth and only wait for her to be home. After a few fast minutes he does what he has been taught, and all starts to slow down again.

To spite the old man, and to bleed to death in fashion, he wraps the cut in the most expensive-looking shirt he sees. He curses, only curses, beds down in the master suite, trying to calm himself with long division. Three digits into three digits: 582 into 619, 349 by 422, and so on.

After a few solutions he is bored with it: mathematics is not for young men. At Alexei's age his duties are ridicule, violence, nationalism. He does not understand the reason but the urges are clear. Arithmetic is true objective order but as for the early teenaged years, those are the highest expression of the subjective. Remember: it is the necessary pride that breaks our hearts.

With other cuts like this he soaks through a cloth in no time. It might be the quantity of material but he does not believe that; after a half-hour he should sense blood on his lower arm, the shirt should be heavy. Sodden.

—Bear? Mama said that in the most dangerous hour of his hemorrhaging, after the peasant struck his elbow with the rifle. He stirred but did not answer, so she said, —My bear?

—Yes?

—Nothing.

Five words in all, four were hers. He longs for them now. They are the tiny, few seams in his material.

Revekka would not have it but he unravels the shirt. Best to die here, with mama, in a way. Not with Evgeny and Konstantin, or the perplexing Nikita.

No fresh blood pours through. What blood has spilled is very dark.

It is chalky in texture, as if becoming dirt. There are places in Russia where the earth and water take on a color like this. High concentrations of iron, mama explained, hence the taste. Alexei drew an unnecessary link: "Doesn't blood have iron, too?" She answered that yes it does, but that was not the reason for the similar color. In the case of soil, the iron oxidized to red.

Ten minutes ago he figured he would be dead by now. Who knows, it could be that a hallucinating fever has seized him, but he does not think so. He is clotting like a normal patient.

Alexei finds a knife and produces a second cut. He has never looked so closely at blood before: it is a brilliant red, and his hand glistens with sweat. Such a vibrant display could never mean illness, quite the opposite.

He watches for about eight minutes while the blood spills and clots, the new incision stops bleeding. That he is cured is a minor revolution in a place that is expert on revolutions.

Chapter Fourteen
Shlisselburg

CHEHREH HEARD wonderful tales of the Romanovs, from not so long ago, either. Unless she had lost count this year was 1763. If the house first came into power in 1613, that was 150 years ago, almost exactly. The imperial house was a mere child, at least compared to the age of the world.

The empire began with a tragedy. The one who would have been the first tsarevich drowned, in the same way as told by an oracle. The birds of Russia were heartbroken, and sang in every language of the world, with hopes that at least one priest would understand, then bless the infant for his passage. A sickly archer assumed the throne and the late tsarevich returned three times, although most Russians called them false.

The land itself was in revolt. Wheat stalks froze in summer, breaking in half and pointing, all of them, toward Moscow. The period of legal anarchy led to war with Sweden and Poland. What crops had not died from frost went unharvested. Between sickness and battle, there was no one left to work.

Chehreh was never sure about the sequence, which event preceded what, but the stories were important to her, they spoke of a Russian state that was months from collapse. In time, after a generation of troubles, the son of an exiled monk and Orthodox nun was crowned as tsar. He was named Michael, and was the first, unwilling head in a new house of emperors. Even his father did not know of the coronation.

#

She loved the scriptures more than she remembered. Or maybe it was like the man away from home, who, when asked of his wife, forgot many of the details and had to fill in his own. He cherished her, but this was more than that. He knew the woman he described, her shape and features, were too exquisite to be true.

Worship and bickering, it was all Chehreh and Ivan could do, and she preferred not to bicker. When autumn wind came from under the walls, she said: "Her children are not afraid of the cold weather, because they wear scarlet, the color of being warm. Such is the essence of faith, because the Lord will provide. They take this warmth to other homes, nor is there any want of blankets."

Of the inmates coughing, and the rumor that two had died; that there were rats in their hair, scurrying through the crotch of their pants, she said: "The Lord will bless your food and water. He will take away all sickness and your fields will not be barren. He will send storms ahead of you and make your enemies confused. Submit to God and the devil will run away. He will choke on his lies then starve from the blight."

Of tsars: "Your throne is built on righteous acts. Like a river, your way is known, and you will bear others along. They will never thirst nor will their teeth ache from the cold."

At times Chehreh would giggle from her inventions. The boy would ask why she laughed and she would say, "It is nothing, *souverain*. I am giddy from the scriptures."

At times he would correct her: "No, you said He spent the night praying to the Father. When morning came he chose 12 of the 40. Luke 6, you said."

"You are right, *souverain*. He chose in the morning." This way the gospels became eight books, 16, an entire shelf's worth of stories.

Her conversations with Ivan, unlike those with any warden or guard, were, in the end, only one exchange, and it took years to finish. It only briefly waited for naps, eating, the occasional bad mood. For this reason it became weird, was at times quite bizarre. Once, when he was 17, Chehreh started asking the boy the colors of various words. Not the things in themselves, but the pigmentation of only the words. He was unwell enough to answer, without the stutter:

She said, "Learning?"

"The word learning is yellow."

"I agree although I do not know why."

"You agree because it is right. A man's study, too. Mama once told me men had studies where the boys were not allowed. The walls were made out of Bibles and that is what held up the roof."

"Tomorrow?"

"Tomorrow is red."

"Do you say that because of Russians and the red color?"

"No, Russia is not tomorrow. What comes when we wake up, that is tomorrow and that is red."

"And music?"

"Music is yellow."

"Music and learning are the same color?"

"Not just that. Music and learning are the same thing."

"And why is that?

"They are built of the same things. The way homes and churches are."

"Are homes and churches the same color?"

"No, because they have different things inside. Thoughts and music have the same things inside."

"What about starling? What color is starling?"

"What is starling?"

"It is a bird, from where I was born."

"What color is the bird?"

"It is blue."

"Then the word starling is blue."

"Because it is the same as the bird?"

"No, because it is the same as everything from where you were born."

It exhausted both of them. In the end she would tousle his hair, so he knew it was a quiet hour.

#

She would miss him dearly. One of the last things he said was, "I'm trying to work through your accent."

"Mine? Yours is the odd one, not mine. You must have heard one of the guards tell me that."

"I did. But when I thought about it I knew, I needed to work through it, too."

"And what have you decided?"

"I decided that your voice and my voice are the same."

"No, *souverain*. Yours is more interesting. I hear your mother in your voice, and it is said that she was very well-read. But I also hear the guards, who are rustics and have never read a book or even seen a book."

"We are talking about yours."

"Before I say anything else, do you know what an accent is? It is one way of speaking a word, which may be different from the way another man speaks the same word, even if the meaning is the same."

"Like the reds and blues?"

"Like the colors, yes. The red and blues."

Her idea to grow herbs, free herself by poisoning the boy, had barely lasted a year. Elizaveta demanded the prisoner be moved to the Shlisselburg fortress, a sudden exodus that took a month, claimed two lives. Besides, after healing Anatoly Fedorovich, Chehreh was free enough. She had as much as she had hoped for, as much as they had promised 12 years ago. Stone floors, stone walls, blankets in the winter.

Now that she and Ivan had shared cold, hunger, worship and study together, the boy was probably right. Their voices were exactly one. Here was only an example among many: he had asked —Like the reds and blues? and she knew exactly what he meant.

No matter. Catherine would put an end to it in a few days.

Chehreh said, "I might say *chien*," she pronounced it quickly, moving only her lips, "which you know is dog. You might say *chien*," she pushed her lower jaw out, an ugly impression of a steppe rancher. "I might barely understand the word, but know you mean dog."

"But I say *chien* the way you say it."

"Because I have taught you most of your French. My Russian is much like your Russian because we have learned it together. At the same time, from the same people."

Her argument was coming apart. The boy was right, there was no chance of denying it. They had spent too much time together for it to be otherwise.

Ivan said, "If I err and call myself tsar again and the men kill me, will you keep your voice like it is now? Will you never change it so you will still talk the way I talk?"

"Who said you cannot call yourself tsar? No one is going to kill you, *souverain*."

"You cannot promise me that. You can only promise you will keep my voice. I have been a good tsar, have I not? I always have the son in my thoughts. I share my food with you. I touch at your arm when you cry."

"You have been the finest."

Men always snored around them, even when she believed it was late morning, but all of that was quiet now.

#

Soon Vasili took Chehreh by the elbow and put words in her ear. They were low but firm: "The tsar is here. Tsar Peter. It would not do if you and Ivan were up to your silliness again."

Dear Vasili, returned as a young man after a tavern fight. As solemn as before, the calm and humor of middle age lost with a pistol-shot.

Chehreh kept what was left of the first Vasili, the sleepier one, in a barrel. He would not look in it, he had to rub his hands together when she talked about it.

His remark was not only a warning, but an expression of dread.

She said, "He is here? Why?"

"He wants to speak with the boy."

They always called him that, but today Ivan was the tallest one here. He was a true madman with blond hair and an itchy, red beard. It was a mistake to allow him to speak with a tsar but there was nothing Vasili could do.

#

To her eyes, Peter III was effeminate, white as bone, with tired eyes and chin. In the end the warden asked Chehreh to keep away from Ivan's cell while the tsar addressed the boy and anyway, the Romanov's uniformed loyalists would have forbidden her from sitting in. But she caught a few words:

"Do you know who I am?"

"You are my brother, Peter?"

"No, cousin, but you are right, my name is Peter. No, believe me! I am telling you the truth. Only our grandfathers were brothers. Their father was Tsar Alexei, the most gentle of the kings."

Something in Ivan's look had made his suspicions plain to see. What the tsar did not know was that it was a thing of the child's bad senses. Everything was a lie to him, all of his experience was cause for suspicion. Even his Bible was mostly narrated by a French-speaking woman, who used to feign knowledge of Russian, just to keep him from complaining.

"Then hello, Peter. Some believe I am Ivan, the unpretending tsar of Russia."

"I have heard. I would ask you to be careful, do not cause offense. The title you are claiming is my title. I trust that, whatever you say about it, these are not your words. They are the lies of your keepers."

"Words are for everyone, they do not belong to me. Other than this, I do not know how to answer your question."

Chehreh felt something in her chest. A snake, perhaps, put down her throat while she slept. It felt like a snake, it licked at her heart when she was supposed to be alarmed. She could calm the thing by calming her chest, which she did.

Anyway, Catherine was here. Her brown hair and blue eyes were striking, but her dead chin, so similar to that of Peter, made her appear to be the tsar's sister. In fact she was his wife.

Chehreh heard Ivan say, "I am a different Ivan. The one you are looking for is at peace. He was at peace years ago."

"Are you saying Ivan VI is dead?"

Catherine said, "Do not worry about them. You are the woman from Chad? The boy's keeper?"

"I am his keeper, but I am from Oridinnes. I have never seen Chad."

"Come, then. It is pleasant outside. We should enjoy the air while we can."

#

They walked, with grooms and armed men, although the arms were unnecessary. Catherine had brought a dagger, was dressed for horseback. She said, "I have Elizaveta's notes, her poor soul. They date from January back to your arrest, 12 years ago."

"At least you call it what it was. The men who came said it was for my protection."

"You were 20 years old, and unmarried, on the day the Prisoner Number One was born."

The fortress was built on a small island at the top of the Neva, split into two bastions, one inside the other. The outermost complex, roughly the shape of a honeycomb cell, was for the more common inmates: thieves, agitators, those brought in for assault. The inner facility was a small but blind maze of cells, living catacombs for Ivan, his guards and Chehreh. Presently she and the empress were circling the inner bastion, making way to the gate tower, which accessed the outer complex, and the river.

"If you do not use his name, I cannot say for sure. But my assault was on the day you introduced Ivan, yes."

"Your assault. Please tell me, the papers are unclear."

"I do not remember it any more. My wounds bled all day, even before the men came. There were five at least. They left me in a stream bed. It is said I died before I rose again."

That had been one of Chehreh's lies to Vasili. It was a woman who attacked her, only one woman, one whose face was like that of Chehreh. Their appearance was as close as sisters. The attacker died, and those who saw the body mistook one combatant for the other.

Catherine said, "Your story is impossible. But then, I understand there are many impossible things now. The dead, for example, come back in Chad, in Oridinnes, in Shlisselburg, in everywhere but Saint Petersburg."

"Only one of us will rise from the dead, mama. And he has already."

Catherine turned to her men, nodded them back. They remained at the flag tower, opposite from the exit. As they circled around Ivan's prison, they would fall out of view.

The wind was loud but Catherine brought her voice down anyway, quiet and close. She said, "There are whispers about the legitimacy of my son. I trust you have heard them, I am sure you treat them discreetly. But I wonder, if Ivan had not been born to the throne. If he was born to the comfort of the Winter Palace, with an understanding father, a brother who loves him. Of course with me as his mother."

"Impossible to say, mama."

"Yes. As I remarked, so much is impossible right now."

Catherine took Chehreh's right hand, put the blade to the outside of the wrist. Chehreh whimpered a little but Catherine shushed her. Besides, the grip was soft, the blade came in at a slow diagonal. She was looking for hair, not life.

She said, "Trust me, child."

"As God commands it, mama."

Catherine sliced at the hair on Chehreh's lower arm. They watched it come loose, change, lift away with the wind. The empress breathed in at length. She said, "Is it true about Vasili Mirovich?"

"Is what true?"

"The stupid dog found himself in a brawl with two men. He got the better of them for a while, and then a brick was the end of it."

The way the rumor had changed made Chehreh glare. No brick would ever finish him, not the wily Mirovich. She said, "You've seen Vasili. He is fat and well."

"Young one, please. My son will be eight. At 13 his face will change the last it is going to change. It was Elizaveta who brought you here, not Peter. Peter does not care if you live contented or miserable or if you die this afternoon. He is indifferent. He will free you with a signature, at my request. I am asking you, is it true what I have heard about your lover?"

Catherine had not returned the dagger. It was shaking with wind, effort. Chehreh could not help but stare at it, and it was clear that the tsar's wife saw her looking.

"Are you offering me my home again? If I tell you the truth of Vasili and put a Romanov in your stomach, a true Romanov birth, you will free me? And what if I fail? You will put that knife in my stomach?"

"You will not fail. It is said all over, your only first demands were a place built of stone and a box of Chadian dirt. Imagine all of Russia, with its thousands of farms, and our one fable is about 300 pounds of dirt. African dirt!"

"The dirt by itself is nothing. It is the crop that is important, and I have fed it to both Vasili and Ivan. They have not responded."

It was a lie, it took a change in her face to say it, but Catherine had to guess which part was not true. All she said before drawing the blade was, "Vasili has not responded?"

She slashed hard, taken aback by such thick tendons, the report of muscle and voice. But the blow was enough. Chehreh put a hand to her throat, checked her palm, sobbed once. Blood dripped from her knuckles. Should she have agreed to Catherine's terms? No, the empress was going to kill her either way.

It always overcomes, how abrupt it is. One common morning the Romanovs arrive at the fortress and in a moment, after a rather dull exchange, the wife of the tsar cuts her neck open.

Chehreh fled: the murderous woman was not going to claim her relics. She sought the Neva but the river was past the outer ring of cells. A simple walk, but in this case too far. Anyway, some sort of cloud blocked out her sight, her view of the courtyard. She was losing the two bastions, and the many paths between them.

"My daughter! Do you believe that Catherine Alexeievna Romanova, Tsaritsa of all the Russias, will respond?"

Once Chehreh promised the Russian earth would never see her blood, not one drop. But look at the sheer pints of it, and in so disgusting a place! It is a story she would tell over and again how, in her final minute, she started to remove her trousers, in order to soak up the blood, keep it in her hands.

#

As Chehreh gave up the ghost, Peter was still speaking to the young man. He said, "There is another way than this, cousin. You might not be a prisoner for good. You could choose the brotherhood, say, at Simonov, which is in Moscow."

"Moscow?"

"You are devout in your studies, are you not? I see your Bible is worn all the way through."

"We read—if we have time. But we are—quite occupied."

"You wound me, cousin. You do not mean to wound your sovereign, do you? You need only to give up your hair, and only part of it. You would never see a fortress again. You would live the rest of your days in sunlight."

"What of my friends?"

"Never mind them, they think of themselves as your advisors. Only a politician needs advisors. Those two have each other and that is enough. Leave the politics to us, Ivanushka. Give up any claims to the crown. Choose to be faithful, live as a free man in cloister."

The young man had already turned his back on the tsar. It was sedition, but the room was too dark for Peter to know that. He heard only the shift in Ivan's clothes.

Chapter Fifteen

ONE MINUTE WERE the dreams of adulthood. Long life and yes, a long sexual life. Just look at the man in the reflections! His beard was full and dark. The cuff of his shirt was taut, ready to break a seam.

But the next minute, he is a frail teenager again. Awake. Thirsty and disoriented.

Evgeny's home is a wreck; did they not spend all last night cleaning it? An irritable stranger is here, with the boy's old companion Freyja. Those two are handing him bread and water—the golem is at work, just as Little Sergei would be. Standing, moving, speaking. And when it seems Alexei will topple to one side, the automaton asks for the water back.

Their questions do not stop. Alexei cannot hear well but even those he hears, he does not answer: When was the first sting? What was the last you heard of Nikita? How much have you eaten?

When was the last you saw your grandfather, or the host?

They are speaking of the others as you do of the dead. So be it, Alexei wanted to throw up anyway and the fact that a man has died is all he needed to hear. He rushes to the toilet but there is no toilet. The wall is missing. The view outside is of rubble but no snow.

The conditions are pleasant. It is a warm, one might say an oppressively warm Moscow winter. It is the weather of legend, and we all know what becomes of legend if we do not refute it in time. Alexei turns an ankle in the ruin, now vomits on summer grass.

He says, with eyes closed, "What is the date?"

The golem says, "You have asked me three times. Will you remember now, are you finally awake? It is August, much has happened."

"August, ridiculous."

"The bee venom is potent, Alexei. Nikita is dead, he called out to me, he was the reason we found you. And when the dead lose their voices they do this." He nods at the missing stonework and Alexei thinks, *They do what? Break through walls? Is that not what death is, a dark wall?*

The golem says, "We only followed the mess."

Another tornado has hit, Alexei knows better than to question it.

The device says, "I am sorry, but your grandfather is gone. We are not sure what will come of Evgeny. Were you close to him?"

Again the boy does not hear. He says, "One thing is true, the sting is potent. I am awake but must be dreaming still. You are Freyja, are you not? Alexander Mamontov built you at Tsarskoye Selo? Little Sergei?"

"I do not know any Mamontov but it is true, I am from Tsarskoye Selo. This one calls me Gabriel."

The boy's eyes are coming back and he takes a more complete look. The device's components are different, of more expensive origin. Not foraged, procured. It is taller than Freyja, with a masculine voice.

He says, "You came because you think I am Alexei Romanov. You are taking me home?"

It is the stranger who answers, the gruff one: "It has been years of this and at least one grave for me. I do not remember your plan in full, or even my full part in it. When you say home, at least tell us which country you mean."

Alexei is not too drunk to spot the paradox: full part.

The man goes on: "Yes, I knew your mother, and your girlfriend's mother. She healed me. So many years ago, I was a child, a different child. I guess she did not heal me after all."

There is nothing here to respond to and for this the boy is quiet.

The man says, "She had help there. We could try to find the brethren but they were idiots, useless, all of them. Easy to forget, except they had the same name, the same face."

"And what name was that?"

"Vasili, Vasili, Vasili."

Alexei still does not have his thoughts together, but he half-remembers the time he asked his father of the man's patronymic, Vasilievich. They were taking a walk along the gulf, and the man wrote in the sand, seemed as if he were mocking himself for a family tree of one name. He started with, "You call me father. But if we look at the line from here, it is grandfather. From there, you can call me great-grandfather." Then he stopped, keen on the waves rinsing his sketch away. A lousy joke, poorly told. Even so, Alexei was smiling wide.

The stranger says, "What? Your parents told you none of this? I do not blame them. But when you cut your hair. Or when you lost—"

Would Alexei have asked that question if things were the other way around, and it was the stranger with a metal prosthesis? He has interrupted the man, says, "My hair does not change when she cuts it. My arm did not change when the surgeon cut it off. But I know some of it. Papa changed when he died, and we keep his relics in a box. Mama says when she passes, she will change."

"But as to why they look like the tsar and empress? Why so many Romanovs look like each other? You know nothing of what we were doing?"

The man, who seems to be Russian, barely pronounces his words. Even the golem is better-suited for questions, making a point. The slurred, almost oily delivery lends his testimony a rather bottomless feel.

Words that always come forth, always bleed into those before and after.

It is akin to damnation, Alexei thinks, although he could not explain how.

The man talks on and on: "Alexanders the Second and Third. The tsar, your father, the grand duke, his brothers Vladimir and—"

"My father is not a Romanov."

"Neither are you. Yet you are identical to the tsesarevich. Why?"

"I suppose you should tell me."

"Look at the women, then. You are acting thickheaded again and, if I am being frank, you inherit that from your mother."

"Rodolfo, please."

So that is his accuser's name, Rodolfo? Not a terribly Russian name, yet the man has come here on Russian business, seems to have devoted himself to Russian matters.

(Within a day he will introduce himself as Rodolfo Gadda, from Novara. Not a Russian-sounding place, either, but it is not as if the man is a spy, not anymore. The old Romanov secrets are blown wide open and the new ones have something to do with the new Russia, the pledge that there are no secrets at all.)

"Alix of Hesse, German and British. Marie Sophie of Denmark. The Brasova woman, from Moscow. Different places of birth but all identical to your mother. Not the same age but the same faces and voices at least. I need you to say it for me, because it would be ridiculous for me to say it any more. My whole life, keeping a tsar on the throne, in the most odd and laborious way."

"You are trying to get me to say the men are all one man, and the women are all one woman. I cannot imagine how, and I am not about to spend my afternoon guessing."

"No? And why is that, do you have urgent things somewhere? You spent nine months sleeping off a honey-drunk and only now, you realize you have things to do?"

Gabriel, who is, to the boy, a grandfather of sorts, says, "Leave him." It is the same as Konstantin would have said.

"You can have no doubt, *amico mio*. I will leave him right here."

Even the man's Italian is unconvincing.

The golem says, "You ask if we are taking you home. By home you mean Karl's land, I am sure. Tsarskoye Selo is not what you would expect and the imperial family is shot. We hear Alexei and Anastasia are alive, and that the tsesarevich lived by catching bullets in his hands, playing dead."

While the golem explained, Alexei adjusted once, again. Now he vomits a second time. It is a hot, black gravy he had no reason to keep.

He bawls, too: a second coma! He had only just woken from the first. Such a waste, he will never agree to sleep again.

Rodolfo says, "What's the use in that, Alexei? Stop it. You win nothing with this."

"I have only one home."

"And you keep carrying on like a baby, you'll never see it."

"The hell with you."

"Listen, we will find your mother and settle you in Finland. You will be safe there for now. You are as important to Russia as anyone."

Finland. Too bad the brute Mamontov knew best all along. But how do they know his mother is home? What if she is away, searching all over, or has fled the farm for good? How do they know she has not turned to mineral, or to empty things, just like her miracles?

#

They have a car, a second-year Moyer that lurches with the terrain. Alexei hates it already, knows it will take them days to get back. For hours and hours, this will be his lot. The northeast of Moscow is an overcast, wooded place, which seems to him both horizontal and vertical. The roads are slow, poor. In some places unfinished. But rail travel would be a mistake.

The boy cannot decide if he is starved or off-kilter.

Rodolfo and the golem found traces of food preparation. Alexei does not remember cooking, nor once eating or drinking anything, yet he would not have held on these last months without it. For now he can only fight the jostling road by taking in water. (They have containers for that and juice, as well as combustible and engine oil. Alexei daydreams of confusing those, of drinking grease instead of cider, of fueling the car with water, not gasoline. If they are in the Moyer long enough, he knows one of those will not be a daydream.)

By Elnya they have to stop to let him off and by Pokrov, he would like to stop again. He does not say anything the second time, he will piss the seat if he has to. He tries to distract himself with conversation and asks the golem: "Do you dream? Do you see things?"

"I am sure that dream is not the word."

You think he is going to explain further but he is quiet. Alexei thinks, *Well, then. I will make up the answer and make up other things, too. I will think of you frozen up with rust, a sickly ice that is born inside you and is always there. Who would trust a creature like that? Who would expect me to?*

The boy's silence only makes it worse, and he has to say, "How did you come to life? Did they only take the cloth from your face?"

"No, it was the residual. Just as with any other like me."

"Residual?"

The golem stares with clear glass and says, "You of all people know what the residual is."

"Does it run out?"

"Run out, you say?"

So the golem would rather waltz than answer. Amen, fellows like Rodolfo would rather brawl than answer. At least this way Gabriel and the boy are on equal footing. One is too young to dance and the other, not the right composition.

By the city of Vladimir they stop for the night. There is a recent and muddy campsite with a structural steel pen. (Exotic animals, or God forbid some manner of outdoor cell.) The nearby barn has given in to its own weight, and because of fire the house is open at the top-north. A rubbish bin is here and Rodolfo drags it toward the pen, now checks his palms for cuts. He finds hay in the barn and fashions a bed in the steel cages. What is left of the hay, he burns.

To the boy's amazement it is the man, not the golem, who will keep watch. Gabriel says he will stay with the car. Alexei believes him, and believes he will look like part of the car.

There are bugs out and the automaton, who is the farthest from the burning trash, takes the worst of it. He swats metal on metal for hours. It is a lengthy percussion solo that Alexei does not recognize as music, even while they are in the first years of jazz.

His motion sickness has not passed, despite hours away from the car. Then again, he may be ill in some other way. Eating has done nothing for his hunger, water does not help. For most of the night he is alert; his eyes are wide and his voice does not sound tired. Gabriel speaks to Rodolfo at times but Alexei responds in his place. Once, before midnight, the golem says, "How is the tsesarevich?"

"Your friend is asleep but I am not well. My stomach is moving around, and there is something happening to my hands."

"You are nervous. You have to relax."

No, it is not nervousness. It is worse than that: an itch he cannot reach. Did that wretched Evgeny give him polio? Yellow fever? If not the old man, was it something in the foul air of his house?

At least he feels safe in the pen, and the breeze through the iron is calming. He says, "I am still sick from the car. I fear I am sick."

"Nine months with the bees. I wonder if you are dependent."

The boy's upper arms, but especially his one lower arm, are plastered with stings, redness. As much histamine as skin. But the sensation is not limited to that. It comes from inside, above his belt, the same place as when he jumped from the roof. The instant before his face struck the metal corrugations and everything changed: Anastasia's con. Natalia's positive response to the salt. Her further treatments. The wheat, the fight, the train to Moscow.

Damn that idea! Save for a stupid act—and he knew better at the time—he would be well and they would have fled the Volga region with the Baratovs. Andrei would be alive. He and mama would have met Little Sergei no matter what, maybe the exile would have been to Finland. But they are all scattered now, and he does not even know how to long for that place, or any other place. Does Helsinki have mountains, grasslands, cities? Is there a tsar, a soviet, or does Finland decide matters like the British decide them?

At last, at four in the morning, he dulls himself off. He dreams of Gabriel speaking in another man's voice, saying things that scare him. The sentences more frightening than war.

In the morning Gabriel is no worse but the others have heavy eyebrows, swollen faces. As if in response to Alexei's dream, Rodolfo takes the golem in widening circles around the car until they find something. It is a dead peasant, frozen in mid-step by the cold of hunger, toppled to the side. Barely dusty, a word half-spoken on his lip.

Rodolfo says, "Is this what you were going on about all night?"

"Not that I'm aware."

"Well, the boy and I are aware."

When Gabriel does not answer Rodolfo says, "Minstrel? We should be moving again. You remember your storms."

"It is my preference you do not call me that."

"A walking bagpipe, drumming all night? Did I say something untrue? Alexei?"

There are flies around the corpse, which reminds the boy of last night's racket. He is reluctant to mention it but he does not have to. Rodolfo disputes the point here and there for 20 miles: "It is not as if you feel them, you louse. It is not as if you're allergic to the bites."

Gabriel says, "Does a fly bite hurt the cattle? Or the horses? Of course not, but you see their tails swatting all the time. It's for keeping the insects away."

"But they don't keep the herd awake with it."

"You don't know that. We call it plague for a reason. They ruin our crops and bring disease."

It looks as if Rodolfo is nodding but that is his bodily momentum, the bouncing of wheels on cheap road. He says, "But you do not get disease. These things could crawl inside you, all throughout you. Your eyes and mouth, to no effect."

"It would have a great effect on you two."

"And that is what the fire was for."

"Then you are forgetting 3,000 years of instinct."

The subject makes Alexei frown, look off. Rodolfo has made a fair point, why did a work of metal choose the stale summer air over a campfire? Were his parts not forged by fire? Leave it to a thing of the elements to shun the elements, but no, he is about to make the same point as Anastasia's psalms. He will leave the rest of that argument unsaid.

After the second day of driving they stop at a river. There is a church on one bank and a monastery across from it, in a competing architectural style from the first building. The bank has a narrow dirt road with houses pushed to the edge of the slope, a hideous town. The first home is an entirely red house and the second, only meters away, is a mostly blue one. There is a third house near, in the exact color of rubble.

The river is dry and a man has stranded his car on the bed. The passenger door is open and he only stands, gazing their way. Because of the man's staring, and his own vanity, Alexei thinks, *All his life this man has known ugly churches, ugly houses, ugly rivers. We must be the ugliest things he has seen. Or worse, we might all three be beautiful to him.*

Of the accommodations, you know what Rodolfo will say and he does, almost word for word: "The kid and I will sleep in the monastery. This one here can pound on himself all night if he wants to. I don't need to hear it again."

Alexei misses the juvenile double entendre. He has spent his pubescent years with a father off at war, while his friends only talk about girls and cigarettes, not about being alone. Mama and Anastasia do not joke that way and Little Sergei is, to the boy, a newcomer.

Yet when he hears the man's chuckle Alexei can enjoy its healthy timbre.

He takes part by smiling, meeting their glances. It is good to have levity with a rather uncouth fellow like this. Rodolfo made the golem laugh a few hours ago and the glass eyes, the unmoving mouth left the boy wanting more. He was going to remark on the automaton's steely chuckle, but most people you know laugh the same way that Gabriel does.

#

The monastery door is standing open. The interior is inexpensive, amateur in hand, but impossibly ornate. They seem to have come in at the rear, through an antechamber and now, to an empty prayer room. It is squat and dark. They knew they left the domes on the opposite side of the river but this is worse than it looked from the outside. Box-shaped, realist, socialist; and here is the problem with that, it was built long before 1848.

The walls are divided into private, modular seats—the boy would have to climb up to sit in one— each with a painted icon behind. Christ and monk, Christ and monk, in exact repetition. The sheer beauty, red and gold, makes him say an atheist curse, yet he is prompt in taking it back.

In a way, to profane is to celebrate life and a monastery reminds him that our lives are quick. Afterward, the celebration, and beyond that, nothing to swear at, swear about. Whether he is devout, superstitious, unbeliever, it is best not to curse here.

"Rough sex, good at guessing. Likes to wear robes and hats. I'd be the best monk of them all." Rodolfo laughs hard, smacks hard on the shoulder blade.

Alexei wonders if the statement would annoy him less if the man did not hit so well.

He can only be speaking of Grigori Novykh, taking one monk's fraud and applying it to every monk in Russia, all the while going through a monk's home for a floor to sleep on. Do all Italians behave like this?

Make general statements, with so little charity? Look, he even has Alexei doing it now.

They bed down at the front of a silly iconostasis. The Messiah is rendered as brown, stooped over, very nearly feminine. A ranching woman. If it is true that she tends to animals the lifetime of work has left her infirm. Or he.

Anastasia would chide Alexei for thinking that but he would say, —If it comforts me, if it helps me sleep, it is good.

To which she would say, —Christ is good on his own, without you saying that he comforts you.

Even here, quiet and separate, they argue. Her statements self-contradict and no, he does not think it is unfair to hold that against her.

#

Overnight he thinks of monks copying Bibles. Not replacing the books, say, after they were burned or wrecked by moisture. But rewriting them while they were still in good condition. Duplicating them, with identical covers, page counts, contents.

One book becomes two, two becomes four; it is only a matter of raw material stock. Perhaps one printing is more scuffed than the others, while another may still reek of ink. But that aside, they are indistinguishable.

Once they are complete Anastasia might suggest that the monastery exhibit them spine-in, with the paper showing out, not the leather. That way the scriptures would come together the way her novels do, as one chapter, eons in scope.

At last the boy understands what the girl's mother was up to.

#

In the morning, setting out for their last time, he has little to say. Mostly he wants to know of Alexei Romanov, who, he assumes now, is the ideal for how he is supposed to live.

But the golem will only speak of Alexei Karlovich Shafirov, and of the precautions the boy should take from today on. At least that is how he will remember it, in words almost identical to Revekka's.

"Nikita said there was a farm seized, immediate to yours. Those men killed your father and neighbor."

"Nikita also said I was the tsesarevich and heir to the throne, and the only hope for Russia."

"We should move your family to the east. An exile without fully leaving the country. There are places where you will be safe."

"And you told me Alexei and Anastasia had survived. I did not believe in fables until men turned to oil while I watched. They went up in flames, and an elevator car took me to Moscow. This trip we are making now, this three-day drive, I made it in an instant."

Their conversation isn't quite as much drivel as this, but close enough.

As the lapses between words become greater, the hours start to log, and by mid-afternoon he comes to a place he does not recognize. It is a flourishing wheat farm, with a house once damaged by a storm, a baby blue lake at the back of the property. Whether or not he knows the land does not matter. His mother is running up, her face beaten into heartbreak and worry, and when Alexei gets it he slumps into the same look exactly.

She is shouting something but what with the roaring in his ears he does not hear. He arm-jumps from the car, no time for the door. He catches a toe again, down on both knees. No matter, and when she screams again—it was his name all along—he can tell her, "It doesn't matter."

She lifts him high, her arms like vices all over, and in the confusion of hair and tears he senses the wonderful cost.

"Careful, my pigeon. Your legs. I've had you back for one second and your legs."

"No, mama. I'm healed. You healed me. It was the salt, always."

Mostly they just embrace. They try not to promise much, or shush each other. Best not to add up the lost time.

#

Natalia Baratova is here and her treatment looks to have stalled. She has taken Alexei's bed and bedroom; the place smells of wet clothes or another, more foul musk, which he will try not to sniff at again. She locks an elbow around his neck, wrenches him in until they are ear to ear. She is in pain and her fever is high. The woman begs pardon in many ways. The boy can barely make out a word.

The one word he can is Anastasia.

He snarls with her mention, his first broken heart. Yet it is best if that happens over mundane things. You see, there are always wars out and in those a town can be consumed whole, in only a day. People wiped out, their languages forgotten. Better then for Alexei to fret about teenaged love, being jilted, a girl who does not visit enough, a blade between his legs that he never gets to draw on someone. That way the much larger scenes of battle, famine, epidemic, you have no time for those.

Little Sergei is here: "Hello, boy." With this third embrace is a third, unique scent, the whiff of a soldier's adventure. That progression—mama's restlessness, Natalia's illness, the warrior's sweat—makes Alexei shudder. Wanderlust, becoming infirm, violent death. His last year has been almost that.

You can only hope the odyssey is figurative and not the final, literal one.

That was a strange word to choose, odyssey, and now that he has renounced Anastasia for good he will have to be the one to cut into their words. Odyssey, from Odyssasthai, one who grieves. The sufferer of pain, *odyne*. The opposite is *anodyne*, a painkiller or mute work of art. It sounds like a worthless idea, art that does not wound, however, works like that are all around us. The numbing patterns of a rug, the non-scandalous masonry walls of a library, or church. Not all work needs to cut us away from others, our families. Cut our skin, watch what happens to our thick when we drop.

Anyway, we will see. Alexei would rather not cut, not be cut, yet the peasants are still at the Kabanov home. They are only a few yards from here, and their last visit will be soon.

Freyja is awake, just as Alexei thought. Mama tired of waiting for Little Sergei to come and tracked down the golem. She poured Karl's salt into the mouth and within a day the automaton was awake. It spoke in a man's voice and went by the name Raphael. There is something with the Oridinnes dirt, it is responsible for many things, but Alexei will have to hear about those second-hand.

Raphael stayed close, oxidizing near the Kabanov house. It shouted out at times, never sleeping, the picture of insomnia. If tornados followed him here it was better to lead them to Oskar, not to Revekka.

When Raphael sees Alexei he only nods, his expression chosen in advance. After the brief gesture he retreats to a private room. All passion, but without the nerve endings to prove it. For this, he is ashamed. The golem is ready for any kind of a fight, but not for a son's numb touch.

He will let Natalia speak for Karl these days, the fleshy Karl.

Rodolfo vows to stay and fight. If only for that reason, the shootout will be soon. Besides, no one here will endure his blasphemy for long. He still boasts of death and rebirth; in the old way, not with Chehreh's salt trickery. Moreover he speaks of a decade-old plot to kill Nicholas II. By that he means Chehreh's plot, not that of the anarchists. His every sentence begins with — After Sarov, after Sarov.

Maybe Revekka is afraid of him. Say mama can put up with Rodolfo for seven days. If that is right, the fighting will be in eight days.

You would think she fears Gabriel, too, but no, she walks straight up to him. She says, "The man on the train, the one the agents beat up? He called to you, like on a radio?"

Gabriel says, "I am the one he called. The rest is hidden from me. How do you know, did he call you, too?" Alexei would not notice the Russian part were it not for his study of French. Russian verbs—to call, to know—are gendered in the past tense, neutral in the present and future tenses.

Revekka says, "No, I have a wireless of my own."

At least two of them will need a bath. Alexei has just the place, and has meant to ask it all sorts of things. He has become an addicted boy of riddles and knows just what to write.

Chapter Sixteen

IT IS MORNING and Raphael is still quiet with him. Continuing shame, or something more than that. But what is deeper than shame? Disorientation, the balancing of accounts?

Alexei will not mention the bees yet. He should give mama some time, at least a day, if he can endure as long. But if he cannot find a hive soon he will have to tell her.

There used to be a rotting heap at his school; the peach skins and syrupy bites brought in flies. Also gnats, and the engine noise of bees. In those days Alexei stood back, so far that his friends made fun of him, but if it were today he would walk right in, put a bare leg in.

After breakfast he searches the property for nasty fruit, rubbish, anything that would become sugar or compost. His hand shakes, especially when he gestures above the waist. This way he mostly lets his arms hang to the side, a kind of statuette with clothes.

The golems are out: statuettes without clothes. Their metal surfaces are hot and reflective, cloaked in sun. Maybe they deserve the archangel names and, if they do, Alexei will have to find a way to tell them. They pass through Revekka's crops without a glance at the wheat. Alexei seems to have found them in an early conspiracy; by all means they have caught him, too, trying to draw a hive out. They agree without speaking of it, neither will ask the other, nor tell Revekka about it. But the boy can hear their strange metal voices longer than they think. It is the echo of a jinni, which speaks in terrible volume from inside a small, metal lantern.

He listens after they pass.

Raphael says, "If you look at those dead limbs, see? Only a haze from here. There were murders there when I was a boy."

"When you were a boy I was a boy, and if it was that long ago those murders are bones already."

"It is the closest grave I can think of. The cemetery is miles past there."

"We can try. But I will tell you, when the cadavers know we have stopped listening, they stop speaking. And from there we have failed, and the weather—"

"Of course."

If you have seen a cat follow a girl you know its expression of disinterest, and the indirect, often silly route it takes to track her. Alexei has to treat them the same as a cat would; walking apart from them, pretending to be unaware, but eventually coming to the same place.

Along the way there is the occasional bouquet, and one of every few flowers buzzes with a drone. He cannot help but reach out, yet the bees avoid him: a child coming in close, the pest keeping a distance. It is such a reversal that he must have made it up. But if that is so, the glen, too, is invented, as is this tree, and the sound in his ears, as of the wind on his shirt.

The golems are disappointed with the thicket but despite that, they choose to sit and wait. Strange that their artisan hearing has not picked up Alexei's noisy boots. Or more likely, they know he has come and are ignoring him. Or they would like for him to eavesdrop.

Gabriel says, "You do not need to listen or try. Maybe if you try it doesn't leave room for voices."

"If you listen, do you hear anything?"

"As I said, you do not need to listen."

Alexei is hungry, and mama will worry about him if he is away for too long. Back at the house, the air is savory, they are healed with only its scent. He hopes, on a day like this in, for example, 1922, she will scratch at his beard for the first time, unpack an old-world saying about clean face, clean soul, and they both will be rebuilt.

He eats and eats but the cravings are worse. It is time for him to admit it, food is not what nourishes him anymore. Sergei is off to buy bread, wine, ammunition. He is always off somewhere, buying or selling, readying them for combat. He was this way already but with

Raphael awake, it is more than ever. One of them has thick in his arms, chest, and can do something to Revekka with only his fingertips. But the other has a promise from her, which she whispered to him before the new century. She tickled his ear with the sound, when he had ears.

Neither is sure how to act and for this Sergei behaves as he always did. Each morning, a new mission. Maneuvers, objectives, every day you survive you win. A soldier's practical way.

Alexei does not attempt to unravel it, that one of them has built the other.

What with the late hour, Raphael and Gabriel must have gone from thicket to church. Mama is cleaning up and Alexei is quiet. That leaves only Rodolfo for Natalia, and the man has already made her angry:

"I had my thoughts about him, too, but he has protected the child for a year."

Alexei only listens. Are they speaking of Little Sergei? If so, it has been two years. For some of that, Little Sergei did not know.

Rodolfo says, "I meet too many of his kind. Drunk, heathens, with whore mothers, the sons of johns. I will say this, they are strong for their size and if you get them working you will never get them to stop. But that is not the man you want protecting a boy."

He turns to Alexei, "You saw the metal pens, we slept in one after Moscow. You think those were for dogs? Or khans? Or do you not understand the difference?"

"I have been the full length of Russia and seen those pens only once. The men for whom they are built, no sum of iron will keep them in."

Natalia will never prove that remark, although Karl might. She says, "We could not stop them if we tried, if indeed they still live. Mamontov says he will watch Alexei, it would be ridiculous not to trust him, to give in to prejudice."

Rodolfo says, "Russia has been on the brink for so many years, you want a Mongol to guard Alexei when he is all we have? A sick, skinny boy with one arm left? It is not prejudice, it is the truth."

For a newcomer, a common stranger to speak of their friend this way, Alexei and Natalia are appalled until silence. The man goes on, "I may be wrong about him. He seems agreeable. But we have so much to do."

"And what is it we have to do, Gadda?" Before Natalia lets him answer she dismisses the question with her hands, "No, forget that. What I should say is how do you respond that Tsar Nicholas II assigned Mamontov to himself, personally? They went all throughout the war front together, among the towns to Malaya Vishera, where I understand you have relatives, and a lover?"

Alexei thinks, *Christ and blood! One of the golems will not speak a word and the other will not stop telling people things.*

Rodolfo says, "The Mongol was a fellow of the tsar's personal security? I must doubt that."

Alexei doubts it, too, if for nothing than Mamontov's inventions on the train. The man's lies were quick and complete. Mostly convincing. What's more, deceiving, covering up, those are ways of life for the Romanovs. Sergei might have learned it from the best of the liars.

Natalia says, "In my travels I find that only the dishonest make accusations of lying."

"Travels! My little black doll will speak to me of her travels? You aristocrats travel like cattle. You run when I say and you graze when I say. When the coyotes come, I will shoot. You sit back and graze some more."

The remark appears to have stung her. Natalia is in too much pain to stand; Revekka has to bring her food, drink and wine, every time she asks. Her body is swollen and her face, unrecognizable. If the peasants returned Natalia could not hold a rifle.

But her answer is brave, "No. It is Mamontov who will shoot. Our ugly little Mongol drives the cattle from ranch to ranch, just like you say. But you, who says he wants to reclaim the country for one boy. Where have you been since Women's Day? There have been two uprisings and a tornado. The Romanovs were in arrest at Tsarskoye Selo, and imprisoned in Yekaterinburg. They were shot, all of them, and here you are, a whole week from Moscow. A week from Petrograd, shouting at a sick cow."

"Alexei Romanov is gone, like you say. Alexei Shafirov is all we have."

"You have nothing. Nicholas abdicated for himself and his son. It is a secular throne now."

The man considers it at length and says, "There is no such thing as a secular throne. It is like saying a creek runs with solid instead of water."

Alexei has heard enough but the man's closing point is more than he can take. There are rivers all over the world that turn from water to solid mass to water again. And between the freezes and thaws, they are both ice and liquid at the same time. Not nonsense, not fable, only the fable of cold weather.

The boy stands and says, "I want no part of this. I never have." He hurries from the room, from the house, now sits at the dead lake and tries not to ask it anything. He longs for something to throw, and shatter, out of rage. The grass does not shatter but it will have to do.

In time, the smell of nicotine. Rodolfo is here, sitting down, a nasal exhale. He pats Alexei on the shoulder. It is too hard again, like a grandfather's touch. Then again, all Alexei knows of grandfathers is Konstantin, who pats too hard.

"We are not here long, my boy. News is slow and the truth is slow. That is uncommon, I think. The dead are quicker to speak than this. Our golems will know what to do soon."

"It is fine. All is fine."

"When they tell us it is time to leave, we will. You can come along or stay, but even if you stay you are still the tsesarevich. No one can control that, only God."

He says, "How can you see these things and believe they are God's will?"

"Like what things? Revolutions, storms? You think the Bible is quiet about storms?"

"Gabriel, bees, the yearner's salt?"

"The Bible mentions everything you say. No, the Bible mentions everything."

The golems are home soon, and they tell of another death in the Buirimov family. The others take it as news, the time to act, but for Alexei it is proof. No god would create a loudspeaker for the Buirimovs. They are crazy, haggard people with liver maps instead of faces.

Good, the boy can have his disbelief again. When it and Anastasia left him he had almost nothing. A march of static, or perhaps that was only the tinnitus.

He will make a lousy automaton, always putting fingers in his ears when the sounds are coming from the inside.

#

Natalia has avoided the question too often. And every time she replies, her answers differ. Alexei reminds her of that and tells her he will ask again, the last time.

He says, "Why were you never detained? Petrograd to here, here to Petrograd. And, like you say, you have been all over the country, even to the east."

She says, although she knows it will not be enough, "The new government has no reason to suspect me."

When the boy continues to stare she says, "I don't know. My first trip, when Revekka was in Petrograd, I cannot say. I suppose even chaos needs time to take hold."

"I can accept that. But the others?"

She closes her eyes and, at the same time, reaches for his hand. Because of this she briefly misses, grabs only at air. It is a touching gesture. The boy knows he will gesture like this always. Searching for what is between them, which neither can quite see.

Now that their hands are together she has her reply: "A soldier knows what to tell another soldier. That is the most I can say for now."

"A soldier!"

"Don't make me explain, Alexei."

"Then how did you come to join the court?"

"My great-grandfather took a job on a ship. Those were the only jobs at the time: ship, rail, infantry. One of Alexander's men found us on board. The tsar kept 20 African men among his guards. With every departure he employed another. We became quite prominent."

Anastasia has told him similar things, with nearly the exact words: "Twenty Sudanese infantrymen, never more or fewer. It was Alexander's promise." Alexei knows to doubt stories such as these, especially when they come from the same printing edition.

He dislikes talk of boats, anyway, because they leave out the shipwreck, murder and scurvy. They tell only of mariners and ghosts, as if no man ever dies, he only rises in rank.

#

Sophie, who lost Boris a year ago, is dead. There is no sadness in the news, only the profound ache that she endured so long.

Raphael will not visit her. The de Morny sisters, if he can call them that, are sure to attend the funeral, and whatever words they had for the golem would be unkind. Nor would Revekka take Sergei if Raphael were to stay back.

As for Alexei, he is angry with Rodolfo again, and has issued his mother an impossible choice. He will not attend services with the man nor agree to stay here with him.

Raphael would like to send the old woman off somehow, and it seems Gabriel has been preparing him for something close to that. The boy would like to see the loudspeaker trick again and Revekka will not let him go anywhere without her. Natalia vows that she will be well for the short time they are away and, given that, Rodolfo should make the trip, too.

So all of those who should attend tomorrow will instead have their own funeral right now, in the deep night behind the Buirimov place. They will approach the house as thieves, but the songs coming from inside, perhaps a radio voice, are all they might steal.

Mama treats it like a long visit to Konstantin's, talking about food, water, extra clothes, rifles. As for the last of those, she does not need to ask. Mamontov behaves as if this is another of his military patrols. Get civilians to the Buirimov place, get them back, no one is lost.

Raphael, who has mostly hidden himself from Alexei, takes the boy aside, "I would rather you stay with Natalia." His hands are on the child's face. They are a father's words and gestures, though the metal palms are cold.

The boy says, "I want to see it. Sophie will speak through you, is that the hope? I saw it once with Gabriel."

"Who knows what you saw or if those two would tell the truth."

Such peril in his voice! He speaks of their lies as if they were an act of violence and perhaps they are. If a lying man wants to conceal himself, does it not follow he will strike out if he is found?

Alexei nearly says —Papa, I saw it. Instead he only says, "I saw it."

"Natalia may need you to heal her. It is best. Also, it is dangerous here. It is not the same place you remember."

"You are the one who needs to remember. I never once left here."

But it is no use: the man was rigid before, and now his body is made out of rigid parts. Very well, Alexei will only track them like he did yesterday. As for his ability to heal, he has accepted that he owes it to the purveyor. Any simpleton can leave a bag of salt in Natalia's reach, he does not have to stay behind to administer it. She is going to sleep through all of this, besides.

The door squeaks shut. He is preparing to go when the Baratova woman calls out: "Alexei?"

You see? It is right there in her voice, which is hoarse again, as deep as Mamontov's voice. She is about to nod off. Alexei ignores her, tickles at his chest the way the men do, lets himself out through the front.

Only minutes into the walk and he knows this will be hard to cover up. His shoes are becoming ruined, he has gained height from mud accumulating. By the time he is home again, his trousers will be streaked to the knee. In the distance and dark he sees Raphael struggling with it, too. For a time the golem stops, puts out a hand that means Gabriel should stop. The shorter one reaches down, breaks the mud free from his heel. The way he braces himself on the other one's arm looks like a wife and husband. It is affectionate, even.

A startling moment. The soldier turned to metal, in the shape and gestures of a mother. Alexei tastes the grief in his throat. Outrage, too. One mother is all he needs.

"Alexei, when you are grown, this mess will be yours and you can be rich making ceramic."

The boy stops in place, crouches low. None of them have turned back or paused to listen. Is Raphael speaking to him directly, or en absentia, ghost to ghost? Hard to say, until Revekka answers with, "And as many years as we have left, you can name us as the heirs."

Rodolfo laughs: "Such rotten fate, to have to joke about that."

It pains Alexei to agree with the man. That was macabre for Revekka to say and moreover, this is an unwanted power he wields, to hear them speak of him, when they do not know he is there. No magic at work, not one of the fables that have plagued his last year. Only the power of hiding well, staying quiet, even when your name comes up.

They press on, he presses on. There is an uphill portion that leaves them winded. The golems are winded, too, although it is psychological, not pulmonary.

They arrive. The Buirimov house is old and humble, too small for anything except mourning. The others stop and sit within sniffing distance of the place. All Alexei needs is to hear; this way he can stay back in a triangle of birch.

"Do you feel anything?"

"You never feel anything." Rodolfo has asked Raphael but it is Gabriel who answers. The Italian bangs a knuckle on Gabriel's arm, a dunce-tone in reply. He says, "I don't mean feel like he feels something. I mean, do you feel you're about to become a wireless?"

"I don't. But then I never do. This one, who knows?"

"Then maybe you let him answer."

It is the sort of response that means no one should speak further. Yet Raphael, as Karl, was used to taking orders as they were stated. He says, "I don't know what I feel. I don't know what I don't feel."

Alexei sees three cigarettes, a failed constellation.

Sergei turns to Raphael, "If this is a success I might ask you to come to my father's place. We never had a chance to finish things. The last he knew I was hurt; he left us wondering if I would survive. His house has room for all of us."

Of course it is Rodolfo who contests that: "It is not a thing of success or failure. If there are sounds little Freyja will broadcast them. If not, she will be quiet, at least to the extent a woman can be quiet."

Is he trying to insult them all? No matter, it is Raphael who answers: "Signore Gadda, I will remind you, you are a guest in my house. You will respect my family and me and I will not remind you again. It is no more complicated than that."

"Your house, you say? From here, your house looks like a muddy yard with a morgue."

"I have said what I will say."

"And you talk about family, your family is back in France, healing ranchers with leaf disease, kissing their necks so they can bleed again and get back to work. Your family sends monks and salesmen to Petrograd to fight. Between all of them there was one warrior, and it was you. But look at you today, metal legs. Evening shoes."

The others have been trying to interrupt but he is not quite finished: "Whatever family you have now is that metal box sitting next to you. He answers to me and, as to your rank, your assumptions are your own."

"I will remind you that you can burn, I cannot."

One of the glowing cigarette ends plunges to the ground, stomps out with a boot. To the extent that the ashes still resemble stars it is a celestial cataclysm, yet too far away for us to despair.

Rodolfo says, "And you can rust, I cannot. What if we hung you from a tree by the neck? You would never die, only wear out. Your mind drips away a speck at a time. It takes years, just like rust."

"Both of you, quiet."

Little Sergei says, "To the contrary, we are here to listen to Raphael, and to you. As for your Italian friend, he can hang them from every tree in Russia. I have an axe. I will follow him around and we can take the forests down together."

"That is just like a khan, declaring war on spring syrup."

"A war? I offered you a place where your hunters do not think to look. Instead of accept it you are degrading my hosts, threatening things. If it were my property, I would put you out. My offer, you can still take it. We could leave tonight. Within 10 or 20 days we would be safe for good."

Hunters, enemies, heathens. Mama has been speaking this way for years, and not of the revolutionaries, either. The tall men were visiting long before the revolutions, with their fists and beards and familiar ways. No Bolshevik ever frightened her into changing her name.

It is an older problem than the soviets, one they will not resolve tonight, with more arguing.

Rodolfo says, "I will say it again, because the smoke has done work on your mind. This godawful place does not belong to us, it is the property of Russia. And because Russia belongs to God and the Romanovs, everything you see goes to God, who would speak to us through the boy if anyone would listen."

Alexei has heard all of the bickering he can. The one they have come to hear—Sophie Buirimov, speaking from the shell of Raphael—is the only silent voice. He departs ahead of the others, but it is absolute dark now. He is briefly lost, approaches the glacial lake from the west instead of east, and now has to avoid the old Kabanov property.

Because of that mama nearly discovers him. They left briefly after he did and he wasted that time with a disoriented return. They, as well as he, reenter the house through the back. The child only has enough time to strip from his shoes and pants, toss them in a wheelbarrow, which she never moved after the storm.

Revekka says, "Alexei, we had such success! Her voice was bell-clear. It was tragic to hear, but a miracle!"

Something has roused her, she has yet to notice that he is bare from the waist. But what she is saying has to be a lie. He waited and waited and heard only disputes. As he chooses between replies, she says, "And how is our patient?"

"Natalia? She is asleep, like we thought." But no, the sick woman is just inside the door, awake, clothes drenched, crawling toward the sounds. She has been bawling and defecating and her voice has fallen in pitch again.

It is too familiar to deny anymore. Alexei used to think his old man's words sounded like locusts, which meant, more than not, the boy wanted to keep Revekka for himself.

Mama says, "What is this?"

Both Natalia and Alexei offer their regrets but it is the woman who says it: "I'm sorry, love. I called and called. I lost track of time, I feared you were killed."

There will be no thoughts of discipline for the boy, no grief for the Buirimov house, wrecked again.

Chapter Seventeen

MAMA DID NOT speak of the arrangement. Alexei had mostly divined it anyway; she was apportioning Karl's remains two parts land, one part treatment. (By point of fact it was three to one, but his guess was close enough.) Natalia's listlessness continued until Rodolfo brought Alexei and Gabriel home. Then, the late-night visit to the Buirimov property and only days after, the gunfight.

Oskar came with the first peasant, the handsome one, as well as rows and columns of others. Little Sergei knew the day was close and had a garden of rifles waiting.

No one had made allowances for the wide Russian mysticism. At the sight of the golems, two of the intruders left. Those men turned their eyes away, lowered their guns and backed off.

Oskar called out to them, "What is this? Metal people make you afraid? Weld them to each other, rivet them to a press, they are nothing."

Alexei found the image stirring but thought, *No, friend. Tear most of a golem away he is still a golem. You cannot say that of a man.*

Oskar continued, "Take shroud and cover heads like corpses, they will be corpses."

There were too many ghosts here, the place stank of Andrei Kabanov and others. Another peasant fled, which meant good odds for Sergei and his spare-parts battalion. The handsome one was negotiating with Revekka about it, even months later. He said, "You have new contract with Oskar and you break that, too. I told you, no armies. But your army is bigger than before."

Alexei was counting: he and mama, Little Sergei and Rodolfo, the two automatons. Also Natalia, moaning from a bed about her insides. She was cursing the paradox of healing, that how a virus rarely kills, but the treatment often does.

Opposite them, 15 peasants, three of whom were gone but within shouting range. Six on 12 or, depending on Natalia's progress, eight on 12. If the others came back, eight on 15.

This is how it ended: the handsome peasant said, "I am a man of my word," then aimed a rifle at the boy. Alexei scarcely had time to duck before the man said, "I finish what I start."

There were two rifle shots. The first, because Oskar had not come to murder a child. He fired shoulder-to-shoulder from his companion and turned the man's skull to snow, which did not melt but rather mixed in with grass and blood.

The other shot, that of the dead man. Alexei felt his senses wake as his hand flashed up and forward, plucking the bullet from the air. The slug was neither hot nor injurious so he had to look to be sure. He could not have done that with his metal side, but he checked all the same.

Revekka shrieked and hurried him in. Natalia was there, frightened of everything. New gunshots rang out but the women only thought of the bullet in Alexei's hand.

He came forward and Natalia would have run from the room if she could. True horror, knowing you are the agent of this. But as he approached she had nowhere to go and when he gave her the slug he only said, "Sorry, papa."

The gunfire kept on. Revekka said, "Mamontov."

Her voice was unsure but the infantryman would live through it, with bullet holes to the forearm and the fat near his belt. The golems would take a score of rifle shots each, nothing beyond repair.

Oskar would fall and the handsome peasant was already cold. Three of their companions were dead. The rest would disarm and run. One of them managed a bullet high on Gadda's chest, just under the throat. A fatal wound? Perhaps, though a day ago Revekka whispered to her son that the Italian kept his heart in a money case.

From today Karl, Little Sergei and Natalia would watch Alexei here, with two of the region's automatons (if the boy was right, last year's storm meant the de

Mornys had one, too). The golems dug a massive wound through the ground, a sheer ditch from the bottom of the glacial lake through the thick of the bank, into the front, which led out to a stream.

The excavation took a year, and they spent the first months of 1919 trying to sift mineral from mineral. Why? A fraction of the sediment was precious to them, and it might help to bring a woman back, although they did not allow themselves much hope.

They kept at it until the de Morny family left Russia. Charlotte preferred to be within reach of glacial water, like she had when she was here. When Karl emptied the lake she chose to resettle in Denver, in a plain, contemporary house on Ogden Street, not worth the name.

When Karl's lake was dry they found a number of slates on the silty bottom, questions he never answered his first time.

Summoned or not, Karl would decide on Colorado. Charlotte had met a man named Jeremy, taken a new name again. They had children. Yet because Charlotte was Revekka almost exactly, Karl was set on following her.

Alexei, too. Also, Little Sergei would come.

#

Only weeks before they left, Anastasia found him. He rarely asked how she knew things, but this time was an exception. She had come to make love with him, as promised, now that they were 17. But had she waited, say, another month, she would have found an empty house, or perhaps a very crowded stinking, profane house.

Karl was in Petrograd, making arrangements. Sergei had taken the golems to a blacksmith, turning their welds to bolts, for easier freight. It was the perfect time. Indeed, the only time.

Alexei wondered about the girl's breath and her choice of skirt, but their skin was warm together and he would always remember the moist purring in his ear.

It was short and he was never sure if he had finished. She was quick to leave for the toilet, the same as you would with, heaven forbid, a cousin's seed among the eggs. After, they stayed close. He was ready to cover his sex but she left her body bare, untaut, with dried sweat. She must have learned that from her mother, when the woman was in her abdomen. Or was it from a man inside her, say, a man close to the Shafirovs?

How do you bid farewell after something like that? Alexei was blunt about it, and reflective. He said, "We were not as I thought we would be, which I can only say about the best friendships."

The compliment was more than he intended. He could not name another friend.

Anastasia said, "You speak of it like a goodbye."

"I think it is."

"With our families and yours, and with the de Morny family, it is never goodbye."

Before, maybe. Yet now they used men built of clock parts to tell time. Everything was different today.

#

For years, the reel of his mother's death played every night. It plays even now sometimes, in 1945, despite that he is an old man. He will dream it again in a few hours, the same day when his youngest sister Rosanna, now an adult, tells him Raphael has wandered off, perhaps to a better climate.

Alexei says, "Such a mess," but our pasts are supposed to be like that, as disheveled as bed linen. It is no surprise then, that pasts and bedding are so inclined to one another.

#

Tonight he sleeps, falls into the memory-dream. That old horizon is rifle smoke again, and he hands the bullet to Natalia. Her palms weigh hard at the bedding, the only kind of motion she has left.

He says, "Sorry, papa."

Revekka says, "Mamontov."

"Alexei, stay here with me."

"And they'll kill them."

"Alexei!" Natalia is reaching out but he is quick, with wet arms. The Baratova woman, despite that she is casting a trained soldier from her body, has never been weaker. It is too strange to watch, it becomes horrible if you do not look away, but there, between her fingers, are five more fingers. Natalia is shedding Karl like skin, leaving both of them whole, fully grown. A woman delivering an adult man.

Alexei will see it three times in all and look away every time, never fully get it. This will be the worst time and he flees the room, breaks toward the chaos outside.

The first one he sees is Oskar, who has a moment to express small relief. Good: the boy is alive. They are not murderers, only poor farmers in search of fairness.

The next second an exploded fruit is above Oskar's heart and he falls, no word or gesture. Raphael fires again and kills again. Rodolfo cries out and kicks up dust, not quite a dervish.

Little Sergei is on a knee, twisting into a pitiful angle, trying to examine the wound as if a hornet stung him in the back.

The golems are perforated with bullets, stained with gunpowder, speaking in nearly everyone's voice. It is the sound of a riot, although their gestures are mostly calm.

Mama is bent over. Raphael is the first to notice. "Revekka? Revekka!"

His voice is reedy and loud, a harmonica giving in to panic.

She chews hard on the bottom lip. This will be the only reassuring sign, that the redness in her face means a good supply of blood. That for now, biology is working as it should.

Raphael says, "Darling, please. Anywhere but in there."

Revekka is hurrying to the lake and answers with her hand. The palm is crimson. Raphael and Alexei follow her in, but only the boy is tall enough to go that far. The golem stands in leg-deep water, some four meters from the shore. Their son is chest-deep and does not care to look at it, his mother's blue water becoming red.

What is it she wants again, to die young? Her chance for that was too many lifetimes ago.

"Mama, it's a bullet, isn't it? At least tell me you're shot."

"My beautiful child."

"You have to say if you are. You have to lie flat."

"So beautiful. My one boy with his one beautiful life."

She arches her chest up, rising to level, her hand moored in with Alexei's hand. It is her last effort; there are no more obligations than this. She has endured 80 years already. No one should have to live in this time anymore.

Alexei chokes on his next words: "All those days you told me to get back in bed, you should know it by heart." The statement, at least on cardiovascular grounds, is meaningless.

Raphael implores Little Sergei to tow her back in, but at last Mamontov understands it, the simple house, sterile land, their lake without life. Never mind her dreadful cough; he still has time to bring her in.

Alexei says, "Your two lunatics—" but she does not hear. One of them has just died. He knows if only by the way his right hand falls through her left. Or is it the other way around, and he is the one to become salt? Was it her hand, instead, that pushed through her son's? Without a mother to ask he will never be sure.

In her last moment Revekka gasped; the boy looked briefly to Raphael when her exhale became chemistry. A farewell reaction. One last, small measurement of heat.

Before he could guess it he looked back, hollered something. Their interlaced fingers were coming apart and his fist closed in. All the boy had left were the white grains sinking down. Minerals lost among minerals. This is why the yearners live nearby.

One of the terrible things about being a son is that, in time, your worries become fact. Your mother's lies—say, the one about saltwater fixing everything—are laid bare.

Alexei wakes before he dreams the part about the loudspeakers. It is August. All around him is warm autumn. From today the storm wreckage is most of the world.

Saint Petersburg
September 15, 1764

IVAN VI WAS GONE and Vasili Mirovich waited for an execution pardon. His composure was striking, a part of history. Such demeanor itself was cause for rumor, and it threatened Catherine's claim. She was empress, now, and German-born. Moreover, she was forced to state that her once-impotent husband was Paul's true father.

For those who doubted, Paul was illegitimate, with little Romanov blood, or perhaps none at all, not even Russian blood. Yet even for those who defended her, the fact that the accused was unafraid meant he held incriminating secrets. If those were disclosed, now or after his death, they might damage the empress. Catherine would step in and stop the execution, which she would not have done without duress.

In a way, even Mirovich's condemnation was a disclosure. An unnamed detention had haunted three consecutive autocrats for 20 years. To look at the boy, he was a living ghost in a dark room, never quite warm, always ranting in the mad things of the dead. Only few knew that he was the descendant of Ivan V, Peter's brother and fellow tsar. (While Peter had been more fit to govern, Ivan was older, and his grandchildren had truer petitions to the throne.)

During Peter III's brief reign, Ivan heard the tsar's offer for freedom in a monastery. But in those last years two officers were assigned to guard him, with positions not unlike Chehreh's post at Kholmogory. No light, no exit, no visitors. Prisoners in fact if not in sentence. They were paid lavishly, and knew the end of their commission was soon. Yet their twice-monthly warden reports read more and more like letters from convicts: "We are desperate. We implore you for new consideration, to take our requisition to the empress."

Catherine's mandate was that, any attempt at freeing Ivan, even one to which the prisoner was ignorant, should be his immediate execution. The empress wanted as few conspirators as possible: the two officers, Vlasev and Chekin, and a commander in the outer bastion, Panin. Mirovich's trial and harsh sentence had brought that closer to light.

#

That May, Vasili's finances were ruined. He was of aristocratic birth, but his sisters were out of money again. His wife always reworked their old, stinking clothes, they had to mind their quantities of food. His first plan was for Ivan's peaceful release but his partner, Appolon Ushakov, drowned while doing other things.

In July he convinced other soldiers of the great wealth at stake; what restored tsar would fail to reward his liberators? That day they knocked out the fortress commander with a musket blow to the jaw. They exchanged fire with Vlasev and Chekin, in time brought a cannon from the river bank. The men surrendered but Ivanushka was already dead, as Catherine had ordered. On his pale body were seven puncture wounds, a sword still in the upper back.

Even dead, the prisoner seemed crazy. His face was swollen and frightful, as if holding back breath until the shooting stopped. His pose was one of considerable effort: stomach to floor, the chest turned slightly upward at the left side, his right hand resting at the waist. On the cell floor were two large bloodstains, one was far from the body.

Vasili wept, kissed the boy on the hand. He proclaimed Ivan the tsar for the last time, and exonerated the other soldiers. "You did not know the identity of the child and were ignorant to my plot. I am responsible and I, alone, will endure their punishments."

He was condemned in early September and beheaded after a week. An official's report stated how the onlookers gasped in one voice, but it omitted the detail of Mirovich's corpse, that it shifted in composition, made for difficult cleaning of the execution scaffolding. There was no mention that, in the condition of the remains, there might have been another explanation for his calm.

One last omission: the internment and questioning of a young woman—a rather lovely, nervous visitor of African descent. Army officers found her near the scaffolding after the crowd had dispersed. She was inspecting the platform, taking a knee on the yard, tasting something which had been ground underfoot.

She offered the name Maria Ivanovna, which she claimed to have taken after her Orthodox conversion and baptism.

The infantrymen doubted the particulars but, in general, found no further cause for detention.

F.N.
July 2017